KATHERINE
MANSFIELD

Twelve Stories

selected and introduced by
J ANE M ILLER

Drawings by
J ENNIFER C AMPBELL

◊

London
THE FOLIO SOCIETY

1978

Printed in Great Britain by W & J Mackay Limited, Chatham

Twelve Stories

Contents

◊ ◊ ◊
◊ ◊
◊

ERRATA

The illustrations facing pages 201 and 216 are transposed and the listing on page 5 should read:

Katherine Mansfield: *Twelve Stories*

Twelve Stories

Illustrations

◇ ◇ ◇
◇ ◇
◇

Introduction

It is customary when making a selection from a writer's
work to insist on the difficulty of the task, the dilemma
posed by having to decide what to include and what to
leave out. I chose the twelve of Katherine Mansfield's
stories I like best and read again with most pleasure. Of
course there are others which might have been included, but I am happy with these. Having made my
selection I was surprised to find that it represented her
range and versatility with a completeness I might have
intended, though I did not. *Germans at Meat* was
written when she was nineteen and included in the
1911 edition of her first book, *In a German Pension*.
When, some years later, she was pressed to have it re-
printed she described it as 'far too *immature*' and con-
sented only reluctantly to its reissue. She thought its
humour crude and embarrassingly anti-German, and
in some ways she was right, but it is an accomplished
and witty story all the same and well worth including
here. *The Little Governess, An Indiscreet Journey* and
Je ne parle pas français were written between 1915
and 1918, and though they are unalike in tone and
purpose they have in common the bewilderment of
travellers abroad, a condition of isolation and vulnera-
bility which Katherine Mansfield experienced for most
of her adult life. *Prelude* is, in my view, her master-
piece, the longest of her stories and the finest example

7

of the New Zealand fiction, while *At the Bay* and *The Doll's House* are in important ways extensions of it. *Marriage à la Mode* and the unfinished and extraordinary *A Married Man's Story* are inspired by two of the writers she most admired, Chekhov and Tolstoy respectively. Her journal shows her to have been a superbly creative reader, who responded to the work of other writers in a powerful and personal way, so that these two stories can be read as tributes to their models (*The Grasshopper* and *Family Happiness*) for being as well so totally her own. *The Daughters of the Late Colonel* and *The Fly* are late stories and painful ones. Both contain fathers who are older, more malevolent versions of the father in the New Zealand stories, and both are about death and its ambiguous meanings for survivors.

So the stories span the whole of Katherine Mansfield's short working life and contain samples of her most insistent preoccupations. They reflect the events of her life and memories of her childhood and family in New Zealand. There are stories written out of her first turbulent years in England and in Europe and others which look at marriages and make use of her difficult relationship with John Middleton Murry to invent alternatives. These periods of her life, and her last years, spent mostly alone and in France looking for a cure for her debilitating illness, are there in the stories, though few of them are in any simple way autobiographical. It is always illuminating to read her letters and journal with the stories, principally for what they reveal about her approach to working on experience to produce her fiction. Murry, for instance, of whom she could write, 'I *do* lament that he is not warm, ardent, eager, full of quick response, careless, spendthrift of himself, vividly alive, *high-spirited*. But it makes no difference to my love,' is transformed by

fiction into versions of himself which go beyond such explicitness and speak with voices of their own.

Katherine Mansfield was thirty-four when she died on 9 January 1923, and she had been seriously ill with TB since 1917. This alone might explain why she never wrote a novel. Yet there were plans to write one which would include material used in the stories set in France, and she refers several times in her journal of 1921 to 'my novel, *Karori*' of which, it seems, *Prelude*, which was started in 1916, and *At the Bay*, written in 1921, were to have formed parts. Another plan, to write a novel about a liar, quickly died: 'I couldn't write a whole novel about anything,' she wrote. Perhaps it is perverse to discuss a writer as gifted as Katherine Mansfield in terms of what she did not write. She produced, after all, more than ninety stories and fragments of stories, as well as poems, book reviews, several volumes of letters and her journal. Yet it does seem worth considering the absence of a novel in her work, because there is evidence that she wanted to write one and because it has a bearing on the nature of the fiction she did write and, more particularly, on the fact that her memories of her New Zealand childhood produced a different sort of fiction, which she at one point felt inclined to develop into a novel.

Many of the stories embody and account for contradictions and dividedness, more openly discussed in her journal and her letters as a sense of duality in herself which produced and was reshaped by her escape from New Zealand and, perhaps more urgently, participated in her talents as a writer. In moments of despair she could write as she did less than a year before her death, 'Nothing of any worth can come from a disunited being.' Yet some of her best stories deal subtly and truthfully with the possibilities of that other self,

secret, 'submerged', even 'false', yet requiring accommodation. The journal and the letters testify to a continual wavering between a view of her work as constricted, exiguous, 'little' (a word she often used to describe what was most moving to her as well as what was fraudulent or unimportant), and a belief in compression and selection as vital to her vision. She writes in her journal: 'What I chiefly admire in Jane Austen is that what she promises, she performs, i.e. if Sir T is to arrive, we have his arrival at length, and it's excellent and excels our expectations. This is rare; it is also my very weakest point. Easy to see why . . .', and in a letter of 1921 to Countess Russell: 'She makes modern episodic people like me, as far as I go, look very incompetent ninnies.' The tone is cheerfully self-disparaging and only partly serious, as in another letter where she writes, 'I want much more material; I am tired of my little stories like birds bred in cages.' She could, at times, deplore her own fluency, and yet something she wrote about Chekhov at the end of her life says a good deal about her own work and the value she put on it: 'Chekhov made a mistake in thinking that if he had had more time he would have written more fully, described the rain, and the midwife and the doctor having tea. The truth is one can get only *so much* into a story: there is always a sacrifice. One has to leave out what one knows and longs to use. Why? I haven't any idea, but there it is. It's always a kind of race to get in as much as one can before it *disappears*.' There was nothing self-disparaging about her associating herself with Chekhov.

In her shortest, most compact stories, *Miss Brill*, for instance, or *The Fly*, it is possible to infer a past and a lifetime's habit of thought from the details of a single episode. Miss Brill, with her mangy fox fur and her gentility, has been induced by loneliness to believe her-

self invisible. She scrutinizes 'other people' in the park
and finds 'something funny about nearly all of them'.
Her delighted discovery that 'she was part of the
performance, after all,' is shockingly reinforced by over-
hearing a young couple laughing at her. The discre-
pancy between an individual's view of himself and the
character other people attribute to him and his actions
is the territory of many of the stories, and it is en-
larged here by Miss Brill's extreme isolation. The boss
and bereaved father of *The Fly* is intact and impressive
to his retired employee, Mr Woodifield. He nurses his
grief privately, so that his inner and outer selves have
lost touch. His elaborate destruction of the fly serves
less to re-enact the pointless death of his son than to
demonstrate the withering away of his grief, its reduction to barely more than a nagging disappointment,
though he has held to his loss as a truth about himself
long after it has ceased to be a reality for him. Both
stories expose people at moments which break roughly
into their settled views of themselves, so painstakingly
built up to protect them from an earlier dismay.

So that what is left out of stories like these is docu-
mented history. Instead, a split second rearranges a
life's accumulation of attitudes, but it does so for us
rather than for Miss Brill or the father. *The Little
Governess* has a plot, and the relationship between the
girl and the old man allows for a different kind of
revelation. The 'charming old grandfather' was never
that; he was always the leering wolf the girl expects all
strange men to be, so that we are not taken aback by
his behaviour. The story's ferocity has to do with the
girl's failure to understand or make use of her own pre-
judices, so that her innocence becomes something sinister, and her nature deformed by a generalized distrust
which is unable to protect her from the simplest
blandishments. She is easily won with magazines and

strawberries and ice-cream, and it is her terrified self-absorption which permits that and which brings out the beast in men and in her creator. The heroine of *An Indiscreet Journey*, on the other hand, has the bravado of the fugitive, and it is hard to imagine her inviting exploitation. The story is based on a bizarre trip Katherine Mansfield made to Paris during the First World War to visit a lover, and the story she made from the affair, which did not survive the escapade, catches the side of her which could delight in other people; the old woman reading her son's letter, for instance, 'Slowly, slowly she sipped a sentence'. It is a sketch with no ending, and yet its pace and the private happiness it suggests defy the war the story is partly about, just as her visit defied it.

Few, if any, of the stories could be said to celebrate the charms of family life and marriage and parturition. Katherine Mansfield was not a feminist though, and one of her few journal entries on the subject of women, written in 1908, is restrained and judicious: 'I feel that I do now realize, dimly, what women in the future will be capable of. They truly as yet have never had their chance. Talk of our enlightened days and our emancipated country, pure nonsense! We are firmly held with the self-fashioned chains of slavery. Yes, now I see that they *are* self-fashioned, and must be self-removed.' Men are blamed no more than women are for unhappy marriages. One of her most successful impersonations is as the waspish, androgynous narrator of *Je ne parle pas français*, a writer with a 'submerged life' who speaks for Katherine Mansfield's sense of the writer's ruthless cannibalizing of other people's sensibilities. And it is a story whose telling combines assurance with its callousness. Women are seen to be callous too, like the treacherous wife of *Marriage à la Mode*. Yet if men in general escape

blame, fathers in particular scarcely do. *The Daughters of the Late Colonel* belongs with the stories about childhood and fathers. She was particularly fond of it and feared it would be misunderstood, read as a sneering comedy, perhaps, when she wished to express the deepest affection for the two elderly sisters engaged in preparing for their monstrous dead father a funeral – 'A good one that will last' – while they tentatively wonder whether life might now be lived, postponed dreams realized, away from their father's consuming tyranny. The sisters *are* laughed at, but they are also pitied. The father of the New Zealand stories, a bully but still a charming one, is no longer indulged. Here he has obstructed his daughters' vision, wasted their lives, just as Beryl in *At the Bay* fears she may be obliged to waste hers. Life for the sisters 'seemed to have happened in a kind of tunnel', so that they are now old children, shrivelled versions of Kezia and Lottie in *Prelude*. Stanley Burnell, the father of the childhood stories, contains the vigour and self-satisfaction of the New Zealand from which Katherine Mansfield had to escape. The irony of her life was that it was the world of her youth, so enclosing and constrained, which was transformed by her sufferings in Europe and by her imagination into a kind of paradise.

Prelude, *At the Bay* and *The Doll's House* are more than memories or exercises in nostalgia. When her young brother was killed in 1915 Katherine Mansfield returned to the scenes and characters of her childhood with a new expectation of them. At the beginning of 1916 she wrote in her journal, 'The people who lived or whom I wished to bring into my stories don't interest me any more. The plots of my stories leave me perfectly cold. Granted that these people exist and all the differences, complexities and resolutions are true to them – why should *I* write about them? They are not

13

near me. All the false threads that bound me to them are cut away quite.

'Now – now I want to write recollections of my own country. Yes, I want to write about my own country till I simply exhaust my store. Not only because it is "a sacred debt" that I pay to my country because my brother and I were born there, but also because in my thoughts I range with him over all the remembered places. I am never far away from them. I long to renew them in writing.'

She had put what turned out to be an irreducible distance between herself and New Zealand, and the effort of returning there and to her childhood, of renewing the past, required a multiple focus. This explains the particular texture of the stories. The characters dance separately into view, change places, confront one another, so that events and landscape are watched by one character from a particular inner world, populated by dreams and feelings unguessed at or ignored by the others, who then get their turn. *Prelude* is about the Burnell family's move to a larger house outside the city. The three little girls travel on their own in the storeman's dray, missing the first moments in the new house, so the day is different for them. Young Aunt Beryl has been working all day and is already dreaming of men she might meet in the new house, while the girls' mother waits languidly for the bustle of arranging her furniture to be over. Her husband anxiously congratulates himself on the successful deal he's made. Beryl 'was watching herself playing and singing', while Alice, the maid, cheers herself with imaginary retorts should Beryl address her too sharply. There is a gliding from dream to thought to speech, and Kezia is there as our childhood selves are watched in memory: contained, remote and impenetrable for most of the time, then suddenly, as if imbued involuntarily

with life the memory lights up, is real, so that the scene
of the duck's decapitation changes from a remembered
tableau, complete and uninvolving, to a moment when
the adult writer is nudged into genuine recall and the
child reacts with abrupt, passionate horror. The characters are self-sufficient, distinct, yet forced by the place
and their predicament to respond to one another. Beryl
is the watchful, hungry girl Katherine Mansfield might
have been had she stayed in Wellington. 'If she had
been happy and leading her own life, her false life
would cease to be,' Beryl thinks to herself. Perhaps it
was that 'false life' which made her creator write
fiction. Beryl is at the centre of the story, sensitive to
the exact quality of what is going on around her,
dreaming of something more, trying to dismiss the life
of the imagination which tormented Katherine Mansfield and made a writer of her. 'In a way, of course,'
Beryl says to herself, 'it was all perfectly true, but it
was all the greatest rubbish and she didn't believe a
word of it.' Or, as Katherine Mansfield wrote of *Prelude*
to Dorothy Brett in 1918, 'And won't the "Intellectuals"
just hate it. They'll think it's a New Primer for Infant
Readers. Let 'em.'

At the Bay is about the family again, this time on
holiday by the sea. 'It's (I hope) full of sand and sea-
weed, bathing dresses hanging over verandas, and
sandshoes on window sills, and little pink "sea" convolvulus, and rather gritty sandwiches and the tide coming
in,' Katherine Mansfield wrote to a friend. The characters are watched against the landscape, the baby
brother just born, the grandmother expanded as a
character who provides a kind of funnel into the past.
An uncle, Jonathan, is glimpsed for a moment and
understood, an opaque adult to the children, a talented
failure to himself and his contemporaries. Beryl's final
dream is shattered by the propositions of an alarming

neighbour. *The Doll's House* is less tantalizing because it feels like a complete story, not a chapter of something else. The Burnell girls go to school, where they avoid, like everyone else, any contact with the poverty-stricken Kelvey children. When they are ejected airily from the uppity Burnell home by Beryl, a disembodied voice wonders about the Kelveys: 'What were their thoughts?' – a query truer to Katherine Mansfield's somewhat perfunctory treatment of social injustice and inequality than stories like *The Garden Party* and *Life of Ma Parker* are. Perhaps her need occasionally to notice indifference or cruelty of that sort was an honourable one, but too often it is accompanied by an apparent belief in the incapacity of the poor to think, except in the crudest concepts and an impoverished dialect.

I have spoken of Katherine Mansfield's range and versatility, and plainly this is not just a question of subject matter. The intensity and compression of her most anthologized and shorter stories move outward from a gesture, some words, to animate a person or a relationship, so that every detail can suggest strands into the past or the future, into their lives elsewhere. What will remain so tantalizing about that absent novel is that when she wrote longer stories she found herself needing another dimension, other voices, variety of pace. *Prelude* and *At the Bay* together make something very like that novel, in fact; a highly original one, which creates a small, dense world through the perceptions of its inhabitants, who are locked in dependency, yet allowed space and time enough to flourish in individual isolation too.

JANE MILLER

◊ ◊
◊

1

Germans at Meat

Bread soup was placed upon the table. 'Ah,' said the Herr Rat, leaning upon the table as he peered into the tureen, 'that is what I need. My "magen" has not been in order for several days. Bread soup, and just the right consistency. I am a good cook myself' – he turned to me.

'How interesting,' I said, attempting to infuse just the right amount of enthusiasm into my voice.

'Oh yes – when one is not married it is necessary. As for me, I have had all I wanted from women without marriage.' He tucked his napkin into his collar and blew upon his soup as he spoke. 'Now at nine o'clock I make myself an English breakfast, but not much. Four slices of bread, two eggs, two slices of cold ham, one plate of soup, two cups of tea – that is nothing to you.'

He asserted the fact so vehemently that I had not the courage to refute it.

All eyes were suddenly turned upon me. I felt I was bearing the burden of the nation's preposterous breakfast – I who drank a cup of coffee while buttoning my blouse in the morning.

'Nothing at all,' cried Herr Hoffmann from Berlin. 'Ach, when I was in England in the morning I used to eat.'

He turned up his eyes and his moustache, wiping the soup drippings from his coat and waistcoat.

'Do they really eat so much?' asked Fräulein Stiege-lauer. 'Soup and baker's bread and pig's flesh, and tea and coffee and stewed fruit, and honey and eggs, and cold fish and kidneys, and hot fish and liver? All the ladies eat, too, especially the ladies?'

'Certainly. I myself have noticed it, when I was living in a hotel in Leicester Square,' cried the Herr Rat. 'It was a good hotel, but they could not make tea – now . . .'

'Ah, that's one thing I *can* do,' said I, laughing brightly. 'I can make very good tea. The great secret is to warm the teapot.'

'Warm the teapot,' interrupted the Herr Rat, push-ing away his soup plate. 'What do you warm the teapot for? Ha! ha! that's very good! One does not eat the teapot, I suppose?'

He fixed his cold blue eyes upon me with an expres-sion which suggested a thousand premeditated invasions.

'So that is the great secret of your English tea? All you do is to warm the teapot.'

I wanted to say that was only the preliminary canter, but could not translate it, and so was silent.

The servant brought in veal, with sauerkraut and potatoes.

'I eat sauerkraut with great pleasure,' said the Traveller from North Germany, 'but now I have eaten so much of it that I cannot retain it. I am immedi-ately forced to . . .'

'A beautiful day,' I cried, turning to Fräulein Stiegelauer. 'Did you get up early?'

'At five o'clock I walked for ten minutes in the wet grass. Again in bed. At half-past five I fell asleep, and woke at seven, when I made an "overbody" washing! Again in bed. At eight o'clock I had a cold-water poul-tice, and at half past eight I drank a cup of mint tea. At nine I drank some malt coffee, and began my "cure".

Pass me the sauerkraut, please. You do not eat it?'

'No, thank you. I still find it a little strong.'

'Is it true,' asked the Widow, picking her teeth with a hairpin as she spoke, 'that you are a vegetarian?'

'Why, yes; I have not eaten meat for three years.'

'Im – possible! Have you any family?'

'No.'

'There now, you see, that's what you're coming to! Who ever heard of having children upon vegetables? It is not possible. But you never have large families in England now; I suppose you are too busy with your suffragetting. Now I have had nine children, and they are all alive, thank God. Fine, healthy babies – though after the first one was born I had to . . .'

'How *wonderful*!' I cried.

'Wonderful,' said the Widow contemptuously, replacing the hairpin in the knob which was balanced on the top of her head. 'Not at all! A friend of mine had four at the same time. Her husband was so pleased he gave a supper-party and had them placed on the table. Of course she was very proud.'

'Germany,' boomed the Traveller, biting round a potato which he had speared with his knife, 'is the home of the Family.'

Followed an appreciative silence.

The dishes were changed for beef, red currants and spinach. They wiped their forks upon black bread and started again.

'How long are you remaining here?' asked the Herr Rat.

'I do not know exactly. I must be back in London in September.'

'Of course you will visit München?'

'I am afraid I shall not have time. You see, it is important not to break into my "cure".'

'But you *must* go to München. You have not seen

19

Germany if you have not been to München. All the Exhibitions, all the Art and Soul life of Germany are in München. There is the Wagner Festival in August, and Mozart and a Japanese collection of pictures – and there is the beer! You do not know what good beer is until you have been to München. Why, I see fine ladies every afternoon, but fine ladies, I tell you, drinking glasses so high.' He measured a good washstand pitcher in height, and I smiled.

'If I drink a great deal of München beer I sweat so,' said Herr Hoffmann. 'When I am here, in the fields or before my baths, I sweat, but I enjoy it; but in the town it is not at all the same thing.'

Promoted by the thought, he wiped his neck and face with his dinner napkin and carefully cleaned his ears.

A glass dish of stewed apricots was placed upon the table.

'Ah, fruit!' said Fräulein Stiegelauer, 'that is so necessary to health. The doctor told me this morning that the more fruit I could eat the better.'

She very obviously followed the advice.

Said the Traveller: 'I suppose you are frightened of an invasion, too, eh? Oh, that's good. I've been reading all about your English play in a newspaper. Did you see it?'

'Yes.' I sat upright. 'I assure you we are not afraid.'

'Well, then, you ought to be,' said the Herr Rat. 'You have got no army at all – a few little boys with their veins full of nicotine poisoning.'

'Don't be afraid,' Herr Hoffmann said. 'We don't want England. If we did we would have had her long ago. We really do not want you.'

He waved his spoon airily, looking across at me as though I were a little child whom he would keep or dismiss as he pleased.

'We certainly do not want Germany,' I said.

'This morning I took a half bath. Then this afternoon I must take a knee bath and an arm bath,' volunteered the Herr Rat; 'then I do my exercises for an hour, and my work is over. A glass of wine and a couple of rolls with some sardines . . .'

They were handed cherry cake with whipped cream.

'What is your husband's favourite meat?' asked the Widow.

'I really do not know,' I answered.

'You really do not know? How long have you been married?'

'Three years.'

'But you cannot be in earnest! You would not have kept house as his wife for a week without knowing that fact.'

'I really never asked him; he is not at all particular about his food.'

A pause. They all looked at me, shaking their heads, their mouths full of cherry stones.

'No wonder there is a repetition in England of that dreadful state of things in Paris,' said the Widow, folding her dinner napkin. 'How can a woman expect to keep her husband if she does not know his favourite food after three years?'

'Mahlzeit!'

'Mahlzeit!'

I closed the door after me.

2

The Little Governess

Oh, dear, how she wished that it wasn't night-time.
She'd have much rather travelled by day, much much
rather. But the lady at the Governess Bureau had said:
'You had better take an evening boat and then if you
get into a compartment for "Ladies Only" in the train
you will be far safer than sleeping in a foreign hotel.
Don't go out of the carriage; don't walk about the corri-
dors and *be sure* to lock the lavatory door if you go
there. The train arrives at Munich at eight o'clock, and
Frau Arnholdt says that the Hotel Grunewald is only
one minute away. A porter can take you there. She
will arrive at six the same evening, so you will have a
nice quiet day to rest after the journey and rub up
your German. And when you want anything to eat I
would advise you to pop into the nearest baker's and
get a bun and some coffee. You haven't been abroad
before, have you?' 'No.' 'Well, I always tell my girls
that it's better to mistrust people at first rather than
trust them, and it's safer to suspect people of evil
intentions rather than good ones. . . . It sounds rather
hard but we've got to be women of the world, haven't
we?'

It had been nice in the Ladies' Cabin. The stewardess
was so kind and changed her money for her and tucked
up her feet. She lay on one of the hard pink-sprigged
couches and watched the other passengers, friendly and

natural, pinning their hats to the bolsters, taking off their boots and skirts, opening dressing-cases and arranging mysterious rustling little packages, tying their heads up in veils before lying down. *Thud, thud, thud,* went the steady screw of the steamer. The stewardess pulled a green shade over the light and sat down by the stove, her skirt turned back over her knees, a long piece of knitting on her lap. On a shelf above her head there was a water-bottle with a tight bunch of flowers stuck in it. 'I like travelling very much,' thought the little governess. She smiled and yielded to the warm rocking.

But when the boat stopped and she went up on deck, her dress-basket in one hand, her rug and umbrella in the other, a cold, strange wind flew under her hat. She looked up at the masts and spars of the ship black against a green glittering sky and down to the dark landing stage where strange muffled figures lounged, waiting; she moved forward with the sleepy flock, all knowing where to go to and what to do except her, and she felt afraid. Just a little – just enough to wish – oh, to wish that it was daytime and that one of those women who had smiled at her in the glass, when they both did their hair in the Ladies' Cabin, was somewhere near now. 'Tickets, please. Show your tickets. Have your tickets ready.' She went down the gangway balancing herself carefully on her heels. Then a man in a black leather cap came forward and touched her on the arm. 'Where for, Miss?' He spoke English – he must be a guard or a stationmaster with a cap like that. She had scarcely answered when he pounced on her dress-basket. 'This way,' he shouted, in a rude, determined voice, and elbowing his way he strode past people. 'But I don't want a porter.' What a horrible man! 'I don't want a porter. I want to carry it myself.' She had to run to keep up with him, and her anger, far

stronger than she, ran before her and snatched the bag out of the wretch's hand. He paid no attention at all, but swung on down the long dark platform, and across a railway line. 'He is a robber.' She was sure he was a robber as she stepped between the silvery rails and felt the cinders crunch under her shoes. On the other side – oh, thank goodness! – there was a train with Munich written on it. The man stopped by the huge lighted carriages. 'Second class?' asked the insolent voice. 'Yes, a Ladies' compartment.' She was quite out of breath. She opened her little purse to find something small enough to give this horrible man while he tossed her dress-basket into the rack of an empty carriage that had a ticket, *Dames Seules*, gummed on the window. She got into the train and handed him twenty centimes. 'What's this?' shouted the man, glaring at the money and then at her, holding it up to his nose, sniffing at it as though he had never in his life seen, much less held, such a sum. 'It's a franc. You know that, don't you? It's a franc. That's my fare!' A franc! Did he imagine that she was going to give him a franc for playing a trick like that just because she was a girl and travelling alone at night? Never, never! She squeezed her purse in her hand and simply did not see him – she looked at a view of St Malo on the wall opposite and simply did not hear him. 'Ah, no. Ah, no. Four sous. You make a mistake. Here, take it. It's a franc I want.' He leapt on to the step of the train and threw the money on to her lap. Trembling with terror she screwed herself tight, tight, and put out an icy hand and took the money – stowed it away in her hand: 'That's all you're going to get,' she said. For a minute or two she felt his sharp eyes pricking her all over, while he nodded slowly, pulling down his mouth: 'Ve-ry well. *Trrrès bien.*' He shrugged his shoulders and disappeared into the dark. Oh, the relief! How

simply terrible that had been! As she stood up to feel if
the dress-basket was firm she caught sight of herself in
the mirror, quite white, with big round eyes. She un-
tied her 'motor veil' and unbuttoned her green cape.
'But it's all over now,' she said to the mirror face, feeling in some way that it was more frightened than she.

People began to assemble on the platform. They
stood together in little groups talking; a strange light
from the station lamps painted their faces almost
green. A little boy in red clattered up with a huge tea
wagon and leaned against it, whistling and flicking his
boots with a serviette. A woman in a black alpaca
apron pushed a barrow with pillows for hire. Dreamy
and vacant she looked – like a woman wheeling a
perambulator – up and down, up and down – with a
sleeping baby inside it. Wreaths of white smoke floated
up from somewhere and hung below the roof like
misty vines. 'How strange it all is,' thought the little
governess, 'and the middle of the night, too.' She
looked out from her safe corner, frightened no longer
but proud that she had not given that franc. 'I can look
after myself – of course I can. The great thing is not
to . . .' Suddenly from the corridor there came a stamping of feet and men's voices, high and broken with
snatches of loud laughter. They were coming her way.
The little governess shrank into her corner as four
young men in bowler hats passed, staring through the
door and window. One of them, bursting with the joke,
pointed to the notice *Dames Seules* and the four bent
down the better to see the one little girl in the corner.
Oh dear, they were in the carriage next door. She
heard them tramping about and then a sudden hush
followed by a tall thin fellow with a tiny black moustache who flung her door open. 'If mademoiselle cares
to come in with us,' he said, in French. She saw the
others crowding behind him, peeping under his arm

and over his shoulder, and she sat very straight and still. 'If mademoiselle will do us the honour,' mocked the tall man. One of them could be quiet no longer; his laughter went off in a loud crack. 'Mademoiselle is serious,' persisted the young man, bowing and grimacing. He took off his hat with a flourish, and she was alone again.

'*En voiture. En voi-ture!*' Some one ran up and down beside the train. 'I wish it wasn't night-time. I wish there was another woman in the carriage. I'm frightened of the men next door.' The little governess looked out to see her porter coming back again – the same man making for her carriage with his arms full of luggage. But – but what *was* he doing? He put his thumb nail under the label *Dames Seules* and tore it right off and then stood aside squinting at her while an old man wrapped in a plaid cape climbed up the high step. 'But this is a ladies' compartment.' 'Oh, no, mademoiselle, you make a mistake. No, no, I assure you. Merci, Monsieur.' '*En voi-turre!*' A shrill whistle. The porter stepped off triumphant and the train started. For a moment or two big tears brimmed her eyes and through them she saw the old man unwinding a scarf from his neck and untying the flaps of his Jaeger cap. He looked very old. Ninety at least. He had a white moustache and big gold-rimmed spectacles with little blue eyes behind them and pink wrinkled cheeks. A nice face – and charming the way he bent forward and said in halting French: 'Do I disturb you, Mademoiselle? Would you rather I took all these things out of the rack and found another carriage?' What! that old man have to move all those heavy things just because she . . . 'No, it's quite all right. You don't disturb me at all.' 'Ah, a thousand thanks.' He sat down opposite her and unbuttoned the cape of his enormous coat and flung it off his shoulders.

The train seemed glad to have left the station. With a long leap it sprang into the dark. She rubbed a place in the window with her glove but she could see nothing – just a tree outspread like a black fan or a scatter of lights, or the line of a hill, solemn and huge. In the carriage next door the young men started singing '*Un, deux, trois.*' They sang the same song over and over at the tops of their voices.

'I never could have dared to go to sleep if I had been alone,' she decided. '*I couldn't* have put my feet up or even taken off my hat.' The singing gave her a queer little tremble in her stomach and, hugging herself to stop it, with her arms crossed under her cape, she felt really glad to have the old man in the carriage with her. Careful to see that he was not looking she peeped at him through her long lashes. He sat extremely upright, the chest thrown out, the chin well in, knees pressed together, reading a German paper. That was why he spoke French so funnily. He was a German. Something in the army, she supposed – a colonel or a general – once, of course, not now; he was too old for that now. How spick and span he looked for an old man. He wore a pearl pin stuck in his black tie and a ring with a dark red stone on his little finger; the tip of a white silk handkerchief showed in the pocket of his double-breasted jacket. Somehow, altogether, he was really nice to look at. Most old men were so horrid. She couldn't bear them doddery – or they had a disgusting cough or something. But not having a beard – that made all the difference – and then his cheeks were so pink and his moustache so very white. Down went the German paper and the old man leaned forward with the same delightful courtesy: 'Do you speak German, Mademoiselle?' '*Ja, ein wenig, mehr als Französisch,*' said the little governess, blushing a deep pink colour that spread slowly over her cheeks and made her blue

eyes look almost black. 'Ach, so!' The old man bowed graciously. 'Then perhaps you would care to look at some illustrated papers.' He slipped a rubber band from a little roll of them and handed them across. 'Thank you very much.' She was very fond of looking at pictures, but first she would take off her hat and gloves. So she stood up, unpinned the brown straw and put it neatly in the rack beside the dress-basket, stripped off her brown kid gloves, paired them in a tight roll and put them in the crown of the hat for safety, and then sat down again, more comfortably this time, her feet crossed, the papers on her lap. How kindly the old man in the corner watched her bare little hand turning over the big white pages, watched her lips moving as she pronounced the long words to herself, rested upon her hair that fairly blazed under the light. Alas! how tragic for a little governess to possess hair that made one think of tangerines and marigolds, of apricots and tortoiseshell cats and champagne! Perhaps that was what the old man was thinking as he gazed and gazed, and that not even the dark ugly clothes could disguise her soft beauty. Perhaps the flush that licked his cheeks and lips was a flush of rage that anyone so young and tender should have to travel alone and unprotected through the night. Who knows he was not murmuring in his sentimental German fashion: '*Ja, es ist eine Tragœdie!* Would to God I were the child's grandpapa!'

'Thank you very much. They were very interesting.' She smiled prettily handing back the papers. 'But you speak German extremely well,' said the old man. 'You have been in Germany before, of course?' 'Oh no, this is the first time' – a little pause, then – 'this is the first time that I have ever been abroad at all.' 'Really! I am surprised. You gave me the impression, if I may say so, that you were accustomed to travelling.' 'Oh, well – I have been about a good deal in England, and to Scot-

land, once.' 'So. I myself have been in England once, but I could not learn English.' He raised one hand and shook his head, laughing. 'No, it was too difficult for me. . . . "Ow-do-you-do. Please vich is ze vay to Leicestaire Squaare?".' She laughed too. 'Foreigners always say . . .' They had quite a little talk about it. 'But you will like Munich,' said the old man. 'Munich is a wonderful city. Museums, pictures, galleries, fine buildings and shops, concerts, theatres, restaurants – all are in Munich. I have travelled all over Europe many, many times in my life, but it is always to Munich that I return. You will enjoy yourself there.' 'I am not going to *stay* in Munich,' said the little governess, and she added shyly, 'I am going to a post as governess to a doctor's family in Augsburg.' 'Ah, that was it.' Augsburg he knew. Augsburg – well – was not beautiful. A solid manufacturing town. But if Germany was new to her he hoped she would find something interesting there too. 'I am sure I shall.' 'But what a pity not to see Munich before you go. You ought to take a little holiday on your way' – he smiled – 'and store up some pleasant memories.' 'I am afraid I could not do *that*,' said the little governess, shaking her head, suddenly important and serious. 'And also, if one is alone . . .' He quite understood. He bowed, serious too. They were silent after that. The train shattered on, baring its dark, flaming breast to the hills and to the valleys. It was warm in the carriage. She seemed to lean against the dark rushing and to be carried away and away. Little sounds made themselves heard; steps in the corridor, doors opening and shutting – a murmur of voices – whistling. . . . Then the window was pricked with long needles of rain. . . . But it did not matter . . . it was outside . . . and she had her umbrella . . . she pouted, sighed, opened and shut her hands once and fell fast asleep.

'Pardon! Pardon!' The sliding back of the carriage
door woke her with a start. What had happened?
Some one had come in and gone out again. The old
man sat in his corner, more upright than ever, his
hands in the pockets of his coat, frowning heavily. 'Ha!
ha! ha!' came from the carriage next door. Still half
asleep, she put her hands to her hair to make sure it
wasn't a dream. 'Disgraceful!' muttered the old man
more to himself than to her. 'Common, vulgar fellows!
I am afraid they disturbed you, gracious Fräulein,
blundering in here like that.' No, not really. She was
just going to wake up, and she took out her silver
watch to look at the time. Half-past four. A cold blue
light filled the window panes. Now when she rubbed a
place she could see bright patches of fields, a clump of
white houses like mushrooms, a road 'like a picture'
with poplar trees on either side, a thread of river. How
pretty it was! How pretty and how different! Even
those pink clouds in the sky looked foreign. It was cold,
but she pretended that it was far colder and rubbed her
hands together and shivered, pulling at the collar of
her coat because she was so happy.

The train began to slow down. The engine gave a
long shrill whistle. They were coming to a town. Taller
houses, pink and yellow, glided by, fast asleep behind
their green eyelids, and guarded by the poplar trees
that quivered in the blue air as if on tiptoe, listening.
In one house a woman opened the shutters, flung a red
and white mattress across the window frame and stood
staring at the train. A pale woman with black hair and
a white woollen shawl over her shoulders. More women
appeared at the doors and at the windows of the sleeping houses. There came a flock of sheep. The shepherd
wore a blue blouse and pointed wooden shoes. Look!
look what flowers – and by the railway station too!
Standard roses like bridesmaids' bouquets, white gera-

niums, waxy pink ones that you would *never* see out of
a greenhouse at home. Slower and slower. A man with
a watering-can was spraying the platform. 'A-a-a-ah!'
Somebody came running and waving his arms. A huge
fat woman waddled through the glass doors of the
station with a tray of strawberries. Oh, she was thirsty!
She was very thirsty! 'A-a-a-ah!' The same somebody
ran back again. The train stopped.

The old man pulled his coat round him and got up,
smiling at her. He murmured something she didn't
quite catch, but she smiled back at him as he left the
carriage. While he was away the little governess looked
at herself again in the glass, shook and patted herself
with the precise practical care of a girl who is old
enough to travel by herself and has nobody else to
assure her that she is 'quite all right behind.' Thirsty
and thirsty! The air tasted of water. She let down the
window and the fat woman with the strawberries
passed as if on purpose; holding up the tray to her.
'*Nein, dank,*' said the little governess, looking at the
big berries on their gleaming leaves. '*Wie viel?*' she
asked as the fat woman moved away. 'Two marks
fifty, Fräulein.' 'Good gracious!' She came in from the
window and sat down in the corner, very sobered for a
minute. Half a crown! 'H-o-o-o-o-o-e-e-e!' shrieked the
train, gathering itself together to be off again. She
hoped the old man wouldn't be left behind. Oh, it was
daylight – everything was lovely if only she hadn't
been so thirsty. Where *was* the old man – oh, here he
was – she dimpled at him as though he were an old
accepted friend as he closed the door and, turning, took
from under his cape a basket of the strawberries. 'If
Fräulein would honour me by accepting these . . .'
'What for me?' But she drew back and raised her hands
as though he were about to put a wild little kitten on
her lap.

'Certainly, for you,' said the old man. 'For myself it is twenty years since I was brave enough to eat strawberries.' 'Oh, thank you very much. *Danke bestens,*' she stammered, '*sie sind so sehr schön!*' 'Eat them and see,' said the old man looking pleased and friendly. 'You won't have even one?' 'No, no, no.' Timidly and charmingly her hand hovered. They were so big and juicy she had to take two bites to them – the juice ran all down her fingers – and it was while she munched the berries that she first thought of the old man as a grandfather. What a perfect grandfather he would make! Just like one out of a book!

The sun came out, the pink clouds in the sky, the strawberry clouds were eaten by the blue. 'Are they good?' asked the old man. 'As good as they look?'

When she had eaten them she felt she had known him for years. She told him about Frau Arnholdt and how she had got the place. Did he know the Hotel Grunewald? Frau Arnholdt would not arrive until the evening. He listened, listened until he knew as much about the affair as she did, until he said – not looking at her – but smoothing the palms of his brown suède gloves together: 'I wonder if you would let me show you a little of Munich today. Nothing much – but perhaps a picture gallery and the Englischer Garten. It seems such a pity that you should have to spend the day at the hotel, and also a little uncomfortable . . . in a strange place. *Nicht wahr?* You would be back there by the early afternoon or whenever you wish, of course, and you would give an old man a great deal of pleasure.'

It was not until long after she had said 'Yes' – because the moment she had said it and he had thanked her he began telling her about his travels in Turkey and attar of roses – that she wondered whether she had done wrong. After all, she really did not know him. But he was so old and he had been so very kind –

not to mention the strawberries . . . And she couldn't
have explained the reason why she said 'No,' and it was
her *last* day in a way, her last day to really enjoy herself
in. 'Was I wrong? Was I?' A drop of sunlight fell into
her hands and lay there, warm and quivering. 'If I
might accompany you as far as the hotel,' he suggested,
'and call for you again at about ten o'clock.' He took
out his pocket-book and handed her a card. 'Herr
Regierungsrat . . .' He had a title! Well, it was *bound*
to be all right! So after that the little governess gave
herself up to the excitement of being really abroad, to
looking out and reading the foreign advertisement
signs, to being told about the places they came to – having her attention and enjoyment looked after by the
charming old grandfather – until they reached Munich
and the Hauptbahnhof. 'Porter! Porter!' He found her
a porter, disposed of his own luggage in a few words,
guided her through the bewildering crowd out of the
station down the clean white steps into the white road
to the hotel. He explained who she was to the manager
as though all this had been bound to happen, and then
for one moment her little hand lost itself in the big
brown suède ones. 'I will call for you at ten o'clock.' He
was gone.

'This way, Fräulein,' said a waiter, who had been
dodging behind the manager's back, all eyes and ears
for the strange couple. She followed him up two flights
of stairs into a dark bedroom. He dashed down her
dress-basket and pulled up a clattering, dusty blind.
Ugh! what an ugly, cold room – what enormous furniture! Fancy spending the day in here! 'Is this the room
Frau Arnholdt ordered?' asked the little governess.
The waiter had a curious way of staring as if there was
something *funny* about her. He pursed up his lips
about to whistle, and then changed his mind. '*Gewiss*,'
he said. Well, why didn't he go? Why did he stare so?

'*Gehen Sie,*' said the little governess, with frigid English simplicity. His little eyes, like currants, nearly popped out of his doughy cheeks. '*Gehen Sie sofort,*' she repeated icily. At the door he turned. 'And the gentleman,' said he, 'shall I show the gentleman upstairs when he comes?'

Over the white streets big white clouds fringed with silver — and sunshine everywhere. Fat, fat coachmen driving fat cabs; funny women with little round hats cleaning the tramway lines; people laughing and pushing against one another; trees on both sides of the streets and everywhere you looked almost, immense fountains; a noise of laughing from the footpaths or the middle of the streets or the open windows. And beside her, more beautifully brushed than ever, with a rolled umbrella in one hand and yellow gloves instead of brown ones, her grandfather who had asked her to spend the day. She wanted to run, she wanted to hang on his arm, she wanted to cry every minute, 'Oh, I am so frightfully happy!' He guided her across the roads, stood still while she 'looked', and his kind eyes beamed on her and he said 'just whatever you wish.' She ate two white sausages and two little rolls of fresh bread at eleven o'clock in the morning and she drank some beer, which he told her wasn't intoxicating, wasn't at all like English beer, out of a glass like a flower vase. And then they took a cab and really she must have seen thousands and thousands of wonderful classical pictures in about a quarter of an hour! 'I shall have to think them over when I am alone' . . . But when they came out of the picture gallery it was raining. The grandfather unfurled his umbrella and held it over the little governess. They started to walk to the restaurant for lunch. She, very close beside him so that he should have some of the umbrella, too. 'It goes easier,' he remarked in a de-

tached way, 'if you take my arm, Fräulein. And besides
it is the custom in Germany.' So she took his arm and
walked beside him while he pointed out the famous
statues, so interested that he quite forgot to put down
the umbrella even when the rain was long over.

After lunch they went to a café to hear a gipsy band,
but she did not like that at all. Ugh! such horrible men
were there with heads like eggs and cuts on their faces,
so she turned her chair and cupped her burning cheeks
in her hands and watched her old friend instead . . .
Then they went to the Englischer Garten.

'I wonder what the time is,' asked the little governess. 'My watch has stopped. I forgot to wind it in the
train last night. We've seen such a lot of things that
I feel it must be quite late.' 'Late!' He stopped in front
of her laughing and shaking his head in a way she had
begun to know. 'Then you have not really enjoyed
yourself. Late! Why, we have not had any ice cream
yet!' 'Oh, but I have enjoyed myself,' she cried, dis-
tressed, 'more than I can possibly say. It has been
wonderful! Only Frau Arnholdt is to be at the hotel at
six and I ought to be there by five.' 'So you shall. After
the ice cream I shall put you into a cab and you can go
there comfortably.' She was happy again. The chocolate
ice cream melted – melted in little sips a long way
down. The shadows of the trees danced on the table
cloths, and she sat with her back safely turned to the
ornamental clock that pointed to twenty-five minutes to
seven. 'Really and truly,' said the little governess
earnestly, 'this has been the happiest day of my life.
I've never even imagined such a day.' In spite of the
ice cream her grateful baby heart glowed with love for
the fairy grandfather.

So they walked out of the garden down a long alley.
The day was nearly over. 'You see those big buildings
opposite,' said the old man. 'The third storey – that is

where I live. I and the old housekeeper who looks after
me.' She was very interested. 'Now just before I find a
cab for you, will you come and see my little "home"
and let me give you a bottle of the attar of roses I told
you about in the train? For remembrance?' She would
love to. 'I've never seen a bachelor's flat in my life,'
laughed the little governess.

The passage was quite dark. 'Ah, I suppose my old
woman has gone out to buy me a chicken. One moment.' He opened a door and stood aside for her to pass,
a little shy but curious, into a strange room. She did not
know quite what to say. It wasn't pretty. In a way it
was very ugly – but neat, and, she supposed, comfortable for such an old man. 'Well, what do you think of
it?' He knelt down and took from a cupboard a round
tray with two pink glasses and a tall pink bottle. 'Two
little bedrooms beyond,' he said gaily, 'and a kitchen.
It's enough, eh?' 'Oh, quite enough.' 'And if ever you
should be in Munich and care to spend a day or two –
why there is always a little nest – a wing of a chicken,
and a salad, and an old man delighted to be your host
once more and many many times, dear little Fräulein!'
He took the stopper out of the bottle and poured some
wine into the two pink glasses. His hand shook and the
wine spilled over the tray. It was very quiet in the
room. She said: 'I think I ought to go now.' 'But you
will have a tiny glass of wine with me – just one before
you go?' said the old man. 'No, really no. I never drink
wine. I – I have promised never to touch wine or anything like that.' And though he pleaded and though she
felt dreadfully rude, especially when he seemed to take
it to heart so, she was quite determined. 'No, *really*,
please.' 'Well, will you just sit down on the sofa for five
minutes and let me drink your health?' The little governess sat down on the edge of the red velvet couch and
he sat down beside her and drank her health at a gulp.

'Have you really been happy today?' asked the old man, turning round, so close beside her that she felt his knee twitching against hers. Before she could answer he held her hands. 'And are you going to give me one little kiss before you go?' he asked, drawing her closer still.

It was a dream! It wasn't true! It wasn't the same old man at all. Ah, how horrible! The little governess stared at him in terror. 'No, no, no!' she stammered, struggling out of his hands. 'One little kiss. A kiss. What is it? Just a kiss, dear little Fräulein. A kiss.' He pushed his face forward, his lips smiling broadly; and how his little blue eyes gleamed behind the spectacles! 'Never – never. How can you!' She sprang up, but he was too quick and he held her against the wall, pressed against her his hard old body and his twitching knee and, though she shook her head from side to side, distracted, kissed her on the mouth. On the mouth! Where not a soul who wasn't a near relation had ever kissed her before . . .

She ran, ran down the street until she found a broad road with tram lines and a policeman standing in the middle like a clockwork doll. 'I want to get a tram to the Hauptbahnhof,' sobbed the little governess. 'Fräulein?' She wrung her hands at him. 'The Hauptbahnhof. There – there's one now,' and while he watched very much surprised, the little girl with her hat on one side, crying without a handkerchief, sprang on to the tram – not seeing the conductor's eyebrows, nor hearing the *hochwohlgebildete Dame* talking her over with a scandalized friend. She rocked herself and cried out loud and said 'Ah, ah!' pressing her hands to her mouth. 'She has been to the dentist,' shrilled a fat old woman, too stupid to be uncharitable. '*Na, sagen Sie 'mal*, what toothache! The child hasn't one left in her mouth.' While the tram swung and jangled through a world full of old men with twitching knees.

37

When the little governess reached the hall of the Hotel Grunewald the same waiter who had come into her room in the morning was standing by a table, polishing a tray of glasses. The sight of the little governess seemed to fill him out with some inexplicable important content. He was ready for her question; his answer came pat and suave. 'Yes, Fräulein, the lady has been here. I told her that you had arrived and gone out again immediately with a gentleman. She asked me when you were coming back again – but of course I could not say. And then she went to the manager.' He took up a glass from the table, held it up to the light, looked at it with one eye closed, and started polishing it with a corner of his apron. '. . ?' 'Pardon, Fräulein? Ach, no, Fräulein. The manager could tell her nothing – nothing.' He shook his head and smiled at the brilliant glass. 'Where is the lady now?' asked the little governess, shuddering so violently that she had to hold her handkerchief up to her mouth. 'How should I know?' cried the waiter, and as he swooped past her to pounce upon a new arrival his heart beat so hard against his ribs that he nearly chuckled aloud. 'That's it! that's it!' he thought. 'That will show her.' And as he swung the new arrival's box on to his shoulders – hoop! – as though he were a giant and the box a feather, he minced over again the little governess's words, '*Gehen Sie. Gehen Sie sofort.* Shall I! Shall I!' he shouted to himself.

3

An Indiscreet Journey

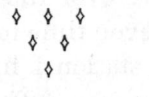

She is like St Anne. Yes, the concierge is the image of St Anne, with that black cloth over her head, the wisps of grey hair hanging, and the tiny smoking lamp in her hand. Really very beautiful, I thought, smiling at St Anne, who said severely: 'Six o'clock. You have only just got time. There is a bowl of milk on the writing table.' I jumped out of my pyjamas and into a basin of cold water like any English lady in any French novel. The concierge, persuaded that I was on my way to prison cells and death by bayonets, opened the shutters and the cold clear light came through. A little steamer hooted on the river; a cart with two horses at a gallop flung past. The rapid swirling water; the tall black trees on the far side, grouped together like negroes conversing. Sinister, very, I thought, as I buttoned on my age-old Burberry. (That Burberry was very significant. It did not belong to me. I had borrowed it from a friend. My eye lighted upon it hanging in her little dark hall. The very thing! The perfect and adequate disguise – an old Burberry. Lions have been faced in a Burberry. Ladies have been rescued from open boats in mountainous seas wrapped in nothing else. An old Burberry seems to me the sign and the token of the undisputed venerable traveller, I decided, leaving my purple peg-top with the real seal collar and cuffs in exchange.)

'You will never get there,' said the concierge, watching me turn up the collar. 'Never! Never!' I ran down the echoing stairs – strange they sounded, like a piano flicked by a sleepy housemaid – and on to the quai. 'Why so fast, *ma mignonne?*' said a lovely little boy in coloured socks, dancing in front of the electric lotus buds that curve over the entrance to the metro. Alas! there was not even time to blow him a kiss. When I arrived at the big station I had only four minutes to spare, and the platform entrance was crowded and packed with soldiers, their yellow papers in one hand and big untidy bundles. The Commissaire of Police stood on one side, a Nameless Official on the other. Will he let me pass? Will he? He was an old man with a fat swollen face covered with big warts. Horn-rimmed spectacles squatted on his nose. Trembling, I made an effort. I conjured up my sweetest early-morning smile and handed it with the papers. But the delicate thing fluttered against the horn spectacles and fell. Nevertheless, he let me pass, and I ran, ran in and out among the soldiers and up the high steps into the yellow-painted carriage.

'Does one go direct to X?' I asked the collector who dug at my ticket with a pair of forceps and handed it back again. 'No, mademoiselle, you must change at X Y Z.'

'At—?'

'X Y Z.'

Again I had not heard. 'At what time do we arrive there if you please?'

'One o'clock.' But that was no good to me. I hadn't a watch. Oh, well – later.

Ah! the train had begun to move. The train was on my side. It swung out of the station, and soon we were passing the vegetable gardens, passing the tall blind houses to let, passing the servants beating carpets. Up

already and walking in the fields, rosy from the rivers
and the red-fringed pools, the sun lighted upon the
swinging train and stroked my muff and told me to take
off that Burberry. I was not alone in the carriage. An
old woman sat opposite, her skirt turned back over her
knees, a bonnet of black lace on her head. In her fat
hands, adorned with a wedding and two mourning
rings, she held a letter. Slowly, slowly she sipped a
sentence, and then looked up and out of the window,
her lips trembling a little, and then another sentence,
and again the old face turned to the light, tasting it . . .
Two soldiers leaned out of the window, their heads
nearly touching – one of them was whistling, the other
had his coat fastened with some rusty safety-pins. And
now there were soldiers everywhere working on the
railway line, leaning against trucks or standing hands
on hips, eyes fixed on the train as though they expected
at least one camera at every window. And now we
were passing big wooden sheds like rigged-up dancing
halls or seaside pavilions, each flying a flag. In and out
of them walked the Red Cross men; the wounded sat
against the walls sunning themselves. At all the bridges,
the crossings, the stations, a *petit soldat*, all boots and
bayonet. Forlorn and desolate he looked, – like a little
comic picture waiting for the joke to be written underneath. Is there really such a thing as war? Are all these
laughing voices really going to the war? These dark
woods lighted so mysteriously by the white stems of
the birch and the ash – these watery fields with the
big birds flying over – these rivers green and blue in
the light – have battles been fought in places like
these?

What beautiful cemeteries we are passing! They flash
gay in the sun. They seem to be full of cornflowers and
poppies and daisies. How can there be so many flowers
at this time of the year? But they are not flowers at all.

They are bunches of ribbons tied on to the soldiers' graves.

I glanced up and caught the old woman's eye. She smiled and folded the letter. 'It is from my son – the first we have had since October. I am taking it to my daughter-in-law.'

'. . . ?'

'Yes, very good,' said the old woman, shaking down her skirt and putting her arm through the handle of her basket. 'He wants me to send him some handker-chieves and a piece of stout string.'

What is the name of the station where I have to change? Perhaps I shall never know. I got up and leaned my arms across the window rail, my feet crossed. One cheek burned as in infancy on the way to the sea-side. When the war is over I shall have a barge and drift along these rivers with a white cat and a pot of mignonette to bear me company.

Down the side of the hill filed the troops, winking red and blue in the light. Far away, but plainly to be seen, some more flew by on bicycles. But really, *ma France adorée*, this uniform is ridiculous. Your soldiers are stamped upon your bosom like bright irreverent transfers.

The train slowed down, stopped . . . Everybody was getting out except me. A big boy, his sabots tied to his back with a piece of string, the inside of his tin wine cup stained a lovely impossible pink, looked very friendly. Does one change here perhaps for X? Another whose képi had come out of a wet paper cracker swung my suit-case to earth. What darlings soldiers are! 'Merci bien, monsieur, vous êtes tout à fait aimable . . .' 'Not this way,' said a bayonet. 'Nor this,' said another. So I followed the crowd. 'Your passport, mademoiselle . . .' *'We, Sir Edward Grey . . .'* I ran through the muddy square and into the buffet.

A green room with a stove jutting out and tables on
each side. On the counter, beautiful with coloured
bottles, a woman leans, her breasts in her folded arms.
Through an open door I can see a kitchen, and the cook
in a white coat breaking eggs into a bowl and tossing
the shells into a corner. The blue and red coats of the
men who are eating hang upon the walls. Their short
swords and belts are piled upon chairs. Heavens! what
a noise. The sunny air seemed all broken up and
trembling with it. A little boy, very pale, swung from
table to table, taking the orders, and poured me out a
glass of purple coffee. *Sssh*, came from the eggs. They
were in a pan. The woman rushed from behind the
counter and began to help the boy. *Toute de suite,
tout' suite!* she chirruped to the loud impatient voices.
There came a clatter of plates and the pop-pop of corks
being drawn.

Suddenly in the doorway I saw someone with a pail
of fish – brown speckled fish, like the fish one sees in a
glass case, swimming through forests of beautiful
pressed sea-weed. He was an old man in a tattered
jacket, standing humbly, waiting for someone to attend
to him. A thin beard fell over his chest, his eyes under
the tufted eyebrows were bent on the pail he carried.
He looked as though he had escaped from some holy
picture, and was entreating the soldiers' pardon for
being there at all . . .

But what could I have done? I could not arrive at X
with two fishes hanging on a straw; and I am sure it is
a penal offence in France to throw fish out of railway-
carriage windows, I thought, miserably climbing into a
smaller, shabbier train. Perhaps I might have taken
them to – *ah, mon Dieu* – I had forgotten the name of
my uncle and aunt again! Buffard, Buffon – what was
it? Again I read the unfamiliar letter in the familiar
handwriting.

'My dear niece,

Now that the weather is more settled, your uncle and I would be charmed if you would pay us a little visit. Telegraph me when you are coming. I shall meet you outside the station if I am free. Otherwise our good friend, Madame Grinçon, who lives in the little toll-house by the bridge, *juste en face de la gare*, will conduct you to our home. *Je vous embrasse bien tendrement,*   JULIE BOIFFARD'

A visiting card was enclosed: *M. Paul Boiffard.*

Boiffard – of course that was the name. *Ma tante Julie et mon oncle Paul* – suddenly they were there with me, more real, more solid than any relations I had ever known. I saw *tante Julie* bridling, with the souptureen in her hands, and *oncle Paul* sitting at the table, with a red and white napkin tied round his neck. Boiffard – Boiffard – I must remember the name. Supposing the Commissaire Militaire should ask me who the relations were I was going to and I muddled the name – Oh, how fatal! Buffard – no, Boiffard. And then for the first time, folding Aunt Julie's letter, I saw scrawled in a corner of the empty back page: *Venez vite, vite.* Strange impulsive woman! My heart began to beat . . .

'Ah, we are not far off now,' said the lady opposite. 'You are going to X, mademoiselle?'

'*Oui, madame.*'

'I also . . . You have been there before?'

'No, madame. This is the first time.'

'Really, it is a strange time for a visit.'

I smiled faintly, and tried to keep my eyes off her hat. She was quite an ordinary little woman, but she wore a black velvet toque, with an incredibly surprised looking sea-gull camped on the very top of it. Its round eyes, fixed on me so inquiringly, were almost too much to bear. I had a dreadful impulse to shoo it away, or to

lean forward and inform her of its presence . . .

'*Excusez-moi, madame,* but perhaps you have not remarked there is an *espèce de* sea-gull *couché sur votre chapeau.*'

Could the bird be there on purpose? I must not laugh . . . I must not laugh. Had she ever looked at herself in a glass with that bird on her head?

'It is very difficult to get into X at present, to pass the station,' she said, and she shook her head with the sea-gull at me. 'Ah, such an affair. One must sign one's name and state one's business.'

'Really, is it as bad as all that?'

'But naturally. You see the whole place is in the hands of the military, and' – she shrugged – 'they have to be strict. Many people do not get beyond the station at all. They arrive. They are put in the waiting-room, and there they remain.'

Did I or did I not detect in her voice a strange, insulting relish?

'I suppose such strictness is absolutely necessary,' I said coldly, stroking my muff.

'Necessary,' she cried. 'I should think so. Why, *mademoiselle,* you cannot imagine what it would be like otherwise! You know what women are like about soldiers' – she raised a final hand – 'mad, completely mad. But –' and she gave a little laugh of triumph – 'they could not get into X. *Mon Dieu,* no! There is no question about that.'

'I don't suppose they even try,' said I.

'Don't you?' said the sea-gull.

Madame said nothing for a moment. 'Of course the authorities are very hard on the men. It means instant imprisonment, and then – off to the firing-line without a word.'

'What are *you* going to X for?' said the sea-gull. 'What on earth are *you* doing here?'

45

'Are you making a long stay in X, *mademoiselle?*'

She had won, she had won. I was terrified. A lamp-post swam past the train with the fatal name upon it. I could hardly breathe – the train had stopped. I smiled gaily at madame and danced down the steps to the platform . . .

It was a hot little room completely furnished with two colonels seated at two tables. They were large grey-whiskered men with a touch of burnt red on their cheeks. Sumptuous and omnipotent they looked. One smoked what ladies love to call a heavy Egyptian cigarette, with a long creamy ash, the other toyed with a gilded pen. Their heads rolled on their tight collars, like big over-ripe fruits. I had a terrible feeling, as I handed my passport and ticket, that a soldier would step forward and tell me to kneel. I would have knelt without question.

'What's this?' said God I, querulously. He did not like my passport at all. The very sight of it seemed to annoy him. He waved a dissenting hand at it, with a *'Non, je ne peux pas manger ça'* air.

'But it won't do. It won't do at all, you know. Look, – read for yourself,' and he glanced with extreme distaste at my photograph, and then with even greater distaste his pebble eyes looked at me.

'Of course the photograph is deplorable,' I said, scarcely breathing with terror, 'but it has been visa-ed and visa-ed.'

He raised his big bulk and went over to God II.

'Courage!' I said to my muff and held it firmly, 'Courage!'

God II held up a finger to me, and I produced Aunt Julie's letter and her card. But he did not seem to feel the slightest interest in her. He stamped my passport idly, scribbled a word on my ticket, and I was on the platform again.

'That way – you pass out that way.'

Terribly pale, with a faint smile on his lips, his hand at salute, stood the little corporal. I gave no sign, I am sure I gave no sign. He stepped behind me.

'And then follow me as though you do not see me,' I heard him half whisper, half sing.

How fast he went, through the slippery mud towards a bridge. He had a postman's bag on his back, a paper parcel and the *Matin* in his hand. We seemed to dodge through a maze of policemen, and I could not keep up at all with the little corporal who began to whistle. From the toll-house 'our good friend, Madame Grinçon,' her hands wrapped in a shawl, watched our coming, and against the toll-house there leaned a tiny faded cab. *Montez vite, vite!* said the little corporal, hurling my suit-case, the postman's bag, the paper parcel and the *Matin* on to the floor.

'A-ie! A-ie! Do not be so mad. Do not ride yourself. You will be seen,' wailed 'our good friend, Madame Grinçon'.

'*Ah, je m'en f . . .*' said the little corporal.

The driver jerked into activity. He lashed the bony horse and away we flew, both doors, which were the complete sides of the cab, flapping and banging

'*Bonjour, mon amie.*'

'*Bonjour, mon ami.*'

And then we swooped down and clutched at the banging doors. They would not keep shut. They were fools of doors.

'Lean back, let me do it!' I cried. 'Policemen are as thick as violets everywhere.'

At the barracks the horse reared up and stopped. A crowd of laughing faces blotted the window.

'*Prends ça, mon vieux,*' said the little corporal, handing the paper parcel.

47

'It's all right,' called someone.

We waved, we were off again. By a river, down a strange white street, with little houses on either side, gay in the late sunlight. 'Jump out as soon as he stops again. The door will be open. Run straight inside. I will follow. The man is already paid. I know you will like the house. It is quite white. And the room is white, too, and the people are . . .'

'White as snow.'

We looked at each other. We began to laugh. 'Now,' said the little corporal.

Out I flew and in at the door. There stood, presumably, my aunt Julie. There in the background hovered, I supposed, my uncle Paul.

'*Bonjour, madame!*' '*Bonjour, monsieur!*'

'It is all right, you are safe,' said my aunt Julie. Heavens, how I loved her! And she opened the door of the white room and shut it upon us. Down went the suit-case, the postman's bag, the *Matin*. I threw my passport up into the air, and the little corporal caught it.

What an extraordinary thing. We had been there to lunch and to dinner each day; but now in the dusk and alone I could not find it. I clop-clopped in my borrowed *sabots* through the greasy mud, right to the end of the village, and there was not a sign of it. I could not even remember what it looked like, or if there was a name painted on the outside, or any bottles or tables showing at the window. Already the village houses were sealed for the night behind big wooden shutters. Strange and mysterious they looked in the ragged drifting light and thin rain, like a company of beggars perched on the hillside, their bosoms full of rich unlawful gold. There was nobody about but the soldiers. A group of wounded stood

under a lamp-post, petting a mangy, shivering dog. Up
the street came four big boys singing:

Dodo, mon homme, fais vit' dodo . . .

and swung off down the hill to their sheds behind the
railway station. They seemed to take the last breath of
the day with them. I began to walk slowly back.

'It must have been one of these houses. I remember
it stood far back from the road – and there were no
steps, not even a porch – one seemed to walk right
through the window.' And then quite suddenly the
waiting-boy came out of just such a place. He saw me
and grinned cheerfully, and began to whistle through
his teeth.

'*Bonsoir, mon petit.*'

'*Bonsoir, madame.*' And he followed me up the café
to our special table, right at the far end by the window,
and marked by a bunch of violets that I had left in a
glass there yesterday.

'You are two?' asked the waiting-boy, flicking the
table with a red and white cloth. His long swinging
steps echoed over the bare floor. He disappeared into
the kitchen and came back to light the lamp that hung
from the ceiling under a spreading shade, like a haymaker's hat. Warm light shone on the empty place
that was really a barn, set out with dilapidated tables
and chairs. Into the middle of the room a black stove
jutted. At one side of it there was a table with a row of
bottles on it, behind which madame sat and took the
money and made entries in a red book. Opposite her
desk a door led into the kitchen. The walls were
covered with a creamy paper patterned all over with
green and swollen trees – hundreds and hundreds of
trees reared their mushroom heads to the ceiling. I
began to wonder who had chosen the paper and why.
Did madame think it was beautiful, or that it was a gay

and lovely thing to eat one's dinner at all seasons in the
middle of a forest . . . On either side of the clock there
hung a picture: one, a young gentleman in black
tights wooing a pear-shaped lady in yellow over the
back of a garden seat, *Premier Rencontre*; two, the
black and yellow in amorous confusion, *Triomphe
d'Amour*.

The clock ticked to a soothing lilt, *C'est ça, c'est ça*.
In the kitchen the waiting-boy was washing up. I
heard the ghostly chatter of the dishes.

And years passed. Perhaps the war is long since over
– there is no village outside at all – the streets are
quiet under the grass. I have an idea this is the sort of
thing one will do on the very last day of all – sit in an
empty café and listen to a clock ticking until . . .

Madame came through the kitchen door, nodded to
me and took her seat behind the table, her plump
hands folded on the red book. 'Ping' went the door. A
handful of soldiers came in, took off their coats and
began to play cards, chaffing and poking fun at the
pretty waiting-boy, who threw up his little round
head, rubbed his thick fringe out of his eyes and
cheeked them back in his broken voice. Sometimes his
voice boomed up from his throat, deep and harsh, and
then in the middle of a sentence it broke and scattered
in a funny squeaking. He seemed to enjoy it himself.
You would not have been surprised if he had walked
into the kitchen on his hands and brought back your
dinner turning a catherine-wheel.

'Ping' went the door again. Two more men came in.
They sat at the table nearest madame, and she leaned
to them with a birdlike movement, her head on one
side. Oh, they had a grievance! The lieutenant was a
fool – nosing about – springing out at them – and
they'd only been sewing on buttons. Yes, that was all –
sewing on buttons, and up comes this young spark.

50

'Now then, what are you up to?' They mimicked the idiotic voice. Madame drew down her mouth, nodding sympathy. The waiting-boy served them with glasses. He took a bottle of some orange-coloured stuff and put it on the table-edge. A shout from the card-players made him turn sharply, and crash! over went the bottle, spilling on the table, the floor – smash! to tinkling atoms. An amazed silence. Through it the drip-drip of the wine from the table on to the floor. It looked very strange dropping so slowly, as though the table were crying. Then there came a roar from the card-players. 'You'll catch it, my lad! That's the style! Now you've done it! . . . *Sept, huit, neuf.*' They started playing again. The waiting-boy never said a word. He stood, his head bent, his hands spread out, and then he knelt and gathered up the glass, piece by piece, and soaked the wine up with a cloth. Only when madame cried cheerfully, 'You wait until *he* finds out,' did he raise his head.

'He can't say anything, if I pay for it,' he muttered, his face jerking, and he marched off into the kitchen with the soaking cloth.

'*Il pleure de colère,*' said madame delightedly, patting her hair with her plump hands.

The café slowly filled. It grew very warm. Blue smoke mounted from the tables and hung about the haymaker's hat in misty wreaths. There was a suffocating smell of onion soup and boots and damp cloth. In the din the door sounded again. It opened to let in a weed of a fellow, who stood with his back against it, one hand shading his eyes.

'Hullo! you've got the bandage off?'

'How does it feel, *mon vieux*?'

'Let's have a look at them.'

But he made no reply. He shrugged and walked unsteadily to a table, sat down and leant against the wall.

Slowly his hand fell. In his white face his eyes showed,
pink as a rabbit's. They brimmed and spilled, brimmed
and spilled. He dragged a white cloth out of his pocket
and wiped them.

'It's the smoke,' said someone. 'It's the smoke
tickles them up for you.'

His comrades watched him a bit, watched his eyes
fill again, again brim over. The water ran down his
face, off his chin on to the table. He rubbed the place
with his coat-sleeve, and then, as though forgetful,
went on rubbing, rubbing with his hand across the
table, staring in front of him. And then he started
shaking his head to the movement of his hand. He gave
a loud strange groan and dragged out the cloth again.

'*Huit, neuf, dix,*' said the card-players.

'*P'tit,* some more bread.'

'Two coffees.'

'*Un Picon!*'

The waiting-boy, quite recovered, but with scarlet
cheeks, ran to and fro. A tremendous quarrel flared up
among the card-players, raged for two minutes, and
died in flickering laughter. 'Ooof!' groaned the man
with the eyes, rocking and mopping. But nobody paid
any attention to him except madame. She made a
little grimace at her two soldiers.

'*Mais vous savez, c'est un peu dégoûtant, ça,*' she said
severely.

'*Ah, oui, madame,*' answered the soldiers, watching
her bent head and pretty hands, as she arranged for
the hundredth time a frill of lace on her lifted bosom.

'*V'là monsieur!*' cawed the waiting-boy over his
shoulder to me. For some silly reason I pretended not
to hear, and I leaned over the table smelling the violets,
until the little corporal's hand closed over mine.

'Shall we have *un peu de charcuterie* to begin with?'
he asked tenderly.

'In England,' said the blue-eyed soldier, 'you drink whisky with your meals. *N'est-ce pas, mademoiselle?* A little glass of whisky neat before eating. Whisky and soda with your *bifteks*, and after, more whisky with hot water and lemon.'

'Is it true, that?' asked his great friend who sat opposite, a big red-faced chap with a black beard and large moist eyes and hair that looked as though it had been cut with a sewing-machine.

'Well, not quite true,' said I.

'*Si, si,*' cried the blue-eyed soldier. 'I ought to know. I'm in business. English travellers come to my place, and it's always the same thing.'

'Bah, I can't stand whisky,' said the little corporal. 'It's too disgusting the morning after. Do you remember, *ma fille*, the whisky in that little bar at Montmartre?'

'*Souvenir tendre,*' sighed Blackbeard, putting two fingers in the breast of his coat and letting his head fall. He was very drunk.

'But I know something that you've never tasted,' said the blue-eyed soldier pointing a finger at me; 'something really good.' *Cluck* he went with his tongue. '*É-patant!* And the curious thing is that you'd hardly know it from whisky except that it's' – he felt with his hand for the word – 'finer, sweeter perhaps, not so sharp, and it leaves you feeling gay as a rabbit next morning.'

'What is it called?'

'Mirabelle!' He rolled the word round his mouth, under his tongue. 'Ah-ha, that's the stuff.'

'I could eat another mushroom,' said Blackbeard. 'I would like another mushroom very much. I am sure I could eat another mushroom if mademoiselle gave it to me out of her hand.'

'You ought to try it,' said the blue-eyed soldier,

leaning both hands on the table and speaking so seriously that I began to wonder how much more sober he was than Blackbeard. 'You ought to try it, and tonight. I would like you to tell me if you don't think it's like whisky.'

'Perhaps they've got it here,' said the little corporal, and he called the waiting-boy. *'P'tit!'*

'Non monsieur,' said the boy, who never stopped smiling. He served us with dessert plates painted with blue parrots and horned beetles.

'What is the name for this in English?' said Blackbeard, pointing. I told him 'Parrot'.

'Ah, *mon Dieu*! . . . Pair-rot . . .' He put his arms round his plate. 'I love you, *ma petite* pair-rot. You are sweet, you are blonde, you are English. You do not know the difference between whisky and mirabelle.'

The little corporal and I looked at each other, laughing. He squeezed up his eyes when he laughed, so that you saw nothing but the long curly lashes.

'Well, I know a place where they do keep it,' said the blue-eyed soldier. *'Café des Amis.* We'll go there – I'll pay – I'll pay for the whole lot of us.' His gesture embraced thousands of pounds

But with a loud whirring noise the clock on the wall struck half-past eight; and no soldier is allowed in a café after eight o'clock at night.

'It is fast,' said the blue-eyed soldier. The little corporal's watch said the same. So did the immense turnip that Blackbeard produced, and carefully deposited on the head of one of the horned beetles.

'Ah, well, we'll take the risk,' said the blue-eyed soldier, and he thrust his arms into his immense cardboard coat. 'It's worth it,' he said. 'It's worth it. You just wait.'

Outside, stars shone between wispy clouds, and the moon fluttered like a candle flame over a pointed spire.

The shadows of the dark plume-like trees waved on the white houses. Not a soul to be seen. No sound to be heard but the *Hsh! Hsh!* of a far-away train, like a big beast shuffling in its sleep.

'You are cold,' whispered the little corporal. 'You are cold, *ma fille.*'

'No, really not.'

'But you are trembling.'

'Yes, but I'm not cold.'

'What are the women like in England?' asked Black-beard. 'After the war is over I shall go to England. I shall find a little English woman and marry her – and her pair-rot.' He gave a loud choking laugh.

'Fool!' said the blue-eyed soldier, shaking him; and he leant over to me. 'It is only after the second glass that you really taste it,' he whispered. 'The second little glass and then – ah! – then you know.'

Café des Amis gleamed in the moonlight. We glanced quickly up and down the road. We ran up the four wooden steps, and opened the ringing glass door into a low room lighted with a hanging lamp, where about ten people were dining. They were seated on two benches at a narrow table.

'Soldiers!' screamed a woman, leaping up from behind a white soup-tureen – a scrag of a woman in a black shawl. 'Soldiers! At this hour! Look at that clock, look at it.' And she pointed to the clock with the dripping ladle.

'It's fast,' said the blue-eyed soldier. 'It's fast, madame. And don't make so much noise, I beg of you. We will drink and we will go.'

'Will you?' she cried, running round the table and planting herself in front of us. 'That's just what you won't do. Coming into an honest woman's house this hour of the night – making a scene – getting the police after you. Ah, no! Ah, no! It's a disgrace, that's what it is.'

'Sh!' said the little corporal, holding up his hand. Dead silence. In the silence we heard steps passing.

'The police,' whispered Blackbeard, winking at a pretty girl with rings in her ears, who smiled back at him, saucy. 'Sh!'

The faces lifted, listening. 'How beautiful they are!' I thought. 'They are like a family party having supper in the New Testament . . .' The steps died away.

'Serve you very well right if you had been caught,' scolded the angry woman. 'I'm sorry on your account that the police didn't come. You deserve it – you deserve it.'

'A little glass of mirabelle and we will go,' persisted the blue-eyed soldier.

Still scolding and muttering she took four glasses from the cupboard and a big bottle. 'But you're not going to drink it in here. Don't you believe it.' The little corporal ran into the kitchen. 'Not there! Not there! Idiot!' she cried. 'Can't you see there's a window there, and a wall opposite where the police come every evening to . . .'

'Sh!' Another scare.

'You are mad and you will end in prison all four of you,' said the woman. She flounced out of the room. We tiptoed after her into a dark smelling scullery, full of pans of greasy water, of salad leaves and meat-bones.

'There now,' she said, putting down the glasses. 'Drink and go!'

'Ah, at last!' The blue-eyed soldier's happy voice trickled through the dark. 'What do you think? Isn't it just as I said? Hasn't it got a taste of excellent – *excellent* whisky?'

4

Je ne parle pas français

I do not know why I have such a fancy for this little café. It's dirty and sad, sad. It's not as if it had anything to distinguish it from a hundred others – it hasn't; or as if the same strange types came here every day, whom one could watch from one's corner and recognize and more or less (with a strong accent on the less) get the hang of.

But pray don't imagine that those brackets are a confession of my humility before the mystery of the human soul. Not at all; I don't believe in the human soul. I never have. I believe that people are like portmanteaux – packed with certain things, started going, thrown about, tossed away, dumped down, lost and found, half-emptied suddenly, or squeezed fatter than ever, until finally the Ultimate Porter swings them on to the Ultimate Train and away they rattle . . .

Not but what these portmanteaux can be very fascinating. Oh, but very! I see myself standing in front of them, don't you know, like a Customs official.

'Have you anything to declare? Any wines, spirits, cigars, perfumes, silks?'

And the moment of hesitation as to whether I am going to be fooled just before I chalk that squiggle, and then the other moment of hesitation just after, as to whether I have been, are perhaps the two most thrilling instances in life. Yes, they are, to me.

But before I started that long and rather far-fetched and not frightfully original digression, what I meant to say quite simply was that there are no portmanteaux to be examined here because the clientele of this café, ladies and gentlemen, does not sit down. No, it stands at the counter, and it consists of a handful of workmen who come up from the river, all powdered over with white flour, lime or something, and a few soldiers, bringing with them thin, dark girls with silver rings in their ears and market baskets on their arms.

Madame is thin and dark, too, with white cheeks and white hands. In certain lights she looks quite transparent, shining out of her black shawl with an extraordinary effect. When she is not serving she sits on a stool with her face turned, always, to the window. Her dark-ringed eyes search among and follow after the people passing, but not as if she was looking for somebody. Perhaps, fifteen years ago, she was; but now the pose has become a habit. You can tell from her air of fatigue and hopelessness that she must have given them up for the last ten years, at least . . .

And then there is the waiter. Not pathetic – decidedly not comic. Never making one of those perfectly insignificant remarks which amaze you so coming from a waiter, (as though the poor wretch were a sort of cross between a coffee-pot and a wine bottle and not expected to hold so much as a drop of anything else). He is grey, flat-footed and withered, with long, brittle nails that set your nerves on edge while he scrapes up your two sous. When he is not smearing over the table or flicking at a dead fly or two, he stands with one hand on the back of a chair, in his far too long apron, and over his other arm the three-cornered dip of dirty napkin, waiting to be photographed in connection with some wretched murder. 'Interior of Café where Body was Found.' You've seen him hundreds of times.

Do you believe that every place has its hour of the day when it really does come alive? That's not exactly what I mean. It's more like this. There does seem to be a moment when you realize that, quite by accident, you happen to have come on to the stage at exactly the moment you were expected. Everything is arranged for you – waiting for you. Ah, master of the situation! You fill with important breath. And at the same time you smile, secretly, slyly, because Life seems to be opposed to granting you these entrances, seems indeed to be engaged in snatching them from you and making them impossible, keeping you in the wings until it is too late, in fact . . . Just for once you've beaten the old hag.

I enjoyed one of these moments the first time I ever came in here. That's why I keep coming back, I suppose. Revisiting the scene of my triumph, or the scene of the crime where I had the old bitch by the throat for once and did what I pleased with her.

Query: Why am I so bitter against Life? And why do I see her as a rag-picker on the American cinema, shuffling along wrapped in a filthy shawl with her old claws crooked over a stick?

Answer: The direct result of the American cinema acting upon a weak mind.

Anyhow, the 'short winter afternoon was drawing to a close', as they say, and I was drifting along, either going home or not going home, when I found myself in here, walking over to this seat in the corner.

I hung up my English overcoat and grey felt hat on that same peg behind me, and after I had allowed the waiter time for at least twenty photographers to snap their fill of him, I ordered a coffee.

He poured me out a glass of the familiar, purplish stuff with a green wandering light playing over it, and shuffled off, and I sat pressing my hands against the glass because it was bitterly cold outside.

Suddenly I realized that quite apart from myself, I was smiling. Slowly I raised my head and saw myself in the mirror opposite. Yes, there I sat, leaning on the table, smiling my deep, sly smile, the glass of coffee with its vague plume of steam before me and beside it the ring of white saucer with two pieces of sugar.

I opened my eyes very wide. There I had been for all eternity, as it were, and now at last I was coming to life . . .

It was very quiet in the café. Outside, one could just see through the dusk that it had begun to snow. One could just see the shapes of horses and carts and people, soft and white, moving through the feathery air. The waiter disappeared and reappeared with an armful of straw. He strewed it over the floor from the door to the counter and round about the stove with humble, almost adoring gestures. One would not have been surprised if the door had opened and the Virgin Mary had come in, riding upon an ass, her meek hands folded over her big belly . . .

That's rather nice, don't you think, that bit about the Virgin? It comes from the pen so gently; it has such a 'dying fall'. I thought so at the time and decided to make a note of it. One never knows when a little tag like that may come in useful to round off a paragraph. So, taking care to move as little as possible because the 'spell' was still unbroken (you know that?), I reached over to the next table for a writing pad.

No paper or envelopes, of course. Only a morsel of pink blotting-paper, incredibly soft and limp and almost moist, like the tongue of a little dead kitten, which I've never felt.

I sat — but always underneath, in this state of expectation, rolling the little dead kitten's tongue round my finger and rolling the soft phrase round my mind while my eyes took in the girls' names and dirty

jokes and drawings of bottles and cups that would not sit in the saucers, scattered over the writing pad.

They are always the same, you know. The girls always have the same names, the cups never sit in the saucers; all the hearts are stuck and tied up with ribbons.

But then, quite suddenly, at the bottom of the page, written in green ink, I fell on to that stupid, stale little phrase: *Je ne parle pas français.*

There! it had come – the moment – the *geste*! And although I was so ready, it caught me, it tumbled me over; I was simply overwhelmed. And the physical feeling was so curious, so particular. It was as if all of me, except my head and arms, all of me that was under the table, had simply dissolved, melted, turned into water. Just my head remained and two sticks of arms pressing on to the table. But, ah! the agony of that moment! How can I describe it? I didn't think of anything. I didn't even cry out to myself. Just for one moment I was not. I was Agony, Agony, Agony.

Then it passed, and the very second after I was thinking: 'Good God! Am I capable of feeling as strongly as that? But I was absolutely unconscious! I hadn't a phrase to meet it with! I was overcome! I was swept off my feet! I didn't even try, in the dimmest way, to put it down!'

And up I puffed and puffed, blowing off finally with: 'After all I must be first-rate. No second-rate mind could have experienced such an intensity of feeling so . . . purely.'

The waiter has touched a spill at the red stove and lighted a bubble of gas under a spreading shade. It is no use looking out of the window, madame; it is quite dark now. Your white hands hover over your dark shawl. They are like two birds that have come home to

roost. They are restless, restless . . . You tuck them, finally, under your warm little armpits.

Now the waiter has taken a long pole and clashed the curtains together. 'All gone,' as children say.

And besides, I've no patience with people who can't let go of things, who will follow after and cry out. When a thing's gone, it's gone. It's over and done with. Let it go then! Ignore it, and comfort yourself, if you do want comforting, with the thought that you never do recover the same thing that you lose. It's always a new thing. The moment it leaves you it's changed. Why, that's even true of a hat you chase after; and I don't mean superficially – I mean profoundly speaking . . . I have made it a rule of my life never to regret and never to look back. Regret is an appalling waste of energy, and no one who intends to be a writer can afford to indulge in it. You can't get it into shape; you can't build on it; it's only good for wallowing in. Looking back, of course, is equally fatal to Art. It's keeping yourself poor. Art can't and won't stand poverty.

Je ne parle pas français. Je ne parle pas français. All the while I wrote that last page my other self has been chasing up and down out in the dark there. It left me just when I began to analyse my grand moment, dashed off distracted, like a lost dog who thinks at last, at last, he hears the familiar step again.

'Mouse! Mouse! Where are you? Are you near? Is that you leaning from the high window and stretching out your arms for the wings of the shutters? Are you this soft bundle moving towards me through the feathery snow? Are you this little girl pressing through the swing-doors of the restaurant? Is that your dark shadow bending forward in the cab? Where are you? Where are you? Which way must I turn? Which way shall I run? And every moment I stand here hesitating you are farther away again. Mouse! Mouse!'

Now the poor dog has come back into the café, his tail between his legs, quite exhausted.

'It was a . . . false . . . alarm. She's nowhere . . . to . . . be seen.'

'Lie down then! Lie down! Lie down!'

My name is Raoul Duquette. I am twenty-six years old and a Parisian, a true Parisian. About my family – it really doesn't matter. I have no family; I don't want any. I never think about my childhood. I've forgotten it.

In fact, there's only one memory that stands out at all. That is rather interesting because it seems to me now so very significant as regards myself from the literary point of view. It is this.

When I was about ten our laundress was an African woman, very big, very dark, with a check handker-chief over her frizzy hair. When she came to our house she always took particular notice of me, and after the clothes had been taken out of the basket she would lift me up into it and give me a rock while I held tight to the handles and screamed for joy and fright. I was tiny for my age, and pale, with a lovely little half-open mouth – I feel sure of that.

One day when I was standing at the door, watching her go, she turned round and beckoned to me, nodding and smiling in a strange secret way. I never thought of not following. She took me into a little outhouse at the end of the passage, caught me up in her arms and began kissing me. Ah, those kisses! Especially those kisses inside my ears that nearly deafened me.

When she set me down she took from her pocket a little round fried cake covered with sugar, and I reeled along the passage back to our door.

As this performance was repeated once a week it is no wonder that I remember it so vividly. Besides, from

that very first afternoon, my childhood was, to put it
prettily, 'kissed away'. I became very languid, very
caressing, and greedy beyond measure. And so quickened,
so sharpened, I seemed to understand everybody and be
able to do what I liked with everybody.

I suppose I was in a state of more or less physical
excitement, and that was what appealed to them. For
all Parisians are more than half – oh, well, enough of
that. And enough of my childhood, too. Bury it under
a laundry basket instead of a shower of roses and
passons oultre.

I date myself from the moment that I became the
tenant of a small bachelor flat on the fifth floor of a tall,
not too shabby house, in a street that might or might
not be discreet. Very useful, that . . . There I emerged,
came out into the light and put out my two horns with
a study and a bedroom and a kitchen on my back. And
real furniture planted in the rooms. In the bedroom a
wardrobe with a long glass, a big bed covered with a
yellow puffed-up quilt, a bed table with a marbled top
and a toilet set sprinkled with tiny apples. In my study
– English writing table with drawers, writing chair
with leather cushions, books, arm-chair, side table with
paper-knife and lamp on it and some nude studies on
the walls. I didn't use the kitchen except to throw old
papers into.

Ah, I can see myself that first evening, after the
furniture men had gone and I'd managed to get rid of
my atrocious old concierge – walking about on tip-toe,
arranging and standing in front of the glass with my
hands in my pockets and saying to that radiant vision:
'I am a young man who has his own flat. I write for
two newspapers. I am going in for serious literature. I
am starting a career. The book that I shall bring out
will simply stagger the critics. I am going to write

about things that have never been touched before. I am going to make a name for myself as a writer about the submerged world. But not as others have done before me. Oh, no! Very naively, with a sort of tender humour and from the inside, as though it were all quite simple, quite natural. I see my way quite perfectly. Nobody has ever done it as I shall do it because none of the others have lived my experiences. I'm rich – I'm rich.'

All the same I had no more money than I have now. It's extraordinary how one can live without money . . . I have quantities of good clothes, silk underwear, two evening suits, four pairs of patent leather boots with light uppers, all sorts of little things, like gloves and powder boxes and a manicure set, perfumes, very good soap, and nothing is paid for. If I find myself in need of right-down cash – well, there's always an African laundress and an outhouse, and I am very frank and *bon enfant* about plenty of sugar on the little fried cake afterwards . . .

And here I should like to put something on record. Not from any strutting conceit, but rather with a mild sense of wonder. I've never yet made the first advances to any woman. It isn't as though I've known only one class of woman – not by any means. But from little prostitutes and kept women and elderly widows and shop girls and wives of respectable men, and even advanced modern literary ladies at the most select dinners and soirées (I've been there), I've met invariably with not only the same readiness, but with the same positive invitation. It surprised me at first. I used to look across the table and think 'Is that very distinguished young lady, discussing *le Kipling* with the gentleman with the brown beard, really pressing my foot?' And I was never really certain until I had pressed hers.

Curious, isn't it? I don't look at all like a maiden's dream . . .

I am little and light with an olive skin, black eyes with long lashes, black silky hair cut short, tiny square teeth that show when I smile. My hands are supple and small. A woman in a bread shop once said to me: 'You have the hands for making fine little pastries.' I confess, without my clothes I am rather charming. Plump, almost like a girl, with smooth shoulders, and I wear a thin gold bracelet above my left elbow.

But, wait! Isn't it strange I should have written all that about my body and so on? It's the result of my bad life, my submerged life. I am like a little woman in a café who has to introduce herself with a handful of photographs. 'Me in my chemise, coming out of an eggshell . . . Me upside down in a swing, with a frilly behind like a cauliflower . . .' You know the things.

If you think what I've written is merely superficial and impudent and cheap you're wrong. I'll admit it does sound so, but then it is not all. If it were, how could I have experienced what I did when I read that stale little phrase written in green ink, in the writing-pad? That proves there's more in me and that I really am important, doesn't it? Anything a fraction less than that moment of anguish I might have put on. But no! That was real.

'Waiter, a whisky.'

I hate whisky. Every time I take it into my mouth my stomach rises against it, and the stuff they keep here is sure to be particularly vile. I only ordered it because I am going to write about an Englishman. We French are incredibly old-fashioned and out of date still in some ways. I wonder I didn't ask him at the same time for a pair of tweed knickerbockers, a pipe, some long teeth and a set of ginger whiskers.

'Thanks, *mon vieux*. You haven't got perhaps a set of ginger whiskers?'

'No, monsieur,' he answers sadly. 'We don't sell American drinks.'

And having smeared a corner of the table he goes back to have another couple of dozen taken by artificial light.

Ugh! The smell of it! And the sickly sensation when one's throat contracts.

'It's bad stuff to get drunk on,' says Dick Harmon, turning his little glass in his fingers and smiling his slow, dreaming smile. So he gets drunk on it slowly and dreamily and at a certain moment begins to sing very low, very low, about a man who walks up and down trying to find a place where he can get some dinner.

Ah! how I loved that song, and how I loved the way he sang it, slowly, slowly, in a dark, soft voice:

> *There was a man*
> *Walked up and down*
> *To get a dinner in the town . . .*

It seemed to hold, in its gravity and muffled measure, all those tall grey buildings, those fogs, those endless streets, those sharp shadows of policemen that mean England.

And then – the subject! The lean, starved creature walking up and down with every house barred against him because he had no 'home'. How extraordinarily English that is . . . I remember that it ended where he did at last 'find a place' and ordered a little cake of fish, but when he asked for bread the waiter cried contemptuously, in a loud voice: 'We don't serve bread with one fish ball.'

What more do you want? How profound those songs are! There is the whole psychology of a people; and how un-French – how un-French!

'Once more, Deeck, once more!' I would plead, clasping my hands and making a pretty mouth at him. He was perfectly content to sing it for ever.

There again. Even with Dick. It was he who made the first advances.

I met him at an evening party given by the editor of a new review. It was a very select, very fashionable affair. One or two of the older men were there and the ladies were extremely *comme il faut*. They sat on cubist sofas in full evening dress and allowed us to hand them thimbles of cherry brandy and to talk to them about their poetry. For, as far as I can remember, they were all poetesses.

It was impossible not to notice Dick. He was the only Englishman present, and instead of circulating gracefully round the room as we all did, he stayed in one place leaning against the wall, his hands in his pockets, that dreamy half smile on his lips, and replying in excellent French in his low, soft voice to anybody who spoke to him.

'Who is he?'

'An Englishman. From London. A writer. And he is making a special study of modern French literature.'

That was enough for me. My little book, *False Coins*, had just been published. I was a young, serious writer who was making a special study of modern English literature.

But I really had not time to fling my line before he said, giving himself a soft shake, coming right out of the water after the bait, as it were: 'Won't you come and see me at my hotel? Come about five o'clock and we can have a talk before going out to dinner.'

'Enchanted!'

I was so deeply, deeply flattered that I had to leave

him then and there to preen and preen myself before
the cubist sofas. What a catch! An Englishman, re-
served, serious, making a special study of French literature . . .

That same night a copy of *False Coins* with a carefully cordial inscription was posted off, and a day or
two later we did dine together and spent the evening
talking.

Talking – but not only of literature. I discovered to
my relief that it wasn't necessary to keep to the
tendency of the modern novel, the need of a new form,
or the reason why our young men appeared to be just
missing it. Now and again, as if by accident, I threw in
a card that seemed to have nothing to do with the
game, just to see how he'd take it. But each time he
gathered it into his hands with his dreamy look and
smile unchanged. Perhaps he murmured: 'That's very
curious.' But not as if it were curious at all.

That calm acceptance went to my head at last. It
fascinated me. It led me on and on till I threw every
card that I possessed at him and sat back and watched
him arrange them in his hand.

'Very curious and interesting . . .'

By that time we were both fairly drunk, and he
began to sing his song very soft, very low, about the
man who walked up and down seeking his dinner.

But I was quite breathless at the thought of what I
had done. I had shown somebody both sides of my life.
Told him everything as sincerely and truthfully as I
could. Taken immense pains to explain things about
my submerged life that really were disgusting and
never could possibly see the light of literary day. On
the whole I had made myself out far worse than I was –
more boastful, more cynical, more calculating.

And there sat the man I had confided in, singing to
himself and smiling . . . It moved me so that real tears

came into my eyes. I saw them glittering on my long silky lashes – so charming.

After that I took Dick about with me everywhere, and he came to my flat, and sat in the arm-chair, very indolent, playing with the paper-knife. I cannot think why his indolence and dreaminess always gave me the impression he had been to sea. And all his leisurely slow ways seemed to be allowing for the movement of the ship. This impression was so strong that often when we were together and he got up and left a little woman just when she did not expect him to get up and leave her, but quite the contrary, I would explain: 'He can't help it, baby. He has to go back to his ship.' And I believed it far more than she did.

All the while we were together Dick never went with a woman. I sometimes wondered whether he wasn't completely innocent. Why didn't I ask him? Because I never did ask him anything about himself. But late one night he took out his pocket-book and a photograph dropped out of it. I picked it up and glanced at it before I gave it to him. It was of a woman. Not quite young. Dark, handsome, wild-looking, but so full in every line of a kind of haggard pride that even if Dick had not stretched out so quickly I wouldn't have looked longer.

'Out of my sight, you little perfumed fox-terrier of a Frenchman,' said she.

(In my very worst moments my nose reminds me of a fox-terrier's.)

'That is my mother,' said Dick, putting up the pocket-book.

But if he had not been Dick I should have been tempted to cross myself, just for fun.

This is how we parted. As we stood outside his hotel

one night waiting for the concierge to release the catch
of the outer door, he said, looking up at the sky: 'I
hope it will be fine tomorrow. I am leaving for
England in the morning.'

'You're not serious.'

'Perfectly. I have to get back. I've some work to do
that I can't manage here.'

'But – but have you made all your preparations?'

'Preparations?' He almost grinned. 'I've none to
make.'

'But – *enfin*, Dick, England is not the other side of
the boulevard.'

'It isn't much farther off,' said he. 'Only a few hours,
you know.' The door cracked open.

'Ah, I wish I'd known at the beginning of the
evening!'

I felt hurt. I felt as a woman must feel when a
man takes out his watch and remembers an appointment that cannot possibly concern her, except that its
claim is the stronger. 'Why didn't you tell me?'

He put out his hand and stood, lightly swaying upon
the step as though the whole hotel were his ship, and
the anchor weighed.

'I forgot. Truly I did. But you'll write, won't you?
Good night, old chap. I'll be over again one of these
days.'

And then I stood on the shore alone, more like a
little fox-terrier than ever . . .

'But after all it was you who whistled to me, you who
asked me to come! What a spectacle I've cut wagging
my tail and leaping round you, only to be left like this
while the boat sails off in its slow, dreamy way . . .
Curse these English! No, this is too insolent altogether.
Who do you imagine I am? A little paid guide to the
night pleasures of Paris? . . . No, monsieur. I am a
young writer, very serious, and extremely interested

71

in modern English literature. And I have been insulted – insulted.'

Two days after came a long, charming letter from him,
written in French that was a shade too French, but
saying how he missed me and counted on our friend-
ship, on keeping in touch.
I read it standing in front of the (unpaid for) wardrobe mirror. It was early morning. I wore a blue
kimono embroidered with white birds and my hair
was still wet; it lay on my forehead, wet and gleaming.
'Portrait of Madame Butterfly,' said I, 'on hearing
of the arrival of *ce cher Pinkerton*.'
According to the books I should have felt immensely
relieved and delighted. '. . . Going over to the window
he drew apart the curtains and looked out at the Paris
trees, just breaking into buds and green . . . Dick!
Dick! My English friend!'
I didn't. I merely felt a little sick. Having been up
for my first ride in an aeroplane I didn't want to go up
again, just now.

That passed, and months after, in the winter, Dick
wrote that he was coming back to Paris to stay indefi-
nitely. Would I take rooms for him? He was bringing
a woman friend with him.
Of course I would. Away the little fox-terrier flew.
It happened most usefully, too; for I owed much money
at the hotel where I took my meals, and two English
people requiring rooms for an indefinite time was an
excellent sum on account.
Perhaps I did rather wonder, as I stood in the larger
of the two rooms with madame, saying 'Admirable',
what the woman friend would be like, but only
vaguely. Either she would be very severe, flat back and
front, or she would be tall, fair, dressed in mignonette

green, name – Daisy, and smelling of rather sweetish lavender water.

You see, by this time, according to my rule of not looking back, I had almost forgotten Dick. I even got the tune of his song about the unfortunate man a little bit wrong when I tried to hum it . . .

I very nearly did not turn up at the station after all. I had arranged to, and had, in fact, dressed with particular care for the occasion. For I intended to take a new line with Dick this time. No more confidences and tears on eyelashes. No, thank you!

'Since you left Paris,' said I, knotting my black silver-spotted tie in the (also unpaid for) mirror over the mantelpiece, 'I have been very successful, you know. I have two more books in preparation, and then I have written a serial story, *Wrong Doors*, which is just on the point of publication and will bring me in a lot of money. And then my little book of poems,' I cried, seizing the clothes-brush and brushing the velvet collar of my new indigo-blue overcoat, 'my little book – *Left Umbrellas* – really did create,' and I laughed and waved the brush, 'an immense sensation!'

It was impossible not to believe this of the person who surveyed himself finally, from top to toe, drawing on his soft grey gloves. He was looking the part; he was the part.

That gave me an idea. I took out my notebook, and still in full view, jotted down a note or two . . . How can one look the part and not be the part? Or be the part and not look it? Isn't looking – being? Or being – looking? At any rate who is to say that it is not? . . .

This seemed to me extraordinarily profound at the time, and quite new. But I confess that something did whisper as, smiling, I put up the note-book: 'You – literary? you look as though you've taken down a bet

on a racecourse!' But I didn't listen. I went out, shutting the door of the flat with a soft, quick pull so as not to warn the concierge of my departure, and ran down the stairs quick as a rabbit for the same reason.

But ah! the old spider. She was too quick for me. She let me run down the last little ladder of the web and then she pounced. 'One moment. One little moment, monsieur,' she whispered, odiously confidential. 'Come in. Come in.' And she beckoned with a dripping soup ladle. I went to the door, but that was not good enough. Right inside and the door shut before she would speak.

There are two ways of managing your concierge if you haven't any money. One is – to take the high hand, make her your enemy, bluster, refuse to discuss anything; the other is – to keep in with her, butter her up to the two knots of the black rag tying up her jaws, pretend to confide in her, and rely on her to arrange with the gas man and to put off the landlord.

I had tried the second. But both are equally detestable and unsuccessful. At any rate whichever you're trying is the worse, the impossible one.

It was the landlord this time . . . Imitation of the landlord by the concierge threatening to toss me out . . . Imitation of the concierge by the concierge taming the wild bull . . . Imitation of the landlord rampant again, breathing in the concierge's face. I was the concierge. No, it was too nauseous. And all the while the black pot on the gas ring bubbling away, stewing out the hearts and livers of every tenant in the place.

'Ah!' I cried, staring at the clock on the mantelpiece, and then, realizing that it didn't go, striking my forehead as though the idea had nothing to do with it. 'Madame, I have a very important appointment with the director of my newspaper at nine-thirty. Perhaps to-morrow I shall be able to give you . . .'

Out, out. And down the metro and squeezed into a full carriage. The more the better. Everybody was one bolster the more between me and the concierge. I was radiant.

'Ah! pardon, monsieur!' said the tall charming creature in black with a big full bosom and a great bunch of violets dropping from it. As the train swayed it thrust the bouquet right into my eyes. 'Ah! pardon, monsieur!'

But I looked up at her, smiling mischievously.

'There is nothing I love more, madame, than flowers on a balcony.'

At the very moment of speaking I caught sight of the huge man in a fur coat against whom my charmer was leaning. He poked his head over her shoulder and he went white to the nose; in fact his nose stood out a sort of cheese green.

'What was that you said to my wife?'

Gare Saint Lazare saved me. But you'll own that even as the author of *False Coins, Wrong Doors, Left Umbrellas,* and two in preparation, it was not too easy to go on my triumphant way.

At length, after countless trains had steamed into my mind, and countless Dick Harmons had come rolling towards me, the real train came. The little knot of us waiting at the barrier moved up close, craned forward, and broke into cries as though we were some kind of many-headed monster, and Paris behind us nothing but a great trap we had set to catch these sleepy innocents.

Into the trap they walked and were snatched and taken off to be devoured. Where was my prey?

'Good God!' My smile and my lifted hand fell together. For one terrible moment I thought this was the woman of the photograph, Dick's mother, walking

75

towards me in Dick's coat and hat. In the effort – and you saw what an effort it was – to smile, his lips curled in just the same way and he made for me, haggard and wild and proud.

What had happened? What could have changed him like this? Should I mention it?

I waited for him and was even conscious of venturing a fox-terrier wag or two to see if he could possibly respond, in the way I said: 'Good evening, Dick! How are you, old chap? All right?'

'All right. All right.' He almost gasped. 'You've got the rooms?'

Twenty times, good God! I saw it all. Light broke on the dark waters and my sailor hadn't been drowned. I almost turned a somersault with amusement.

It was nervousness, of course. It was embarrassment. It was the famous English seriousness. What fun I was going to have! I could have hugged him.

'Yes, I've got the rooms,' I nearly shouted, 'But where is madame?'

'She's been looking after the luggage,' he panted. 'Here she comes, now.'

Not this baby walking beside the old porter as though he were her nurse and had just lifted her out of her ugly perambulator while he trundled the boxes on it.

'And she's not madame,' said Dick, drawling suddenly.

At that moment she caught sight of him and hailed him with her minute muff. She broke away from her nurse and ran up and said something, very quick, in English; but he replied in French: 'Oh, very well. I'll manage.'

But before he turned to the porter he indicated me with a vague wave and muttered something. We were introduced. She held out her hand in that strange boyish way Englishwomen do, and standing very straight

in front of me with her chin raised and making – she
too – the effort of her life to control her preposterous
excitement, she said, wringing my hand (I'm sure she
didn't know it was mine), *Je ne parle pas français.*

'But I'm sure you do,' I answered, so tender, so
reassuring, I might have been a dentist about to draw
her first little milk tooth.

'Of course she does.' Dick swerved back to us. 'Here,
can't we get a cab or taxi or something? We don't want
to stay in this cursed station all night. Do we?'

This was so rude that it took me a moment to
recover; and he must have noticed, for he flung his arm
round my shoulder in the old way, saying: 'Ah, forgive
me, old chap. But we've had such a loathsome, hideous
journey. We've taken years to come. Haven't we?' To
her. But she did not answer. She bent her head and
began stroking her grey muff; she walked beside us
stroking her grey muff all the way.

'Have I been wrong?' thought I. 'Is this simply a
case of frenzied impatience on their part? Are they
merely "in need of a bed", as we say? Have they been
suffering agonies on the journey? Sitting, perhaps, very
close and warm under the same travelling rug?' and
so on and so on while the driver strapped on the boxes.
That done . . .

'Look here, Dick. I go home by metro. Here is the
address of your hotel. Everything is arranged. Come
and see me as soon as you can.'

Upon my life I thought he was going to faint. He
went white to the lips.

'But you're coming back with us,' he cried. 'I
thought it was all settled. Of course, you're coming
back. You're not going to leave us.' No, I gave it up.
It was too difficult, too English for me.

'Certainly, certainly. Delighted. I only thought, perhaps . . .'

'You must come!' said Dick to the little fox-terrier. And again he made that big awkward turn towards her. 'Get in, Mouse.'

And Mouse got in the black hole and sat stroking Mouse II and not saying a word.

Away we jolted and rattled like three little dice that life had decided to have a fling with.

I had insisted on taking the flap seat facing them because I would not have missed for anything those occasional flashing glimpses I had as we broke through the white circles of lamp-light.

They revealed Dick, sitting far back in his corner, his coat collar turned up, his hands thrust in his pockets, and his broad dark hat shading him as if it were a part of him – a sort of wing he hid under. They showed her, sitting up very straight, her lovely little face more like a drawing than a real face – every line was so full of meaning and so sharp cut against the swimming dark.

For Mouse was beautiful. She was exquisite, but so fragile and fine that each time I looked at her it was as if for the first time. She came upon you with the same kind of shock that you feel when you have been drinking tea out of a thin innocent cup and suddenly, at the bottom, you see a tiny creature, half butterfly, half woman, bowing to you with her hands in her sleeves.

As far as I could make out she had dark hair and blue or black eyes. Her long lashes and the two little feathers traced above were most important.

She wore a long dark cloak such as one sees in old-fashioned pictures of Englishwomen abroad. Where her arms came out of it there was grey fur – fur round her neck, too, and her close-fitting cap was furry.

'Carrying out the mouse idea,' I decided.

Ah, but how intriguing it was – how intriguing! Their excitement came nearer and nearer to me, while I ran out to meet it, bathed in it, flung myself far out of my depth, until at last I was as hard put to it to keep control as they.

But what I wanted to do was to behave in the most extraordinary fashion – like a clown. To start singing, with large extravagant gestures, to point out of the window and cry: 'We are now passing, ladies and gentlemen, one of the sights for which *notre Paris* is justly famous,' to jump out of the taxi while it was going, climb over the roof and dive in by another door; to hang out of the window and look for the hotel through the wrong end of a broken telescope, which was also a peculiarly ear-splitting trumpet.

I watched myself do all this, you understand, and even managed to applaud in a private way by putting my gloved hands gently together, while I said to Mouse: 'And is this your first visit to Paris?'

'Yes, I've not been here before.'

'Ah, then you have a great deal to see.'

And I was just going to touch lightly upon the objects of interest and the museums when we wrenched to a stop.

Do you know – it's very absurd – but as I pushed open the door for them and followed up the stairs to the bureau on the landing I felt somehow that this hotel was mine.

There was a vase of flowers on the window sill of the bureau and I even went so far as to rearrange a bud or two and to stand off and note the effect while the manageress welcomed them. And when she turned to me and handed me the keys (the *garçon* was hauling up the boxes) and said: 'Monsieur Duquette will show you your rooms' – I had a longing to tap Dick on the arm

79

with a key and say, very confidentially: 'Look here, old
chap. As a friend of mine I'll be only too willing to
make a slight reduction . . .'

Up and up we climbed. Round and round. Past an
occasional pair of boots (why is it one never sees an
attractive pair of boots outside a door?). Higher and
higher.

'I'm afraid they're rather high up,' I murmured
idiotically. 'But I chose them because . . .'

They so obviously did not care why I chose them
that I went no further. They accepted everything.
They did not expect anything to be different. This was
just part of what they were going through – that was
how I analysed it.

'Arrived at last.' I ran from one side of the passage
to the other, turning on the lights, explaining.

'This one I thought for you, Dick. The other is
larger and it has a little dressing-room in the alcove.'

My 'proprietary' eye noted the clean towels and
covers, and the bed linen embroidered in red cotton. I
thought them rather charming rooms, sloping, full of
angles, just the sort of rooms one would expect to find
if one had not been to Paris before.

Dick dashed his hat down on the bed.

'Oughtn't I to help that chap with the boxes?' he
asked – nobody.

'Yes, you ought,' replied Mouse, 'they're dreadfully
heavy.'

And she turned to me with the first glimmer of a
smile: 'Books, you know.' Oh, he darted such a strange
look at her before he rushed out. And he not only
helped, he must have torn the box off the *garçon's*
back, for he staggered back, carrying one, dumped it
down and then fetched in the other.

'That's yours, Dick,' said she.

'Well, you don't mind it standing here for the

present, do you?' he asked, breathless, breathing hard
(the box must have been tremendously heavy). He
pulled out a handful of money. 'I suppose I ought to
pay this chap.'

The *garçon*, standing by, seemed to think so to.

'And will you require anything further, monsieur?'

'No! No!' said Dick impatiently.

But at that Mouse stepped forward. She said, too
deliberately, not looking at Dick, with her quaint
clipped English accent: 'Yes, I'd like some tea. Tea for
three.'

And suddenly she raised her muff as though her
hands were clasped inside it, and she was telling the
pale, sweaty *garçon* by that action that she was at the
end of her resources, that she cried out to him to save
her with 'Tea. Immediately!'

This seemed to me so amazingly in the picture, so
exactly the gesture and cry that one would expect
(though I couldn't have imagined it) to be wrung
out of an Englishwoman faced with a great crisis,
that I was almost tempted to hold up my hand and
protest.

'No! No! Enough. Enough. Let us leave off there. At
the word – tea. For really, really, you've filled your
greediest subscriber so full that he will burst if he has
to swallow another word.'

It even pulled Dick up. Like someone who has been
unconscious for a long long time he turned slowly to
Mouse and slowly looked at her with his tired, haggard eyes, and murmured with the echo of his dreamy
voice: 'Yes. That's a good idea.' And then: 'You must
be tired, Mouse. Sit down.'

She sat down in a chair with lace tabs on the arms;
he leaned against the bed, and I established myself on a
straight-backed chair, crossed my legs and brushed

some imaginary dust off the knees of my trousers.
(The Parisian at his ease.)

There came a tiny pause. Then he said: 'Won't you
take off your coat, Mouse?'

'No thanks. Not just now.'

Were they going to ask me? Or should I hold up my
hand and call out in a baby voice: 'It's my turn to be
asked.'

No, I shouldn't. They didn't ask me.

The pause became a silence. A real silence.

'. . . Come, my Parisian fox-terrier! Amuse these
sad English! It's no wonder they are such a nation for
dogs.'

But, after all – why should I? It was not my 'job', as
they would say. Nevertheless, I made a vivacious little
bound at Mouse.

'What a pity it is that you did not arrive by daylight.
There is such a charming view from these two windows.
You know, the hotel is on a corner and each window
looks down an immensely long, straight street.'

'Yes,' said she.

'Not that that sounds very charming,' I laughed.
'But there is so much animation oo many absurd little
boys on bicycles and people hanging out of windows and
– oh, well, you'll see for yourself in the morning . . .
Very amusing. Very animated.'

'Oh, yes,' said she.

If the pale, sweaty *garçon* had not come in at that
moment, carrying the tea-tray high on one hand as if
the cups were cannon-balls and he a heavy weight
lifter on the cinema . . .

He managed to lower it on to a round table.

'Bring the table over here,' said Mouse. The waiter
seemed to be the only person she cared to speak to.
She took her hands out of her muff, drew off her gloves
and flung back the old-fashioned cape.

'Do you take milk and sugar?'

'No milk, thank you, and no sugar.'

I went over for mine like a gentleman. She poured out another cup.

'That's for Dick.'

And the faithful fox-terrier carried it across to him and laid it at his feet, as it were.

'Oh, thanks,' said Dick.

And then I went back to my chair and she sank back in hers.

But Dick was off again. He stared wildly at the cup of tea for a moment, glanced round him, put it down on the bed-table, caught up his hat and stammered at full gallop: 'Oh, by the way, do you mind posting a letter for me? I want to get it off by tonight's post. I must. It's very urgent . . .' Feeling her eyes on him, he flung: 'It's to my mother.' To me: 'I won't be long. I've got everything I want. But it must go off tonight. You don't mind? It . . . it won't take any time.'

'Of course I'll post it. Delighted.'

'Won't you drink your tea first?' suggested Mouse softly.

. . . Tea? Tea? Yes, of course. Tea . . . A cup of tea on the bed-table . . . In his racing dream he flashed the brightest, most charming smile at his little hostess.

'No, thanks. Not just now.'

And still hoping it would not be any trouble to me he went out of the room and closed the door, and we heard him cross the passage.

I scalded myself with mine in my hurry to take the cup back to the table and to say as I stood there: 'You must forgive me if I am impertinent . . . if I am too frank. But Dick hasn't tried to disguise it – has he? There is something the matter. Can I help?'

(Soft music. Mouse gets up, walks the stage for a

moment or so before she returns to her chair and pours
him out, oh, such a brimming, such a burning cup that
tears come into the friend's eyes while he sips – while
he drains it to the bitter dregs . . .)

I had time to do all this before she replied. First she
looked in the teapot, filled it with hot water, and stirred
it with a spoon.

'Yes, there is something the matter. No, I'm afraid
you can't help, thank you.' Again I got that glimmer
of a smile. 'I'm awfully sorry. It must be horrid for
you.'

Horrid, indeed! Ah, why couldn't I tell her that it
was months and months since I had been so entertained?

'But you are suffering,' I ventured softly, as though
that was what I could not bear to see.

She didn't deny it. She nodded and bit her under-lip
and I thought I saw her chin tremble.

'And there is really nothing I can do?' More softly
still.

She shook her head, pushed back the table and
jumped up.

'Oh, it will be all right soon,' she breathed, walking
over to the dressing table and standing with her back
towards me. 'It will be all right. It can't go on like
this.'

'But of course it can't.' I agreed, wondering whether
it would look heartless if I lit a cigarette; I had a sudden
longing to smoke.

In some way she saw my hand move to my breast
pocket, half draw out my cigarette case and put it back
again, for the next thing she said was: 'Matches . . .
in . . . candlestick. I noticed them.'

And I heard from her voice that she was crying.

'Ah! thank you. Yes. Yes. I've found them.' I lighted
my cigarette and walked up and down, smoking.

84

It was so quiet it might have been two o'clock in the morning. It was so quiet you heard the boards creak and pop as one does in a house in the country. I smoked the whole cigarette and stabbed the end into my saucer before Mouse turned round and came back to the table.

'Isn't Dick being rather a long time?'

'You are very tired. I expect you want to go to bed,' I said kindly. (And pray don't mind me if you do, said my mind.)

'But isn't he being a very long time?' she insisted.

I shrugged. 'He is, rather.'

Then I saw she looked at me strangely. She was listening.

'He's been gone ages,' she said, and she went with little light steps to the door, opened it, and crossed the passage into his room.

I waited. I listened too, now. I couldn't have borne to miss a word. She had left the door open. I stole across the room and looked after her. Dick's door was open, too. But – there wasn't a word to miss.

You know I had the mad idea that they were kissing in that quiet room – a long comfortable kiss. One of those kisses that not only puts one's grief to bed, but nurses it and warms it and tucks it up and keeps it fast enfolded until it is sleeping sound. Ah! how good that is.

It was over at last. I heard some one move and tiptoed away.

It was Mouse. She came back. She felt her way into the room carrying the letter for me. But it wasn't in an envelope; it was just a sheet of paper and she held it by the corner as though it was still wet.

Her head was bent so low – so tucked in her furry collar that I hadn't a notion – until she let the paper fall and almost fell herself on to the floor by the side of the bed, leaned her cheek against it, flung out her hands as

though the last of her poor little weapons was gone and now she let herself be carried away, washed out into the deep water.

Flash! went my mind. Dick has shot himself, and then a succession of flashes while I rushed in, saw the body, head unharmed, small blue hole over temple, roused hotel, arranged funeral, attended funeral, closed cab, new morning coat . . .

I stooped down and picked up the paper and would you believe it – so ingrained is my Parisian sense of *comme il faut* – I murmured 'pardon' before I read it.

'MOUSE, MY LITTLE MOUSE,
It's no good. It's impossible. I can't see it through. Oh, I do love you. I do love you, Mouse, but I can't hurt her. People have been hurting her all her life. I simply dare not give her this final blow. You see, though she's stronger than both of us, she's so frail and proud. It would kill her – kill her, Mouse. And, oh God, I can't kill my mother! Not even for you. Not even for us. You do see that – don't you.
It all seemed so possible when we talked and planned, but the very moment the train started it was all over. I felt her drag me back to her – calling. I can hear her now as I write. And she's alone and she doesn't know. A man would have to be a devil to tell her and I'm not a devil, Mouse. She musn't know. Oh, Mouse, some-where, somewhere in you don't you agree? It's all so unspeakably awful that I don't know if I want to go or not. Do I? Or is mother just dragging me? I don't know. My head is too tired. Mouse, Mouse – what will you do? But I can't think of that, either. I dare not. I'd break down. And I must not break down. All I've got to do is – just to tell you this and go. I couldn't have gone off without telling you. You'd have been frightened. And you must not be frightened. You won't – will

you? I can't bear – but no more of that. And don't write. I should not have the courage to answer your letters and the sight of your spidery handwriting . . .

Forgive me. Don't love me any more. Yes. Love me. Love me. Dick.'

What do you think of that? Wasn't that a rare find? My relief at his not having shot himself was mixed with a wonderful sense of elation. I was even – more than even with my 'that's very curious and interesting' Englishman . . .

She wept so strangely. With her eyes shut, with her face quite calm except for the quivering eyelids. The tears pearled down her cheeks and she let them fall.

But feeling my glance upon her she opened her eyes and saw me holding the letter.

'You've read it?'

Her voice was quite calm, but it was not her voice any more. It was like the voice you might imagine coming out of a tiny, cold sea-shell swept high and dry at last by the salt tide . . .

I nodded, quite overcome, you understand, and laid the letter down.

'It's incredible! incredible!' I whispered.

At that she got up from the floor, walked over to the wash-stand, dipped her handkerchief into the jug and sponged her eyes, saying: 'Oh, no. It's not incredible at all.' And still pressing the wet ball to her eyes she came back to me, to her chair with the lace tabs, and sank into it.

'I knew all along, of course,' said the cold, salty little voice. 'From the very moment that we started. I felt it all through me, but I still went on hoping – ' and here she took the handkerchief down and gave me a final glimmer – 'as one so stupidly does, you know.'

'As one does.'

Silence.

'But what will you do? You'll go back? You'll see him?'

That made her sit right up and stare across at me.

'What an extraordinary idea!' she said, more coldly than ever. 'Of course I shall not dream of seeing him. As for going back – that is quite out of the question. I can't go back.'

'But . . .'

'It's impossible. For one thing all my friends think I am married.'

I put out my hand – 'Ah, my poor little friend.' But she shrank away. (False move.)

Of course there was one question that had been at the back of my mind all this time. I hated it.

'Have you any money?'

'Yes, I have twenty pounds – here,' and she put her hand on her breast. I bowed. It was a great deal more than I had expected.

'And what are your plans?'

Yes, I know. My question was the most clumsy, the most idiotic one I could have put. She had been so tame, so confiding, letting me, at any rate spiritually speaking, hold her tiny quivering body in one hand and stroke her furry head – and now, I'd thrown her away. Oh, I could have kicked myself.

She stood up. 'I have no plans. But – it's very late. You must go now, please.'

How could I get her back? I wanted her back. I swear I was not acting then.

'Do feel that I am your friend,' I cried. 'You will let me come tomorrow, early? You will let me look after you a little – take care of you a little? You'll use me just as you think fit?'

I succeeded. She came out of her hole . . . timid . . . but she came out.

'Yes, you're very kind. Yes. Do come tomorrow. I shall be glad. It makes things rather difficult because – ' and again I clasped her boyish hand – '*je ne parle pas français.*'

Not until I was half-way down the boulevard did it come over me – the full force of it.

Why, they were suffering . . . those two . . . really suffering. I have seen two people suffer as I don't suppose I ever shall again . . .

Of course you know what to expect. You anticipate, fully, what I am going to write. It wouldn't be me, otherwise.

I never went near the place again.

Yes, I still owe that considerable amount for lunches and dinners, but that's beside the mark. It's vulgar to mention it in the same breath with the fact that I never saw Mouse again.

Naturally, I intended to. Started out – got to the door – wrote and tore up letters – did all those things. But I simply could not make the final effort.

Even now I don't fully understand why. Of course I knew that I couldn't have kept it up. That had a great deal to do with it. But you would have thought, putting it at its lowest, curiosity couldn't have kept my fox-terrier nose away . . .

Je ne parle pas français. That was her swan song for me.

But how she makes me break my rule. Oh, you've seen for yourself, but I could give you countless examples.

. . . Evenings, when I sit in some gloomy café, and an automatic piano starts playing a 'mouse' tune (there are dozens of tunes that evoke just her) I begin to dream things like . . .

A little house on the edge of the sea, somewhere far,

far away. A girl outside in a frock rather like Red Indian women wear, hailing a light, barefoot boy who runs up from the beach.

'What have you got?'

'A fish.' I smile and give it to her.

. . . The same girl, the same boy, different costumes – sitting at an open window, eating fruit and leaning out and laughing.

'All the wild strawberries are for you, Mouse. I won't touch one.'

. . . A wet night. They are going home together under an umbrella. They stop on the door to press their wet cheeks together.

And so on and so on until some dirty old gallant comes up to my table and sits opposite and begins to grimace and yap. Until I hear myself saying: 'But I've got the little girl for you, *mon vieux*. So little . . . so tiny.' I kiss the tips of my fingers and lay them upon my heart. 'I give you my word of honour as a gentleman, a writer, serious, young, and extremely interested in modern English literature.'

I must go. I must go. I reach down my coat and hat. Madame knows me. 'You haven't dined yet?' she smiles.

'No, not yet, madame.'

5

Miss Brill

◊ ◊ ◊
◊ ◊
◊

Although it was so brilliantly fine – the blue sky
powdered with gold and great spots of light like white
wine splashed over the Jardins Publiques – Miss Brill
was glad that she had decided on her fur. The air was
motionless, but when you opened your mouth there
was just a faint chill, like a chill from a glass of iced
water before you sip, and now and again a leaf came
drifting – from nowhere, from the sky. Miss Brill put
up her hand and touched her fur. Dear little thing! It
was nice to feel it again. She had taken it out of its box
that afternoon, shaken out the moth-powder, given it a
good brush, and rubbed the life back into the dim little
eyes. 'What has been happening to me?' said the sad
little eyes. Oh, how sweet it was to see them snap at
her again from the red eiderdown! . . . But the nose,
which was of some black composition, wasn't at all
firm. It must have had a knock, somehow. Never mind
–a little dab of black sealing-wax when the time came –
when it was absolutely necessary. . . . Little rogue!
Yes, she really felt like that about it. Little rogue biting
its tail just by her left ear. She could have taken it off
and laid it on her lap and stroked it. She felt a tingling
in her hands and arms, but that came from walking,
she supposed. And when she breathed, something light
and sad – no, not sad, exactly – something gentle
seemed to move in her bosom.

There were a number of people out this afternoon, far more than last Sunday. And the band sounded louder and gayer. That was because the Season had begun. For although the band played all the year round on Sundays, out of season it was never the same. It was like someone playing with only the family to listen; it didn't care how it played if there weren't any strangers present. Wasn't the conductor wearing a new coat, too? She was sure it was new. He scraped with his foot and flapped his arms like a rooster about to crow, and the bandsmen sitting in the green rotunda blew out their cheeks and glared at the music. Now there came a little 'flutey' bit – very pretty! – a little chain of bright drops. She was sure it would be repeated. It was; she lifted her head and smiled.

Only two people shared her 'special' seat: a fine old man in a velvet coat, his hands clasped over a huge carved walking-stick, and a big old woman, sitting upright, with a roll of knitting on her embroidered apron. They did not speak. This was disappointing, for Miss Brill always looked forward to the conversation. She had become really quite expert, she thought, at listening as though she didn't listen, at sitting in other people's lives just for a minute while they talked round her.

She glanced, sideways, at the old couple. Perhaps they would go soon. Last Sunday, too, hadn't been as interesting as usual. An Englishman and his wife, he wearing a dreadful Panama hat and she button shoes. And she'd gone on the whole time about how she ought to wear spectacles; she knew she needed them; but that it was no good getting any; they'd be sure to break and they'd never keep on. And he'd been so patient. He'd suggested everything – gold rims, the kind that curved round your ears, little pads inside the bridge. No, nothing would please her. 'They'll always be

sliding down my nose!' Miss Brill had wanted to shake her.

The old people sat on the bench, still as statues. Never mind, there was always the crowd to watch. To and fro, in front of the flower-beds and the band rotunda, the couples and groups paraded, stopped to talk, to greet, to buy a handful of flowers from the old beggar who had his tray fixed to the railings. Little children ran among them, swooping and laughing; little boys with big white silk bows under their chins, little girls, little French dolls, dressed up in velvet and lace. And sometimes a tiny staggerer came suddenly rocking into the open from under the trees stopped, stared, as suddenly sat down 'flop', until its small high-stepping mother, like a young hen, rushed scolding to its rescue. Other people sat on the benches and green chairs, but they were nearly always the same, Sunday after Sunday, and – Miss Brill had often noticed – there was something funny about nearly all of them. They were odd, silent, nearly all old, and from the way they stared they looked as though they'd just come from dark little rooms or even – even cupboards!

Behind the rotunda the slender trees with yellow leaves down drooping, and through them just a line of sea, and beyond the blue sky with gold-veined clouds.

Tum-tum-tum tiddle-um! tiddle-um! tum tiddley-um tum ta! blew the band.

Two young girls in red came by and two young soldiers in blue met them, and they laughed and paired and went off arm-in-arm. Two pleasant women with funny straw hats passed, gravely, leading beautiful smoke-coloured donkeys. A cold, pale nun hurried by. A beautiful woman came along and dropped her bunch of violets, and a little boy ran after to hand them to her, and she took them and threw them away as if they'd been poisoned. Dear me! Miss Brill didn't know

whether to admire that or not! And now an ermine toque and a gentleman in grey met just in front of her. He was tall, stiff, dignified, and she was wearing the ermine toque she'd bought when her hair was yellow. Now everything, her hair, her face, even her eyes, was the same colour as the shabby ermine, and her hand, in its cleaned glove, lifted to dab her lips, was a tiny yellowish paw. Oh, she was so pleased to see him – delighted! She rather thought they were going to meet that afternoon. She described where she'd been – everywhere, here, there, along by the sea. The day was so charming – didn't he agree? And wouldn't he, perhaps? . . . But he shook his head, lighted a cigarette, slowly breathed a great deep puff into her face, and, even while she was still talking and laughing, flicked the match away and walked on. The ermine toque was alone; she smiled more brightly than ever. But even the band seemed to know what she was feeling and played more softly, played tenderly, and the drum beat, 'The Brute! The Brute!' over and over. What would she do? What was going to happen now? But as Miss Brill wondered, the ermine toque turned, raised her hand as though she'd seen someone else, much nicer, just over there, and pattered away. And the band changed again and played more quickly, more gaily than ever, and the old couple on Miss Brill's seat got up and marched away, and such a funny old man with long whiskers hobbled along in time to the music and was nearly knocked over by four girls walking abreast.

Oh, how fascinating it was! How she enjoyed it! How she loved sitting here, watching it all! It was like a play. It was exactly like a play. Who could believe the sky at the back wasn't painted? But it wasn't till a little brown dog trotted on solemn and then slowly trotted off, like a little 'theatre' dog, a little dog that had been

drugged, that Miss Brill discovered what it was that
made it so exciting. They were all on the stage. They
weren't only the audience, not only looking on; they
were acting. Even she had a part and came every
Sunday. No doubt somebody would have noticed if she
hadn't been there; she was part of the performance
after all. How strange she'd never thought of it like
that before! And yet it explained why she made such
a point of starting from home at just the same time
each week – so as not to be late for the performance –
and it also explained why she had quite a queer, shy
feeling at telling her English pupils how she spent her
Sunday afternoons. No wonder! Miss Brill nearly
laughed out loud. She was on the stage. She thought of
the old invalid gentleman to whom she read the newspaper four afternoons a week while he slept in the
garden. She had got quite used to the frail head on the
cotton pillow, the hollowed eyes, the open mouth and
the high pinched nose. If he'd been dead she mightn't
have noticed for weeks; she wouldn't have minded.
But suddenly he knew he was having the paper read
to him by an actress! 'An actress!' The old head lifted;
two points of light quivered in the old eyes. 'An actress
– are ye?' And Miss Brill smoothed the newspaper as
though it were the manuscript of her part and said
gently: 'Yes, I have been an actress for a long time.'

The band had been having a rest. Now they started
again. And what they played was warm, sunny, yet
there was just a faint chill – a something what was
it? – not sadness – no, not sadness – a something
that made you want to sing. The tune lifted, lifted,
the light shone; and it seemed to Miss Brill that in
another moment all of them, all the whole company,
would begin singing. The young ones, the laughing
ones who were moving together, they would begin,
and the men's voices, very resolute and brave, would

join them. And then she too, she too, and the others on
the benches – they would come in with a kind of
accompaniment – something low, that scarcely rose or
fell, something so beautiful – moving . . . And Miss
Brill's eyes filled with tears and she looked smiling at
all the other members of the company. Yes, we understand, we understand, she thought – though what they
understood she didn't know.

Just at that moment a boy and a girl came and sat
down where the old couple had been. They were
beautifully dressed; they were in love. The hero and
heroine, of course, just arrived from his father's yacht.
And still soundlessly singing, still with that trembling
smile, Miss Brill prepared to listen.

'No, not now,' said the girl. 'Not here, I can't.'

'But why? Because of that stupid old thing at the
end there?' asked the boy. 'Why does she come here at
all – who wants her? Why doesn't she keep her silly
old mug at home?'

'It's her fu-fur which is so funny,' giggled the girl.
'It's exactly like a fried whiting.'

'Ah, be off with you!' said the boy in an angry
whisper. Then: 'Tell me, *ma petite chère* –'

'No, not here,' said the girl. 'Not *yet*.'

On her way home she usually bought a slice of
honey-cake at the baker's. It was her Sunday treat.
Sometimes there was an almond in her slice, sometimes
not. It made a great difference. If there was an almond
it was like carrying home a tiny present – a surprise –
something that might very well not have been there.
She hurried on the almond Sundays and struck the
match for the kettle in quite a dashing way.

But today she passed the baker's by, climbed the
stairs, went into the little dark room – her room like a
cupboard – and sat down on the red eiderdown. She

sat there for a long time. The box that the fur came out
of was on the bed. She unclasped the necklet quickly;
quickly, without looking, laid it inside. But when she put
the lid on she thought she heard something crying.

6

Prelude

◊ ◊ ◊
◊ ◊
◊

1

There was not an inch of room for Lottie and Kezia in the buggy. When Pat swung them on top of the luggage they wobbled; the grandmother's lap was full and Linda Burnell could not possibly have held a lump of a child on hers for any distance. Isabel, very superior, was perched beside the new handy-man on the driver's seat. Holdalls, bags and boxes were piled upon the floor. 'These are absolute necessities that I will not let out of my sight for one instant,' said Linda Burnell, her voice trembling with fatigue and excitement.

Lottie and Kezia stood on the patch of lawn just inside the gate all ready for the fray in their coats with brass anchor buttons and little round caps with battle-ship ribbons. Hand in hand, they stared with round solemn eyes first at the absolute necessities and then at their mother.

'We shall simply have to leave them. That is all. We shall simply have to cast them off,' said Linda Burnell. A strange little laugh flew from her lips; she leaned back against the buttoned leather cushions and shut her eyes, her lips trembling with laughter. Happily at that moment Mrs Samuel Josephs, who had been watching the scene from behind her drawing-room blind, waddled down the garden path.

'Why nod leave the chudren with be for the after-doon, Brs Burnell? They could go on the dray with the storeban when he comes in the eveding. Those thigs on the path have to go, dod't they?'

'Yes, everything outside the house is supposed to go,' said Linda Burnell, and she waved a white hand at the tables and chairs standing on their heads on the front lawn. How absurd they looked! Either they ought to be the other way up, or Lottie and Kezia ought to stand on their heads, too. And she longed to say: 'Stand on your heads, children, and wait for the store-man.' It seemed to her that would be so exquisitely funny that she could not attend to Mrs Samuel Josephs.

The fat creaking body leaned across the gate, and the big jelly of a face smiled. 'Dod't you worry, Brs Burnell. Loddie and Kezia can have tea with by chudren in the dursery, and I'll see theb on the dray afterwards.'

The grandmother considered. 'Yes, it really is quite the best plan. We are very obliged to you, Mrs Samuel Josephs. Children, say "thank you" to Mrs Samuel Josephs.'

Two subdued chirrups: 'Thank you, Mrs Samuel Josephs.'

'And be good little girls, and – come closer – ' they advanced, 'don't forget to tell Mrs Samuel Josephs when you want to . . .'

'No, granma.'

'Dod't worry, Brs Burnell.'

At the last moment Kezia let go Lottie's hand and darted towards the buggy.

'I want to kiss my granma good-bye again.'

But she was too late. The buggy rolled off up the road, Isabel bursting with pride, her nose turned up at all the world, Linda Burnell prostrated, and the grand-mother rummaging among the very curious oddments she had had put in her black silk reticule at the last

moment, for something to give her daughter. The
buggy twinkled away in the sunlight and fine golden
dust up the hill and over. Kezia bit her lip, but Lottie,
carefully finding her handkerchief first, set up a wail.
'Mother! Granma!'

Mrs Samuel Josephs, like a huge warm black silk
tea cosy, enveloped her.

'It's all right, by dear. Be a brave child. You come
and blay in the dursery!'

She put her arm round weeping Lottie and led her
away. Kezia followed, making a face at Mrs Samuel
Josephs' placket, which was undone as usual, with two
long pink corset laces hanging out of it . . .

Lottie's weeping died down as she mounted the
stairs, but the sight of her at the nursery door with
swollen eyes and a blob of a nose gave great satisfaction
to the S. J.'s, who sat on two benches before a long table
covered with American cloth and set out with immense
plates of bread and dripping and two brown jugs that
faintly steamed.

'Hullo! You've been crying!'

'Ooh! Your eyes have gone right in.'

'Doesn't her nose look funny.'

'You're all red-and-patchy.'

Lottie was quite a success. She felt it and swelled,
smiling timidly.

'Go and sit by Zaidee, ducky,' said Mrs Samuel
Josephs, 'and Kezia, you sid ad the end by Boses.'

Moses grinned and gave her a nip as she sat down;
but she pretended not to notice. She did hate boys.

'Which will you have?' asked Stanley, leaning across
the table very politely, and smiling at her. 'Which will
you have to begin with – strawberries and cream or
bread and dripping?'

'Strawberries and cream, please,' said she.

'Ah-h-h-h.' How they all laughed and beat the table

with their teaspoons. Wasn't that a take in! Wasn't it now! Didn't he fox her! Good old Stan!

'Ma! She thought it was real.'

Even Mrs Samuel Josephs, pouring out the milk and water, could not help smiling. 'You bustn't tease theb on their last day,' she wheezed.

But Kezia bit a big piece out of her bread and dripping, and then stood the piece up on her plate. With the bite out it made a dear little sort of a gate. Pooh! She didn't care! A tear rolled down her cheek, but she wasn't crying. She couldn't have cried in front of those awful Samuel Josephs. She sat with her head bent, and as the tear dripped slowly down, she caught it with a neat little whisk of her tongue and ate it before any of them had seen.

2

After tea Kezia wandered back to their own house. Slowly she walked up the back steps, and through the scullery into the kitchen. Nothing was left in it but a lump of gritty yellow soap in one corner of the kitchen window sill and a piece of flannel stained with a blue bag in another. The fireplace was choked up with rubbish. She poked among it but found nothing except a hair-tidy with a heart painted on it that had belonged to the servant girl. Even that she left lying, and she trailed through the narrow passage into the drawing-room. The Venetian blind was pulled down but not drawn close. Long pencil rays of sunlight shone through and the wavy shadow of a bush outside danced on the gold lines. Now it was still, now it began to flutter again, and now it came almost as far as her feet. Zoom! Zoom! a bluebottle knocked against the ceiling; the carpet-tacks had little bits of red fluff sticking to them.

The dining-room window had a square of coloured glass at each corner. One was blue and one was yellow.

Kezia bent down to have one more look at a blue lawn with blue arum lilies growing at the gate, and then at a yellow lawn with yellow lilies and a yellow fence. As she looked a little Chinese Lottie came out on to the lawn and began to dust the tables and chairs with a corner of her pinafore. Was that really Lottie? Kezia was not quite sure until she had looked through the ordinary window.

Upstairs in her father's and mother's room she found a pill box black and shiny outside and red in, holding a blob of cotton wool.

'I could keep a bird's egg in that,' she decided.

In the servant girl's room there was a stay-button stuck in a crack of the floor, and in another crack some beads and a long needle. She knew there was nothing in her grandmother's room; she had watched her pack. She went over to the window and leaned against it, pressing her hands against the pane.

Kezia liked to stand so before the window. She liked the feeling of the cold shining glass against her hot palms, and she liked to watch the funny white tops that came on her fingers when she pressed them hard against the pane. As she stood there, the day flickered out and dark came. With the dark crept the wind snuffling and howling. The windows of the empty house shook, a creaking came from the walls and floors, a piece of loose iron on the roof banged forlornly. Kezia was suddenly quite, quite still, with wide open eyes and knees pressed together. She was frightened. She wanted to call Lottie and to go on calling all the while she ran downstairs and out of the house. But IT was just behind her, waiting at the door, at the head of the stairs, at the bottom of the stairs, hiding in the passage, ready to dart out at the back door. But Lottie was at the back door, too.

'Kezia!' she called cheerfully. 'The storeman's here.

Everything is on the dray and three horses, Kezia.
Mrs Samuel Josephs has given us a big shawl to wear
round us, and she says to button up your coat. She
won't come out because of asthma.'

Lottie was very important.

'Now then, you kids,' called the storeman. He hooked
his big thumbs under their arms and up they swung.
Lottie arranged the shawl 'most beautifully' and the
storeman tucked up their feet in a piece of old blanket.

'Lift up. Easy does it.'

They might have been a couple of young ponies.
The storeman felt over the cords holding his load, un-
hooked the brakechain from the wheel, and whistling,
he swung up beside them.

'Keep close to me,' said Lottie, 'because otherwise
you pull the shawl away from my side, Kezia.'

But Kezia edged up to the storeman. He towered
beside her big as a giant and he smelled of nuts and
new wooden boxes.

3

It was the first time that Lottie and Kezia had ever
been out so late. Everything looked different – the
painted wooden houses far smaller than they did by
day, the gardens far bigger and wilder. Bright stars
speckled the sky and the moon hung over the harbour
dabbling the waves with gold. They could see the
lighthouse shining on Quarantine Island, and the green
lights on the old coal hulks.

'There comes the Picton boat,' said the storeman,
pointing to a little steamer all hung with bright beads.

But when they reached the top of the hill and began
to go down the other side the harbour disappeared, and
although they were still in the town they were quite lost.
Other carts rattled past. Everybody knew the storeman.

'Night, Fred.'

'Night O,' he shouted.

Kezia liked very much to hear him. Whenever a cart appeared in the distance she looked up and waited for his voice. He was an old friend; and she and her grandmother had often been to his place to buy grapes. The storeman lived alone in a cottage that had a glasshouse against one wall built by himself. All the glasshouse was spanned and arched over with one beautiful vine. He took her brown basket from her, lined it with three large leaves, and then he felt in his belt for a little horn knife, reached up and snapped off a big blue cluster and laid it on the leaves so tenderly that Kezia held her breath to watch. He was a very big man. He wore brown velvet trousers, and he had a long brown beard. But he never wore a collar, not even on Sunday. The back of his neck was burnt bright red.

'Where are we now?' Every few minutes one of the children asked him the question.

'Why, this is Hawk Street, or Charlotte Crescent.'

'Of course it is,' Lottie pricked up her ears at the last name; she always felt that Charlotte Crescent belonged specially to her. Very few people had streets with the same name as theirs.

'Look, Kezia, there is Charlotte Crescent. Doesn't it look different?' Now everything familiar was left behind. Now the big dray rattled into unknown country, along new roads with high clay banks on either side, up steep, steep hills, down into bushy valleys, through wide shallow rivers. Further and further. Lottie's head wagged; she drooped, she slipped half into Kezia's lap and lay there. But Kezia could not open her eyes wide enough. The wind blew and she shivered; but her cheeks and ears burned.

'Do stars ever blow about?' she asked.

'Not to notice,' said the storeman.

'We've got a nuncle and a naunt living near our new house,' said Kezia. 'They have got two children, Pip, the eldest is called, and the youngest's name is Rags. He's got a ram. He has to feed it with a nenamuel teapot and a glove top over the spout. He's going to show us. What is the difference between a ram and a sheep?'

'Well, a ram has horns and runs for you.'

Kezia considered. 'I don't want to see it frightfully,' she said. 'I hate rushing animals like dogs and parrots. I often dream that animals rush at me – even camels – and while they are rushing, their heads swell e-enormous.'

The storeman said nothing. Kezia peered up at him, screwing up her eyes. Then she put her finger out and stroked his sleeve; it felt hairy. 'Are we near?' she asked.

'Not far off, now,' answered the storeman. 'Getting tired?'

'Well, I'm not an atom bit sleepy,' said Kezia. 'But my eyes keep curling up in such a funny sort of way.' She gave a long sigh, and to stop her eyes from curling she shut them. . . . When she opened them again they were clanking through a drive that cut through the garden like a whip lash, looping suddenly an island of green, and behind the island, but out of sight until you came upon it, was the house. It was long and low built, with a pillared verandah and balcony all the way round. The soft white bulk of it lay stretched upon the green garden like a sleeping beast. And now one and now another of the windows leaped into light. Someone was walking through the empty rooms carrying a lamp. From a window downstairs the light of a fire flickered. A strange beautiful excitement seemed to stream from the house in quivering ripples.

'Where are we?' said Lottie, sitting up. Her reefer

cap was all on one side and on her cheek there was the print of an anchor button she had pressed against while sleeping. Tenderly the storeman lifted her, set her cap straight, and pulled down her crumpled clothes. She stood blinking on the lowest verandah step watching Kezia who seemed to come flying through the air to her feet.

'Ooh!' cried Kezia, flinging up her arms. The grandmother came out of the dark hall carrying a little lamp. She was smiling.

'You found your way in the dark?' said she.

'Perfectly well.'

But Lottie staggered on the lowest verandah step like a bird fallen out of the nest. If she stood still for a moment she fell asleep, if she leaned against anything her eyes closed. She could not walk another step.

'Kezia,' said the grandmother, 'can I trust you to carry the lamp?'

'Yes, my granma.'

The old woman bent down and gave the bright breathing thing into her hands and then she caught up drunken Lottie. 'This way.'

Through a square hall filled with bales and hundreds of parrots (but the parrots were only on the wall-paper) down a narrow passage where the parrots persisted in flying past Kezia with her lamp.

'Be very quiet,' warned the grandmother, putting down Lottie and opening the dining-room door. 'Poor little mother has got such a headache.'

Linda Burnell, in a long cane chair, with her feet on a hassock, and a plaid over her knees, lay before a crackling fire. Burnell and Beryl sat at the table in the middle of the room eating a dish of fried chops and drinking tea out of a brown china teapot. Over the back of her mother's chair leaned Isabel. She had a comb in her fingers and in a gentle absorbed fashion

she was combing the curls from her mother's forehead. Outside the pool of lamp and firelight the room stretched dark and bare to the hollow windows.

'Are those the children?' But Linda did not really care; she did not even open her eyes to see.

'Put down the lamp, Kezia,' said Aunt Beryl, 'or we shall have the house on fire before we are out of the packing cases. More tea, Stanley?'

'Well, you might just give me five-eighths of a cup,' said Burnell, leaning across the table. 'Have another chop, Beryl. Tip-top meat, isn't it? Not too lean and not too fat.' He turned to his wife. 'You're sure you won't change your mind, Linda darling?'

'The very thought of it is enough.' She raised one eyebrow in the way she had. The grandmother brought the children bread and milk and they sat up to table, flushed and sleepy behind the wavy steam.

'I had meat for my supper,' said Isabel, still combing gently.

'I had a whole chop for my supper, the bone and all and Worcester sauce. Didn't I, father?'

'Oh, don't boast, Isabel,' said Aunt Beryl.

Isabel looked astounded. 'I wasn't boasting, was I, Mummy? I never thought of boasting. I thought they would like to know. I only meant to tell them.'

'Very well. That's enough,' said Burnell. He pushed back his plate, took a tooth-pick out of his pocket and began picking his strong white teeth.

'You might see that Fred has a bite of something in the kitchen before he goes, will you, mother?'

'Yes, Stanley.' The old woman turned to go.

'Oh, hold on half a jiffy. I suppose nobody knows where my slippers were put? I suppose I shall not be able to get at them for a month or two – what?'

'Yes,' came from Linda. 'In the top of the canvas holdall marked "urgent necessities".'

'Well you might get them for me will you, mother?'

'Yes, Stanley.'

Burnell got up, stretched himself, and going over to the fire he turned his back to it and lifted up his coat tails.

'By Jove, this is a pretty pickle. Eh, Beryl?'

Beryl, sipping tea, her elbows on the table, smiled over the cup at him. She wore an unfamiliar pink pinafore; the sleeves of her blouse were rolled up to her shoulders showing her lovely freckled arms, and she had let her hair fall down her back in a long pig-tail.

'How long do you think it will take to get straight – couple of weeks – eh?' he chaffed.

'Good heavens, no,' said Beryl airily. 'The worst is over already. The servant girl and I have simply slaved all day, and ever since mother came she has worked like a horse, too. We have never sat down for a moment. We have had a day.'

Stanley scented a rebuke.

'Well, I suppose you did not expect me to rush away from the office and nail carpets – did you?'

'Certainly not,' laughed Beryl. She put down her cup and ran out of the dining-room.

'What the hell does she expect us to do?' asked Stanley. 'Sit down and fan herself with a palm leaf fan while I have a gang of professionals to do the job? By Jove, if she can't do a hand's turn occasionally without shouting about it in return for . . .'

And he gloomed as the chops began to fight the tea in his sensitive stomach. But Linda put up a hand and dragged him down to the side of her long chair.

'This is a wretched time for you, old boy,' she said. Her cheeks were very white but she smiled and curled her fingers into the big red hand she held. Burnell became quiet. Suddenly he began to whistle 'Pure as a lily, joyous and free' – a good sign.

'Think you're going to like it?' he asked.

'I don't want to tell you, but I think I ought to, mother,' said Isabel. 'Kezia is drinking tea out of Aunt Beryl's cup.'

4

They were taken off to bed by the grandmother. She went first with a candle; the stairs rang to their climbing feet. Isabel and Lottie lay in a room to themselves, Kezia curled in her grandmother's soft bed.

'Aren't there going to be any sheets, my granma?'

'No, not tonight.'

'It's tickly,' said Kezia, 'but it's like Indians.' She dragged her grandmother down to her and kissed her under the chin. 'Come to bed soon and be my Indian brave.'

'What a silly you are,' said the old woman, tucking her in as she loved to be tucked.

'Aren't you going to leave me a candle?'

'No. Sh–h. Go to sleep.'

'Well, can I have the door left open?'

She rolled herself up into a round but she did not go to sleep. From all over the house came the sound of steps. The house itself creaked and popped. Loud whispering voices came from downstairs. Once she heard Aunt Beryl's rush of high laughter, and once she heard a loud trumpeting from Burnell blowing his nose. Outside the window hundreds of black cats with yellow eyes sat in the sky watching her – but she was not frightened. Lottie was saying to Isabel:

'I'm going to say my prayers in bed tonight.'

'No you can't, Lottie.' Isabel was very firm. 'God only excuses you saying your prayers in bed if you've got a temperature.' So Lottie yielded:

Gentle Jesus meek anmile,

Look pon a little chile.
Pity me, simple Lizzie
Suffer me to come to thee.

And then they lay down back to back, their little
behinds just touching, and fell asleep.

Standing in a pool of moonlight Beryl Fairfield undressed herself. She was tired, but she pretended to be
more tired than she really was – letting her clothes
fall, pushing back with a languid gesture her warm,
heavy hair.

'Oh, how tired I am – very tired.'

She shut her eyes a moment, but her lips smiled.
Her breath rose and fell in her breast like two fanning
wings. The window was wide open; it was warm, and
somewhere out there in the garden a young man, dark
and slender, with mocking eyes, tip-toed among the
bushes, and gathered the flowers into a big bouquet,
and slipped under her window and held it up to her.
She saw herself bending forward. He thrust his head
among the bright waxy flowers, sly and laughing. 'No,
no,' said Beryl. She turned from the window and
dropped her nightgown over her head.

'How frightfully unreasonable Stanley is sometimes,'
she thought, buttoning. And then, as she lay down,
there came the old thought, the cruel thought – ah, if
only she had money of her own.

A young man, immensely rich, has just arrived from
England. He meets her quite by chance . . . The new
governor is unmarried . . . There is a ball at Government House . . . Who is that exquisite creature in *eau
de nil* satin? Beryl Fairfield . . .

'The thing that pleases me,' said Stanley, leaning
against the side of the bed and giving himself a good

scratch on his shoulders and back before turning in, 'is that I've got the place dirt cheap, Linda. I was talking about it to little Wally Bell today and he said he simply could not understand why they had accepted my figure. You see land about here is bound to become more and more valuable . . . in about ten years' time . . . of course we shall have to go very slow and cut down expenses as fine as possible. Not asleep – are you?'

'No, dear, I've heard every word,' said Linda.

He sprang into bed, leaned over her and blew out the candle.

'Good night, Mr Business Man,' said she, and she took hold of his head by the ears and gave him a quick kiss. Her faint far-away voice seemed to come from a deep well.

'Good night, darling.' He slipped his arm under her neck and drew her to him.

'Yes, clasp me,' said the faint voice from the deep well.

Pat the handy man sprawled in his little room behind the kitchen. His sponge-bag coat and trousers hung from the door-peg like a hanged man. From the edge of the blanket his twisted toes protruded, and on the floor beside him there was an empty cane bird-cage. He looked like a comic picture.

'Honk, honk,' came from the servant girl. She had adenoids.

Last to go to bed was the grandmother.

'What. Not asleep yet?'

'No, I'm waiting for you,' said Kezia. The old woman sighed and lay down beside her. Kezia thrust her head under the grandmother's arm and gave a little squeak. But the old woman only pressed her faintly, and sighed again, took out her teeth, and put them in a glass of water beside her on the floor.

In the garden some tiny owls, perched on the branches of a lace-bark tree, called: 'More pork; more pork.' And far away in the bush there sounded a harsh rapid chatter: 'Ha-ha-ha . . . Ha-ha-ha.'

5

Dawn came sharp and chill with red clouds on a faint green sky and drops of water on every leaf and blade. A breeze blew over the garden, dropping dew and dropping petals, shivered over the drenched paddocks, and was lost in the sombre bush. In the sky some tiny stars floated for a moment and then they were gone – they were dissolved like bubbles. And plain to be heard in the early quiet was the sound of the creek in the paddock running over the crown stones, running in and out of the sandy hollows, hiding under clumps of dark berry bushes, spilling into a swamp of yellow water flowers and cresses.

And then at the first beam of sun the birds began. Big cheeky birds, starlings and mynahs, whistled on the lawns, the little birds, the goldfinches and linnets and fan-tails flicked from bough to bough. A lovely kingfisher perched on the paddock fence preening his rich beauty, and a *tui* sang his three notes and laughed and sang them again.

'How loud the birds are,' said Linda in her dream. She was walking with her father through a green paddock sprinkled with daisies. Suddenly he bent down and parted the grasses and showed her a tiny ball of fluff just at her feet. 'Oh, Papa, the darling.' She made a cup of her hands and caught the tiny bird and stroked its head with her finger. It was quite tame. But a funny thing happened. As she stroked it began to swell, it ruffled and pouched, it grew bigger and bigger and its round eyes seemed to smile knowingly at

her. Now her arms were hardly wide enough to hold it
and she dropped it into her apron. It had become a
baby with a big naked head and a gaping bird-mouth,
opening and shutting. Her father broke into a loud
clattering laugh and she woke to see Burnell standing
by the windows rattling the Venetian blind up to the
very top.

'Hullo,' he said. 'Didn't wake you, did I? Nothing
much wrong with the weather this morning.'

He was enormously pleased. Weather like this set a
final seal on his bargain. He felt, somehow, that he had
bought the lovely day, too – got it chucked in dirt
cheap with the house and ground. He dashed off to his
bath and Linda turned over and raised herself on one
elbow to see the room by daylight. All the furniture
had found a place – all the old paraphernalia – as she
expressed it. Even the photographs were on the mantelpiece and the medicine bottles on the shelf above the
wash-stand. Her clothes lay across a chair – her out-
door things, a purple cape and a round hat with a
plume in it. Looking at them she wished that she was
going away from this house, too. And she saw herself
driving away from them all in a little buggy, driving
away from everybody and not even waving.

Back came Stanley girt with a towel, glowing and
slapping his thighs. He pitched the wet towel on top of
her hat and cape, and standing firm in the exact centre
of a square of sunlight he began to do his exercises.
Deep breathing, bending and squatting like a frog and
shooting out his legs. He was so delighted with his
firm, obedient body that he hit himself on the chest
and gave a loud 'Ah'. But this amazing vigour seemed
to set him worlds away from Linda. She lay on the
white tumbled bed and watched him as if from the
clouds.

'Oh, damn! Oh, blast!' said Stanley, who had butted

into a crisp white shirt only to find that some idiot had fastened the neck-band and he was caught. He stalked over to Linda waving his arms.

'You look like a big fat turkey,' said she.

'Fat. I like that,' said Stanley. 'I haven't a square inch of fat on me. Feel that.'

'It's rock – it's iron,' mocked she.

'You'd be surprised,' said Stanley, as though this were intensely interesting, 'at the number of chaps at the club who have got a corporation. Young chaps, you know – men of my age.' He began parting his bushy ginger hair, his blue eyes fixed and round in the glass, his knees bent, because the dressing table was always – confound it – a bit too low for him. 'Little Wally Bell, for instance,' and he straightened, describing upon himself an enormous curve with the hairbrush. 'I must say I've a perfect horror . . .'

'My dear, don't worry. You'll never be fat. You are far too energetic.'

'Yes, yes, I suppose that's true,' said he, comforted for the hundredth time, and taking a pearl pen-knife out of his pocket he began to pare his nails.

'Breakfast, Stanley.' Beryl was at the door. 'Oh, Linda, mother says you are not to get up yet.' She popped her head in at the door. She had a big piece of syringa stuck through her hair.

'Everything we left on the verandah last night is simply sopping this morning. You should see poor dear mother wringing out the tables and the chairs. However, there is no harm done . . .' this with the faintest glance at Stanley.

'Have you told Pat to have the buggy round in time? It's a good six and a half miles to the office.'

'I can imagine what this early start for the office will be like,' thought Linda. 'It will be very high pressure indeed.'

'Pat, Pat.' She heard the servant girl calling. But Pat was evidently hard to find; the silly voice went baa – baaing through the garden.

Linda did not rest again until the final slam of the front door told her that Stanley was really gone.

Later she heard her children playing in the garden. Lottie's stolid, compact little voice cried: 'Ke – zia. Isa – bel.' She was always getting lost or losing people only to find them again, to her great surprise, round the next tree or the next corner. 'Oh, there you are after all.' They had been turned out after breakfast and told not to come back to the house until they were called. Isabel wheeled a neat pramload of prim dolls and Lottie was allowed for a great treat to walk beside her holding the doll's parasol over the face of the wax one.

'Where are you going to, Kezia?' asked Isabel, who longed to find some light and menial duty that Kezia might perform and so be roped in under her government.

'Oh, just away,' said Kezia . . .

Then she did not hear them any more. What a glare there was in the room. She hated blinds pulled up to the top at any time, but in the morning it was intolerable. She turned over to the wall and idly, with one finger, she traced a poppy on the wall-paper with a leaf and a stem and a fat bursting bud. In the quiet, and under her tracing finger, the poppy seemed to come alive. She could feel the sticky, silky petals, the stem, hairy like a gooseberry skin, the rough leaf and the tight glazed bud. Things had a habit of coming alive like that. Not only large substantial things like furniture, but curtains and the patterns of stuffs and the fringes of quilts and cushions. How often she had seen the tassel fringe of her quilt change into a funny procession of dancers with priests attending . . . For

there were some tassels that did not dance at all but walked stately, bent forward as if praying or chanting. How often the medicine bottles had turned into a row of little men with brown top-hats on; and the washstand jug had a way of sitting in the basin like a fat bird in a round nest.

'I dreamed about birds last night,' thought Linda. What was it? She had forgotten. But the strangest part of this coming alive of things was what they did. They listened, they seemed to swell out with some mysterious important content, and when they were full she felt that they smiled. But it was not for her, only, their sly secret smile; they were members of a secret society and they smiled among themselves. Sometimes, when she had fallen asleep in the daytime, she woke and could not lift a finger, could not even turn her eyes to left or right because *they* were there; sometimes when she went out of a room and left it empty, she knew as she clicked the door to that *they* were filling it. And there were times in the evenings when she was upstairs, perhaps, and everybody else was down, when she could hardly escape from them. Then she could not hurry, she could not hum a tune; if she tried to say ever so carelessly – 'Bother that old thimble' – *they* were not deceived. *They* knew how frightened she was; *they* saw how she turned her head away as she passed the mirror. What Linda always felt was that *they* wanted something of her, and she knew that if she gave herself up and was quiet, more than quiet, silent, motionless, something would really happen.

'It's very quiet now,' she thought. She opened her eyes wide, and she heard the silence spinning its soft endless web. How lightly she breathed; she scarcely had to breathe at all.

Yes, everything had come alive down to the minutest, tiniest particle, and she did not feel her bed, she

floated, held up in the air. Only she seemed to be listening with her wide open watchful eyes, waiting for someone to come who just did not come, watching for something to happen that just did not happen.

6

In the kitchen at the long deal table under the two windows old Mrs Fairfield was washing the breakfast dishes. The kitchen window looked out on to a big grass patch that led down to the vegetable garden and the rhubarb beds. On one side the grass patch was bordered by the scullery and washhouse and over this whitewashed lean-to there grew a knotted vine. She had noticed yesterday that a few tiny corkscrew tendrils had come right through some cracks in the scullery ceiling and all the windows of the lean-to had a thick frill of ruffled green.

'I am very fond of a grape vine,' declared Mrs Fairfield, 'but I do not think that the grapes will ripen here. It takes Australian sun.' And she remembered how Beryl when she was a baby had been picking some white grapes from the vine on the back verandah of their Tasmanian house and she had been stung on the leg by a huge red ant. She saw Beryl in a little plaid dress with red ribbon tie-ups on the shoulders screaming so dreadfully that half the street rushed in. And how the child's leg had swelled! 'T – t – t – t!' Mrs Fairfield caught her breath remembering. 'Poor child, how terrifying it was.' And she set her lips tight and went over to the stove for some more hot water. The water frothed up in the big soapy bowl with pink and blue bubbles on top of the foam. Old Mrs Fairfield's arms were bare to the elbow and stained a bright pink. She wore a grey foulard dress patterned with large purple pansies, a white linen apron and a high cap shaped like

117

a jelly mould of white muslin. At her throat there was a silver crescent moon with five little owls seated on it, and round her neck she wore a watchguard made of black beads.

It was hard to believe that she had not been in that kitchen for years; she was so much a part of it. She put the crocks away with a sure, precise touch, moving leisurely and ample from the stove to the dresser, looking into the pantry and the larder as though there were not an unfamiliar corner. When she had finished, everything in the kitchen had become part of a series of patterns. She stood in the middle of the room wiping her hands on a check cloth; a smile beamed on her lips; she thought it looked very nice, very satisfactory.

'Mother! Mother! Are you there?' called Beryl.

'Yes, dear. Do you want me?'

'No. I'm coming,' and Beryl rushed in, very flushed, dragging with her two big pictures.

'Mother, whatever can I do with these awful hideous Chinese paintings that Chung Wah gave Stanley when he went bankrupt? It's absurd to say that they are valuable, because they were hanging in Chung Wah's fruit shop for months before. I can't make out why Stanley wants them kept. I'm sure he thinks them just as hideous as we do, but it's because of the frames,' she said spitefully. 'I suppose he thinks the frames might fetch something some day or other.'

'Why don't you hang them in the passage?' suggested Mrs Fairfield; 'they would not be much seen there.'

'I can't. There is no room. I've hung all the photographs of his office there before and after building, and the signed photos of his business friends, and that awful enlargement of Isabel lying on the mat in her singlet.' Her angry glance swept the placid kitchen. 'I know what I'll do. I'll hang them here. I will tell

118

Stanley they got a little damp in the moving so I have put them in here for the time being.'

She dragged a chair forward, jumped on it, took a hammer and a big nail out of her pinafore pocket and banged away.

'There! That is enough! Hand me the picture, mother.'

'One moment, child.' Her mother was wiping over the carved ebony frame.

'Oh, mother, really you need not dust them. It would take years to dust all those little holes.' And she frowned at the top of her mother's head and bit her lip with impatience. Mother's deliberate way of doing things was simply maddening. It was old age, she supposed, loftily.

At last the two pictures were hung side by side. She jumped off the chair, stowing away the little hammer.

'They don't look so bad there, do they?' said she. 'And at any rate nobody need gaze at them except Pat and the servant girl – have I got a spider's web on my face, mother? I've been poking into that cupboard under the stairs and now something keeps tickling my nose.'

But before Mrs Fairfield had time to look Beryl had turned away. Someone tapped on the window: Linda was there, nodding and smiling. They heard the latch of the scullery door lift and she came in. She had no hat on; her hair stood up on her head in curling rings and she was wrapped up in an old cashmere shawl.

'I'm so hungry,' said Linda: 'where can I get something to eat, mother? This is the first time I've been in the kitchen. It says "mother" all over; everything is in pairs.'

'I will make you some tea,' said Mrs Fairfield, spreading a clean napkin over a corner of the table, 'and Beryl can have a cup with you.'

119

'Beryl, do you want half my gingerbread?' Linda waved the knife at her. 'Beryl, do you like the house now that we are here?'

'Oh yes, I like the house immensely and the garden is beautiful, but it feels very far away from everything to me. I can't imagine people coming out from town to see us in that dreadful jolting bus, and I am sure there is not anyone here to come and call. Of course it does not matter to you because . . .'

'But there's the buggy,' said Linda. 'Pat can drive you into town whenever you like.'

That was a consolation, certainly, but there was something at the back of Beryl's mind, something she did not even put into words for herself.

'Oh, well, at any rate it won't kill us,' she said dryly, putting down her empty cup and standing up and stretching. 'I am going to hang curtains.' And she ran away singing:

> *How many thousand birds I see*
> *That sing aloud from every tree . . .*

'. . . birds I see That sing aloud from every tree . . .' But when she reached the dining-room she stopped singing, her face changed; it became gloomy and sullen.

'One may as well rot here as anywhere else,' she muttered savagely, digging the stiff brass safety-pins into the red serge curtains.

The two left in the kitchen were quiet for a little. Linda leaned her cheek on her fingers and watched her mother. She thought her mother looked wonderfully beautiful with her back to the leafy window. There was something comforting in the sight of her that Linda felt she could never do without. She needed the sweet smell of her flesh, and the soft feel of her cheeks and her arms and shoulders still softer. She

loved the way her hair curled, silver at her forehead, lighter at her neck, and bright brown still in the big coil under the muslin cap. Exquisite were her mother's hands, and the two rings she wore seemed to melt into her creamy skin. And she was always so fresh, so delicious. The old woman could bear nothing but linen next to her body and she bathed in cold water winter and summer.

'Isn't there anything for me to do?' asked Linda.

'No, darling. I wish you would go into the garden and give an eye to your children; but that I know you will not do.'

'Of course I will, but you know Isabel is much more grown up than any of us.'

'Yes, but Kezia is not,' said Mrs Fairfield.

'Oh, Kezia has been tossed by a bull hours ago,' said Linda, winding herself up in her shawl again.

But no, Kezia had seen a bull through a hole in a knot of wood in the paling that separated the tennis lawn from the paddock. But she had not liked the bull frightfully, so she had walked away back through the orchard, up the grassy slope, along the path by the lace bark tree and so into the spread tangled garden. She did not believe that she would ever not get lost in this garden. Twice she had found her way back to the big iron gates they had driven through the night before, and then had turned to walk up the drive that led to the house, but there were so many little paths on either side. On one side they all led into a tangle of tall dark trees and strange bushes with flat velvet leaves and feathery cream flowers that buzzed with flies when you shook them – this was the frightening side, and no garden at all. The little paths here were wet and clayey with tree roots spanned across them like the marks of big fowls' feet.

But on the other side of the drive there was a high

box border and the paths had box edges and all of them led into a deeper and deeper tangle of flowers. The camellias were in bloom, white and crimson and pink and white striped with flashing leaves. You could not see a leaf on the syringa bushes for the white clusters. The roses were in flower – gentlemen's button-hole roses, little white ones, but far too full of insects to hold under anyone's nose, pink monthly roses with a ring of fallen petals round the bushes, cabbage roses on thick stalks, moss roses, always in bud, pink smooth beauties opening curl on curl, red ones so dark they seemed to turn black as they fell, and a certain exquisite cream kind with a slender red stem and bright scarlet leaves.

There were clumps of fairy bells, and all kinds of geraniums, and there were little trees of verbena and bluish lavender bushes and a bed of pelagoniums with velvet eyes and leaves like moths' wings. There was a bed of nothing but mignonette and another of nothing but pansies – borders of double and single daisies and all kinds of tufty plants she had never seen before.

The red-hot pokers were taller than she; the Japanese sunflowers grew in a tiny jungle. She sat down on one of the box borders. By pressing hard at first it made a nice seat. But how dusty it was inside! Kezia bent down to look and sneezed and rubbed her nose.

And then she found herself at the top of the rolling grassy slope that led down to the orchard . . . She looked down at the slope a moment; then she lay down on her back, gave a squeak and rolled over and over into the thick flowery orchard grass. As she lay waiting for things to stop spinning, she decided to go up to the house and ask the servant girl for an empty match-box. She wanted to make a surprise for the grandmother . . . First she would put a leaf inside with a big violet lying on it, then she would put a very small white picotee,

perhaps, on each side of the violet, and then she would sprinkle some lavender on the top, but not to cover their heads.

She often made these surprises for the grandmother, and they were always most successful.

'Do you want a match, my granny?'

'Why, yes, child, I believe a match is just what I'm looking for.'

The grandmother slowly opened the box and came upon the picture inside.

'Good gracious, child! How you astonished me!'

'I can make her one every day here,' she thought, scrambling up the grass on her slippery shoes.

But on her way back to the house she came to that island that lay in the middle of the drive, dividing the drive into two arms that met in front of the house. The island was made of grass banked up high. Nothing grew on the top except one huge plant with thick, grey-green, thorny leaves, and out of the middle there sprang up a tall stout stem. Some of the leaves of the plant were so old that they curled up in the air no longer; they turned back, they were split and broken; some of them lay flat and withered on the ground.

Whatever could it be? She had never seen anything like it before. She stood and stared. And then she saw her mother coming down the path.

'Mother, what is it?' asked Kezia.

Linda looked up at the fat swelling plant with its cruel leaves and fleshy stem. High above them, as though becalmed in the air, and yet holding so fast to the earth it grew from, it might have had claws instead of roots. The curving leaves seemed to be hiding something; the blind stem cut into the air as if no wind could ever shake it.

'That is an aloe, Kezia,' said her mother.

'Does it ever have any flowers?'

'Yes, Kezia,' and Linda smiled down at her, and half shut her eyes. 'Once every hundred years.'

7

On his way home from the office Stanley Burnell stopped the buggy at the Bodega, got out and bought a large bottle of oysters. At the Chinaman's shop next door he bought a pineapple in the pink of condition, and noticing a basket of fresh black cherries he told John to put him a pound of those as well. The oysters and the pine he stowed away in the box under the front seat, but the cherries he kept in his hand.

Pat, the handy-man, leapt off the box and tucked him up again in the brown rug.

'Lift yer feet, Mr Burnell, while I give yer a fold under,' said he.

'Right! Right! First-rate!' said Stanley. 'You can make straight for home now.'

Pat gave the grey mare a touch and the buggy sprang forward.

'I believe this man is a first-rate chap,' thought Stanley. He liked the look of him sitting up there in his neat brown coat and brown bowler. He liked the way Pat had tucked him in, and he liked his eyes. There was nothing servile about him – and if there was one thing he hated more than another it was servility. And he looked as if he was pleased with his job – happy and contented already.

The grey mare went very well; Burnell was impatient to be out of the town. He wanted to be home. Ah, it was splendid to live in the country – to get right out of that hole of a town once the office was closed; and this drive in the fresh warm air, knowing all the while that his own house was at the other end, with its garden and paddocks, its three tip-top cows and enough

fowls and ducks to keep them in poultry, was splendid too.

As they left the town finally and bowled away up the deserted road his heart beat hard for joy. He rooted in the bag and began to eat the cherries, three or four at a time, chucking the stones over the side of the buggy. They were delicious, so plump and cold, without a spot or a bruise on them.

Look at those two, now – black one side and white the other – perfect! A perfect little pair of Siamese twins. And he stuck them in his button-hole . . . By Jove, he wouldn't mind giving that chap up there a handful – but no, better not. Better wait until he had been with him a bit longer.

He began to plan what he would do with his Saturday afternoons and his Sundays. He wouldn't go to the club for lunch on Saturday. No, cut away from the office as soon as possible and get them to give him a couple of slices of cold meat and half a lettuce when he got home. And then he'd get a few chaps out from town to play tennis in the afternoon. Not too many – three at most. Beryl was a good player, too . . . He stretched out his right arm and slowly bent it, feeling the muscle . . . A bath, a good rub-down, a cigar on the verandah after dinner . . .

On Sunday morning they would go to church – children and all. Which reminded him that he must hire a pew, in the sun if possible and well forward so as to be out of the draught from the door. In fancy he heard himself intoning extremely well: 'When thou did overcome the *Sharp*ness of Death Thou didst open the *King*dom of Heaven to *all* Believers.' And he saw the neat brass-edged card on the corner of the pew – Mr Stanley Burnell and family . . . The rest of the day he'd loaf about with Linda . . . Now they were walking about the garden; she was on his arm, and he was

explaining to her at length what he intended doing at the office the week following. He heard her saying: 'My dear, I think that is most wise.' . . . Talking things over with Linda was a wonderful help even though they were apt to drift away from the point.

Hang it all! They weren't getting along very fast. Pat had put the brake on again. Ugh! What a brute of a thing it was. He could feel it in the pit of his stomach.

A sort of panic overtook Burnell whenever he approached near home. Before he was well inside the gate he would shout to anyone within sight: 'Is everything all right?' And then he did not believe it was until he heard Linda say: 'Hullo! Are you home again?' That was the worst of living in the country – it took the deuce of a long time to get back . . . But now they weren't far off. They were on the top of the last hill; it was a gentle slope all the way now and not more than half a mile.

Pat trailed the whip over the mare's back and he coaxed her: 'Goop now. Goop now.'

It wanted a few minutes to sunset. Everything stood motionless bathed in bright, metallic light and from the paddocks on either side there streamed the milky scent of ripe grass. The iron gates were open. They dashed through and up the drive and round the island, stopping at the exact middle of the verandah.

'Did she satisfy yer, sir?' said Pat, getting off the box and grinning at his master.

'Very well indeed, Pat,' said Stanley.

Linda came out of the glass door; her voice rang in the shadowy quiet. 'Hullo! Are you home again?'

At the sound of her his heart beat so hard that he could hardly stop himself dashing up the steps and catching her in his arms.

'Yes, I'm home again. Is everything all right?'

Pat began to lead the buggy round to the side gate

that opened into the courtyard.

'Here, half a moment,' said Burnell. 'Hand me those two parcels.' And he said to Linda, 'I've brought you back a bottle of oysters and a pineapple,' as though he had brought her back all the harvest of the earth.

They went into the hall; Linda carried the oysters in one hand and the pineapple in the other. Burnell shut the glass door, threw his hat down, put his arms round her and strained her to him, kissing the top of her head, her ears, her lips, her eyes.

'Oh, dear! Oh, dear!' said she. 'Wait a moment. Let me put down these silly things,' and she put the bottle of oysters and the pine on a little carved chair. 'What have you got in your button-hole – cherries?' She took them out and hung them over his ear.

'Don't do that, darling. They are for you.'

So she took them off his ear again. 'You don't mind if I save them. They'd spoil my appetite for dinner. Come and see your children. They are having tea.'

The lamp was lighted on the nursery table. Mrs Fairfield was cutting and spreading bread and butter. The three little girls sat up to table wearing large bibs embroidered with their names. They wiped their mouths as their father came in ready to be kissed. The windows were open; a jar of wild flowers stood on the mantelpiece, and the lamp made a big soft bubble of light on the ceiling.

'You seem pretty snug, mother,' said Burnell, blinking at the light. Isabel and Lottie sat one on either side of the table, Kezia at the bottom – the place at the top was empty.

'That's where my boy ought to sit,' thought Stanley. He tightened his arm round Linda's shoulder. By God, he was a perfect fool to feel as happy as this!

'We are, Stanley. We are very snug,' said Mrs Fairfield, cutting Kezia's bread into fingers.

'Like it better than town – eh, children?' asked Burnell.

'Oh, yes,' said the three little girls, and Isabel added as an after-thought: 'Thank you very much indeed, father dear.'

'Come upstairs,' said Linda. 'I'll bring your slippers.'

But the stairs were too narrow for them to go up arm in arm. It was quite dark in the room. He heard her ring tapping on the marble mantelpiece as she felt for the matches.

'I've got some, darling. I'll light the candles.'

But instead he came up behind her and again he put his arms round her and pressed her head into his shoulder.

'I'm so confoundedly happy,' he said.

'Are you?' She turned and put her hands on his breast and looked up at him.

'I don't know what has come over me,' he protested.

It was quite dark outside now and heavy dew was falling. When Linda shut the window the cold dew touched her finger tips. Far away a dog barked. 'I believe there is going to be a moon,' she said.

At the words, and with the cold wet dew on her fingers, she felt as though the moon had risen – that she was being strangely discovered in a flood of cold light. She shivered; she came away from the window and sat down upon the box ottoman beside Stanley.

In the dining-room, by the flicker of a wood fire, Beryl sat on a hassock playing the guitar. She had bathed and changed all her clothes. Now she wore a white muslin dress with black spots on it and in her hair she had pinned a black silk rose.

> *Nature has gone to her rest, love,*
> *See, we are alone.*

Give me your hand to press, love,
  Lightly within my own.

She played and sang half to herself, for she was watching herself playing and singing. The firelight gleamed on her shoes, on the ruddy belly of the guitar, and on her white fingers . . .

'If I were outside the window and looked in and saw myself I really would be rather struck,' thought she. Still more softly she played the accompaniment – not singing now but listening.

 . . . 'The first time that I ever saw you, little girl – oh, you had no idea that you were not alone – you were sitting with your little feet upon a hassock, playing the guitar. God, I can never forget . . .' Beryl flung up her head and began to sing again:

Even the moon is aweary . . .

But there came a loud bang at the door. The servant girl's crimson face popped through.

'Please, Miss Beryl, I've got to come and lay.'

'Certainly, Alice,' said Beryl, in a voice of ice. She put the guitar in a corner. Alice lunged in with a heavy black iron tray.

'Well, I have had a job with that oving,' said she. 'I can't get nothing to brown.'

'Really!' said Beryl.

But no, she could not stand that fool of a girl. She ran into the dark drawing-room and began walking up and down . . . Oh, she was restless, restless. There was a mirror over the mantel. She leaned her arms along and looked at her pale shadow in it. How beautiful she looked, but there was nobody to see, nobody.

'Why must you suffer so?' said the face in the mirror. 'You were not made for suffering . . . Smile!'

Beryl smiled, and really her smile *was* so adorable

that she smiled again – but this time because she could not help it.

8

'Good morning, Mrs Jones.'

'Oh, good morning, Mrs Smith. I'm so glad to see you. Have you brought your children?'

'Yes, I've brought both my twins. I have had another baby since I saw you last, but she came so suddenly that I haven't had time to make her any clothes, yet. So I left her . . . How is your husband?'

'Oh, he is very well, thank you. At least he had a nawful cold but Queen Victoria – she's my godmother, you know – sent him a case of pineapples and that cured it im – mediately. Is that your new servant?'

'Yes, her name's Gwen. I've only had her two days. Oh, Gwen, this is my friend, Mrs Smith.'

'Good morning, Mrs Smith. Dinner won't be ready for about ten minutes.'

'I don't think you ought to introduce me to the servant. I think I ought to just begin talking to her.'

'Well, she's more of a lady-help than a servant and you do introduce lady-helps, I know, because Mrs Samuel Josephs had one.'

'Oh, well, it doesn't matter,' said the servant, carelessly, beating up a chocolate custard with half a broken clothes peg. The dinner was baking beautifully on a concrete step. She began to lay the cloth on a pink garden seat. In front of each person she put two geranium leaf plates, a pine needle fork and a twig knife. There were three daisy heads on a laurel leaf for poached eggs, some slices of fuchsia petal cold beef, some lovely little rissoles made of earth and water and dandelion seeds, and the chocolate custard which she had decided to serve in the pawa shell she had cooked it in.

'You needn't trouble about my children,' said Mrs Smith graciously. 'If you'll just take this bottle and fill it at the tap – I mean at the dairy.'

'Oh, all right,' said Gwen, and she whispered to Mrs Jones: 'Shall I go and ask Alice for a little bit of real milk?'

But someone called from the front of the house and the luncheon party melted away, leaving the charming table, leaving the rissoles and the poached eggs to the ants and to an old snail who pushed his quivering horns over the edge of the garden seat and began to nibble a geranium plate.

'Come round to the front, children. Pip and Rags have come.'

The Trout boys were the cousins Kezia had mentioned to the storeman. They lived about a mile away in a house called Monkey Tree Cottage. Pip was tall for his age, with lank black hair and a white face, but Rags was very small and so thin that when he was undressed his shoulder blades stuck out like two little wings. They had a mongrel dog with pale blue eyes and a long tail turned up at the end who followed them everywhere; he was called Snooker. They spent half their time combing and brushing Snooker and dosing him with various awful mixtures concocted by Pip, and kept secretly by him in a broken jug covered with an old kettle lid. Even faithful little Rags was not allowed to know the full secret of these mixtures . . . Take some carbolic tooth powder and a pinch of sulphur powdered up fine, and perhaps a bit of starch to stiffen up Snooker's coat . . . But that was not all; Rags privately thought that the rest was gun-powder . . . And he never was allowed to help with the mixing because of the danger . . . 'Why if a spot of this flew in your eye, you would be blinded for life,' Pip would say, stirring the mixture with an iron spoon. 'And there's

always the chance – just the chance, mind you – of it exploding if you whack it hard enough . . . Two spoons of this in a kerosene tin will be enough to kill thousands of fleas.' But Snooker spent all his spare time biting and snuffling, and he stank abominably.

'It's because he is such a grand fighting dog,' Pip would say. 'All fighting dogs smell.'

The Trout boys had often spent the day with the Burnells in town, but now that they lived in this fine house and boncer garden they were inclined to be very friendly. Besides, both of them liked playing with girls – Pip, because he could fox them so, and because Lottie was so easily frightened, and Rags for a shameful reason. He adored dolls. How he would look at a doll as it lay asleep, speaking in a whisper and smiling timidly, and what a treat it was to him to be allowed to hold one . . .

'Curve your arms round her. Don't keep them stiff like that. You'll drop her,' Isabel would say sternly.

Now they were standing on the verandah and holding back Snooker who wanted to go into the house but wasn't allowed to because Aunt Linda hated decent dogs.

'We came over in the bus with mum,' they said, 'and we're going to spend the afternoon with you. We brought over a batch of our gingerbread for Aunt Linda. Our Minnie made it. It's all over nuts.'

'I skinned the almonds,' said Pip. 'I just stuck my hand into a saucepan of boiling water and grabbed them out and gave them a kind of pinch and the nuts flew out of the skins, some of them as high as the ceiling. Didn't they, Rags?'

Rags nodded. 'When they make cakes at our place,' said Pip, 'we always stay in the kitchen, Rags and me, and I get the bowl and he gets the spoon and the egg beater. Sponge cake's best. It's all frothy stuff, then.'

He ran down the verandah steps to the lawn, planted his hands on the grass, bent forward, and just did not stand on his head.

'That lawn's all bumpy,' he said. 'You have to have a flat place for standing on your head. I can walk round the monkey tree on my head at our place. Can't I, Rags?'

'Nearly,' said Rags faintly.

'Stand on your head on the verandah. That's quite flat,' said Kezia.

'No, smarty,' said Pip. 'You have to do it on something soft. Because if you give a jerk and fall over, something in your neck goes click, and it breaks off. Dad told me.'

'Oh, do let's play something,' said Kezia.

'Very well,' said Isabel quickly, 'we'll play hospitals. I will be nurse and Pip can be the doctor and you and Lottie and Rags can be the sick people.'

Lottie didn't want to play that, because last time Pip had squeezed something down her throat and it hurt awfully.

'Pooh,' scoffed Pip. 'It was only the juice out of a bit of mandarin peel.'

'Well, let's play ladies,' said Isabel. 'Pip can be the father and you can be all our dear little children.'

'I hate playing ladies,' said Kezia. 'You always make us go to church hand in hand and come home and go to bed.'

Suddenly Pip took a filthy handkerchief out of his pocket. 'Snooker! Here, sir,' he called. But Snooker, as usual, tried to sneak away, his tail between his legs. Pip leapt on top of him, and pressed him between his knees.

'Keep his head firm, Rags,' he said, and he tied the handkerchief round Snooker's head with a funny knot sticking up at the top.

'Whatever is that for?' asked Lottie.

'It's to train his ears to grow more close to his head – see?' said Pip. 'All fighting dogs have ears that lie back. But Snooker's ears are a bit too soft.'

'I know,' said Kezia. 'They are always turning inside out. I hate that.'

Snooker lay down, made one feeble effort with his paw to get the handkerchief off, but finding he could not, trailed after the children, shivering with misery.

9

Pat came swinging along; in his hand he held a little tomahawk that winked in the sun.

'Come with me,' he said to the children, 'and I'll show you how the kings of Ireland chop the head off a duck.'

They drew back – they didn't believe him, and besides, the Trout boys had never seen Pat before.

'Come on now,' he coaxed, smiling and holding out his hand to Kezia.

'Is it a real duck's head? One from the paddock?'

'It is,' said Pat. She put her hand in his hard dry one, and he stuck the tomahawk in his belt and held out the other to Rags. He loved little children.

'I'd better keep hold of Snooker's head if there's going to be any blood about,' said Pip, 'because the sight of blood makes him awfully wild.' He ran ahead dragging Snooker by the handkerchief.

'Do you think we ought to go?' whispered Isabel. 'We haven't asked or anything. Have we?'

At the bottom of the orchard a gate was set in the paling fence. On the other side a steep bank led down to a bridge that spanned the creek, and once up the bank on the other side you were on the fringe of the paddocks. A little old stable in the first paddock had been turned into a fowl house. The fowls had strayed

far away across the paddock down to a dumping ground in a hollow, but the ducks kept close to that part of the creek that flowed under the bridge.

Tall bushes overhung the stream with red leaves and yellow flowers and clusters of blackberries. At some places the stream was wide and shallow, but at others it tumbled into deep little pools with foam at the edges and quivering bubbles. It was in these pools that the big white ducks had made themselves at home, swimming and guzzling along the weedy banks.

Up and down they swam, preening their dazzling breasts, and other ducks with the same dazzling breasts and yellow bills swam upside down with them.

'There is the little Irish navy,' said Pat, 'and look at the old admiral there with the green neck and the grand little flagstaff on his tail.'

He pulled a handful of grain from his pocket and began to walk towards the fowl-house, lazy, his straw hat with the broken crown pulled over his eyes.

'Lid. Lid – lid – lid – lid . . .' he called.

'Qua. Qua – qua – qua – qua . . .' answered the ducks, making for land, and flapping and scrambling up the bank they streamed after him in a long waddling line. He coaxed them, pretending to throw the grain, shaking it in his hands and calling to them until they swept round him in a white ring.

From far away the fowls heard the clamour and they too came running across the paddock, their heads thrust forward, their wings spread, turning in their feet in the silly way fowls run and scolding as they came.

Then Pat scattered the grain and the greedy ducks began to gobble. Quickly he stooped, seized two, one under each arm, and strode across to the children. Their darting heads and round eyes frightened the children – all except Pip.

'Come on, sillies,' he cried, 'they can't bite. They haven't any teeth. They've only got those two little holes in their beaks for breathing through.'

'Will you hold one while I finish with the other?' asked Pat. Pip let go of Snooker. 'Won't I? Won't I? Give us one. I don't mind how much he kicks.'

He nearly sobbed with delight when Pat gave the white lump into his arms.

There was an old stump beside the door of the fowl-house. Pat grabbed the duck by the legs, laid it flat across the stump, and almost at the same moment down came the little tomahawk and the duck's head flew off the stump. Up the blood spurted over the white feathers and over his hand.

When the children saw the blood they were frightened no longer. They crowded round him and began to scream. Even Isabel leaped about crying: 'The blood! The blood!' Pip forgot all about his duck. He simply threw it away from him and shouted, 'I saw it. I saw it,' and jumped round the wood block.

Rags, with cheeks as white as paper, ran up to the little head, put out a finger as if he wanted to touch it, shrank back again and then again put out a finger. He was shivering all over.

Even Lottie, frightened little Lottie, began to laugh and pointed at the duck and shrieked: 'Look, Kezia, look.'

'Watch it!' shouted Pat. He put down the body and it began to waddle – with only a long spurt of blood where the head had been; it began to pad away without a sound towards the steep bank that led to the stream . . . That was the crowning wonder.

'Do you see that? Do you see that?' yelled Pip. He ran among the little girls tugging at their pinafores.

'It's like a little engine. It's like a funny little railway engine,' squealed Isabel.

But Kezia suddenly rushed at Pat and flung her arms round his legs and butted her head as hard as she could against his knees.

'Put head back! Put head back!' she screamed.

When he stooped to move her she would not let go or take her head away. She held on as hard as she could and sobbed: 'Head back! Head back!' until it sounded like a loud strange hiccup.

'It's stopped. It's tumbled over. It's dead,' said Pip.

Pat dragged Kezia up into his arms. Her sun-bonnet had fallen back, but she would not let him look at her face. No, she pressed her face into a bone in his shoulder and clasped her arms round his neck.

The children stopped screaming as suddenly as they had begun. They stood round the dead duck. Rags was not frightened of the head any more. He knelt down and stroked it, now.

'I don't think the head is quite dead yet,' he said. 'Do you think it would keep alive if I gave it something to drink?'

But Pip got very cross: 'Bah! You baby.' He whistled to Snooker and went off.

When Isabel went up to Lottie, Lottie snatched away.

'What are you always touching me for, Isabel?'

'There now,' said Pat to Kezia. 'There's the grand little girl.'

She put up her hands and touched his ears. She felt something. Slowly she raised her quivering face and looked. Pat wore little round gold ear-rings. She never knew that men wore ear-rings. She was very much surprised.

'Do they come on and off?' she asked huskily.

10

Up in the house, in the warm tidy kitchen, Alice, the servant girl, was getting the afternoon tea. She was 'dressed'. She had on a black stuff dress that smelt under the arms, a white apron like a large sheet of paper, and a lace bow pinned on to her hair with two jetty pins. Also her comfortable carpet slippers were changed for a pair of black leather ones that pinched her corn on her little toe something dreadful . . .

It was warm in the kitchen. A blow-fly buzzed, a fan of white steam came out of the kettle, and the lid kept up a rattling jig as the water bubbled. The clock ticked in the warm air, slow and deliberate, like the click of an old woman's knitting needle, and sometimes – for no reason at all, for there wasn't any breeze – the blind swung out and back, tapping the window.

Alice was making water-cress sandwiches. She had a lump of butter on the table, a barracouta loaf, and the cresses tumbled in a white cloth.

But propped against the butter dish there was a dirty, greasy little book, half unstitched, with curled edges, and while she mashed the butter she read:

'To dream of black-beetles drawing a hearse is bad. Signifies death of one you hold near or dear, either father, husband, brother, son, or intended. If beetles crawl backwards as you watch them it means death from fire or from great height such as flight of stairs, scaffolding, etc.

'Spiders. To dream of spiders creeping over you is good. Signifies large sum of money in near future. Should party be in family way an easy confinement may be expected. But care should be taken in sixth month to avoid eating of probable present of shell fish . . .'

How many thousand birds I see.

Oh, life. There was Miss Beryl. Alice dropped the knife and slipped the *Dream Book* under the butter dish. But she hadn't time to hide it quite, for Beryl ran into the kitchen and up to the table, and the first thing her eye lighted on were those greasy edges. Alice saw Miss Beryl's meaning little smile and the way she raised her eyebrows and screwed up her eyes as though she were not quite sure what that could be. She decided to answer if Miss Beryl should ask her: 'Nothing as belongs to you, Miss.' But she knew Miss Beryl would not ask her.

Alice was a mild creature in reality, but she had the most marvellous retorts ready for questions that she knew would never be put to her. The composing of them and the turning of them over and over in her mind comforted her just as much as if they'd been expressed. Really, they kept her alive in places where she'd been that chivvied she'd been afraid to go to bed at night with a box of matches on the chair in case she bit the tops off in her sleep, as you might say.

'Oh, Alice,' said Miss Beryl. 'There's one extra to tea, so heat a plate of yesterday's scones, please. And put on the Victoria sandwich as well as the coffee cake. And don't forget to put little doyleys under the plates – will you? You did yesterday, you know, and the tea looked so ugly and common. And, Alice, don't put that dreadful old pink and green cosy on the afternoon teapot again. That is only for the mornings. Really, I think it ought to be kept for the kitchen – it's so shabby, and quite smelly. Put on the Japanese one. You quite understand, don't you?'

Miss Beryl had finished.

That sing aloud from every tree . . .

she sang as she left the kitchen, very pleased with her firm handling of Alice.

139

Oh, Alice was wild. She wasn't one to mind being told, but there was something in the way Miss Beryl had of speaking to her that she couldn't stand. Oh, that she couldn't. It made her curl up inside, as you might say, and she fair trembled. But what Alice really hated Miss Beryl for was that she made her feel low. She talked to Alice in a special voice as though she wasn't quite all there; and she never lost her temper with her – never. Even when Alice dropped anything or forgot anything important Miss Beryl seemed to have expected it to happen.

'If you please, Mrs Burnell,' said an imaginary Alice, as she buttered the scones, 'I'd rather not take my orders from Miss Beryl. I may be only a common servant girl as doesn't know how to play the guitar, but . . .'

This last thrust pleased her so much that she quite recovered her temper.

'The only thing to do,' she heard, as she opened the dining-room door, 'is to cut the sleeves out entirely and just have a broad band of black velvet over the shoulders instead . . .'

11

The white duck did not look as if it had ever had a head when Alice placed it in front of Stanley Burnell that night. It lay, in beautifully basted resignation, on a blue dish – its legs tied together with a piece of string and a wreath of little balls of stuffing round it.

It was hard to say which of the two, Alice or the duck, looked the better basted; they were both such a rich colour and they both had the same air of gloss and strain. But Alice was fiery red and the duck a Spanish mahogany.

Burnell ran his eye along the edge of the carving

knife. He prided himself very much upon his carving, upon making a first-class job of it. He hated seeing a woman carve; they were always too slow and they never seemed to care what the meat looked like afterwards. Now he did; he took a real pride in cutting delicate shaves of cold beef, little wads of mutton, just the right thickness, and in dividing a chicken or a duck with nice precision . . .

'Is this the first of the home products?' he asked, knowing perfectly well that it was.

'Yes, the butcher did not come. We have found out that he only calls twice a week.'

But there was no need to apologize. It was a superb bird. It wasn't meat at all, but a kind of very superior jelly. 'My father would say,' said Burnell, 'this must have been one of those birds whose mother played to it in infancy upon the German flute. And the sweet strains of the dulcet instrument acted with such effect upon the infant mind . . . Have some more, Beryl? You and I are the only ones in this house with a real feeling for food. I'm perfectly willing to state, in a court of law, if necessary, that I love good food.'

Tea was served in the drawing-room, and Beryl, who for some reason had been very charming to Stanley ever since he came home, suggested a game of crib. They sat at a little table near one of the open windows. Mrs Fairfield disappeared, and Linda lay in a rocking-chair, her arms above her head, rocking to and fro.

'You don't want the light – do you, Linda?' said Beryl. She moved the tall lamp so that she sat under its soft light.

How remote they looked, those two, from where Linda sat and rocked. The green table, the polished cards, Stanley's big hands and Beryl's tiny ones, all seemed to be part of one mysterious movement. Stanley

himself, big and solid, in his dark suit, took his ease, and Beryl tossed her bright head and pouted. Round her throat she wore an unfamiliar velvet ribbon. It changed her, somehow – altered the shape of her face – but it was charming, Linda decided. The room smelled of lilies; there were two big jars of arums in the fireplace.

'Fifteen two – fifteen four – and a pair is six and a run of three is nine,' said Stanley, so deliberately, he might have been counting sheep.

'I've nothing but two pairs,' said Beryl, exaggerating her woe because she knew how he loved winning.

The cribbage pegs were like two little people going up the road together, turning round the sharp corner, and coming down the road again. They were pursuing each other. They did not so much want to get ahead as to keep near enough to talk – to keep near, perhaps that was all.

But no, there was always one who was impatient and hopped away as the other came up, and would not listen. Perhaps the white peg was frightened of the red one, or perhaps he was cruel and would not give the red one a chance to speak . . .

In the front of her dress Beryl wore a bunch of pansies, and once when the little pegs were side by side, she bent over and the pansies dropped out and covered them.

'What a shame,' said she, picking up the pansies. 'Just as they had a chance to fly into each other's arms.'

'Farewell, my girl,' laughed Stanley, and away the red peg hopped.

The drawing-room was long and narrow with glass doors that gave on to the verandah. It had a cream paper with a pattern of gilt roses, and the furniture, which had belonged to old Mrs Fairfield, was dark and plain. A little piano stood against the wall with yellow

pleated silk let into the carved front. Above it hung an oil painting by Beryl of a large cluster of surprised looking clematis. Each flower was the size of a small saucer, with a centre like an astonished eye fringed in black. But the room was not finished yet. Stanley had set his heart on a Chesterfield and two decent chairs. Linda liked it best as it was . . .

Two big moths flew in through the window and round and round the circle of lamplight.

'Fly away before it is too late. Fly out again.'

Round and round they flew; they seemed to bring the silence and the moonlight in with them on their silent wings . . .

'I've two kings,' said Stanley. 'Any good?'

'Quite good,' said Beryl.

Linda stopped rocking and got up. Stanley looked across. 'Anything the matter, darling?'

'No, nothing. I'm going to find mother.'

She went out of the room and standing at the foot of the stairs she called, but her mother's voice answered her from the verandah.

The moon that Lottie and Kezia had seen from the storeman's wagon was full, and the house, the garden, the old woman and Linda – all were bathed in dazzling light.

'I have been looking at the aloe,' said Mrs Fairfield. 'I believe it is going to flower this year. Look at the top there. Are those buds, or is it only an effect of light?'

As they stood on the steps, the high grassy bank on which the aloe rested rose up like a wave, and the aloe seemed to ride upon it like a ship with the oars lifted. Bright moonlight hung upon the lifted oars like water, and on the green wave glittered the dew.

'Do you feel it, too,' said Linda, and she spoke to her mother with the special voice that women use at night to each other as though they spoke in their sleep or

from some hollow cave – 'Don't you feel that it is coming towards us?'

She dreamed that she was caught up out of the cold water into the ship with the lifted oars and the budding mast. Now the oars fell striking quickly, quickly. They rowed far away over the top of the garden trees, the paddocks and the dark bush beyond. Ah, she heard herself cry: 'Faster! Faster!' to those who were rowing.

How much more real this dream was than that they should go back to the house where the sleeping children lay and where Stanley and Beryl played cribbage.

'I believe those are buds,' said she. 'Let us go down into the garden, mother. I like that aloe. I like it more than anything here. And I am sure I shall remember it long after I've forgotten all the other things.'

She put her hand on her mother's arm and they walked down the steps, round the island and on to the main drive that led to the front gates.

Looking at it from below she could see the long sharp thorns that edged the aloe leaves, and at the sight of them her heart grew hard . . . She particularly liked the long sharp thorns . . . Nobody would dare to come near the ship or to follow after.

'Not even my Newfoundland dog,' thought she, 'that I'm so fond of in the daytime.'

For she really was fond of him; she loved and admired and respected him tremendously. Oh, better than anyone else in the world. She knew him through and through. He was the soul of truth and decency, and for all his practical experience he was awfully simple, easily pleased and easily hurt . . .

If only he wouldn't jump at her so, and bark so loudly, and watch her with such eager, loving eyes. He was too strong for her; she had always hated things that rush at her, from a child. There were times when he was frightening – really frightening. When she

144

just had not screamed at the top of her voice: 'You are killing me.' And at those times she had longed to say the most coarse, hateful things . . .

'You know I'm very delicate. You know as well as I do that my heart is affected, and the doctor has told you I may die any moment. I have had three great lumps of children already . . .'

Yes, yes, it was true. Linda snatched her hand from mother's arm. For all her love and respect and admiration she hated him. And how tender he always was after times like those, how submissive, how thoughtful. He would do anything for her; he longed to serve her . . . Linda heard herself saying in a weak voice:

'Stanley, would you light a candle?'

And she heard his joyful voice answer: 'Of course I will, my darling.' And he leapt out of bed as though he were going to leap at the moon for her.

It had never been so plain to her as it was at this moment. There were all her feelings for him, sharp and defined, one as true as the other. And there was this other, this hatred, just as real as the rest. She could have done her feelings up in little packets and given them to Stanley. She longed to hand him that last one, for a surprise. She could see his eyes as he opened that . . .

She hugged her folded arms and began to laugh silently. How absurd life was – it was laughable, simply laughable. And why this mania of hers to keep alive at all? For it really was a mania, she thought, mocking and laughing.

'What am I guarding myself for so preciously? I shall go on having children and Stanley will go on making money and the children and the gardens will grow bigger and bigger, with whole fleets of aloes in them for me to choose from.'

She had been walking with her head bent, looking

at nothing. Now she looked up and about her. They were standing by the red and white camellia trees. Beautiful were the rich dark leaves spangled with light and the round flowers that perch among them like red and white birds. Linda pulled a piece of verbena and crumpled it, and held her hands to her mother. 'Delicious,' said the old woman. 'Are you cold, child? Are you trembling? Yes, your hands are cold. We had better go back to the house.'

'What have you been thinking about?' said Linda. 'Tell me.'

'I haven't really been thinking of anything. I wondered as we passed the orchard what the fruit trees were like and whether we should be able to make much jam this autumn. There are splendid healthy currant bushes in the vegetable garden. I noticed them today. I should like to see those pantry shelves thoroughly well stocked with our own jam . . .'

12

MY DARLING NAN,

Don't think mo a piggy-wig because I haven't written before. I haven't had a moment, dear, and even now I feel so exhausted that I can hardly hold a pen.

Well, the dreadful deed is done. We have actually left the giddy whirl of town, and I can't see how we shall ever go back again, for my brother-in-law has bought this house 'lock, stock and barrel', to use his own words.

In a way, of course, it is an awful relief, for he has been threatening to take a place in the country ever since I've lived with them – and I must say the house and garden are awfully nice – a million times better than that awful cubby-hole in town.

But buried, my dear. Buried isn't the word.

We have got neighbours, but they are only farmers –
big louts of boys who seem to be milking all day, and
two dreadful females with rabbit teeth who brought us
some scones when we were moving and said they would
be pleased to help. But my sister who lives a mile away
doesn't know a soul here, so I am sure we never shall.
It's pretty certain nobody will ever come out from
town to see us, because though there is a bus it's an
awful old rattling thing with black leather sides that
any decent person would rather die than ride in for
six miles.

Such is life. It's a sad ending for poor little B. I'll
get to be a most awful frump in a year or two and come
and see you in a mackintosh and a sailor hat tied on
with a white china silk motor veil. So pretty.

Stanley says that now we are settled – for after the
most awful week of my life we really are settled – he
is going to bring out a couple of men from the club on
Saturday afternoons for tennis. In fact, two are promised as a great treat today. But, my dear, if you could
see Stanley's men from the club . . . rather fattish, the
type who look frightfully indecent without waistcoats –
always with toes that turn in rather – so conspicuous
when you are walking about a court in white shoes.
And they are pulling up their trousers every minute –
don't you know – and whacking at imaginary things
with their rackets.

I used to play with them at the club last summer, and
I am sure you will know the type when I tell you that
after I'd been there about three times they all called
me Miss Beryl. It's a weary world. Of course mother
simply loves the place, but then I suppose when I am
mother's age I shall be content to sit in the sun and
shell peas into a basin. But I'm not – not – not.

What Linda thinks about the whole affair, per usual,
I haven't the slightest idea. Mysterious as ever . . .

My dear, you know that white satin dress of mine.
I have taken the sleeves out entirely, put bands of
black velvet across the shoulders and two big red
poppies off my dear sister's *chapeau*. It is a great success,
though when I shall wear it I do not know.

Beryl sat writing this letter at a little table in her room.
In a way, of course, it was all perfectly true, but in
another way it was all the greatest rubbish and she
didn't believe a word of it. No, that wasn't true. She
felt all those things, but she didn't really feel them like
that.

It was her other self who had written that letter. It
not only bored, it rather disgusted her real self.

'Flippant and silly,' said her real self. Yet she knew
that she'd send it and she'd always write that kind of
twaddle to Nan Pym. In fact, it was a very mild
example of the kind of letter she generally wrote.

Beryl leaned her elbows on the table and read it
through again. The voice of the letter seemed to come
up to her from the page. It was faint already, like a
voice heard over the telephone, high, gushing, with
something bitter in the sound. Oh, she detested it
today.

'You've always got so much animation,' said Nan
Pym. 'That's why men are so keen on you.' And she
had added, rather mournfully, for men were not at all
keen on Nan, who was a solid kind of girl, with fat
hips and a high colour – 'I can't understand how you
can keep it up. But it is your nature, I suppose.'

What rot. What nonsense. It wasn't her nature at
all. Good heavens, if she had ever been her real self
with Nan Pym, Nannie would have jumped out of the
window with surprise . . . My dear, you know that
white satin of mine . . . Beryl slammed the letter-case
to.

She jumped up and half unconsciously, half consciously she drifted over to the looking-glass.

There stood a slim girl in white – a white serge skirt, a white blouse, and a leather belt drawn in very tightly at her tiny waist.

Her face was heart-shaped, wide at the brows and with a pointed chin – but not too pointed. Her eyes, her eyes were perhaps her best feature; they were such a strange uncommon colour – greeny blue with little gold points in them.

She had fine black eyebrows and long lashes – so long, that when they lay on her cheeks you positively caught the light in them, someone or other had told her.

Her mouth was rather large. Too large? No, not really. Her underlip protruded a little; she had a way of sucking it in that somebody else had told her was awfully fascinating.

Her nose was her least satisfactory feature. Not that it was really ugly. But it was not half as fine as Linda's. Linda really had a perfect little nose. Hers spread rather – not badly. And in all probability she exaggerated the spreadiness of it just because it was her nose, and she was so awfully critical of herself. She pinched it with a thumb and first finger and made a little face . . .

Lovely, lovely hair. And such a mass of it. It had the colour of fresh fallen leaves, brown and red with a glint of yellow. When she did it in a long plait she felt it on her backbone like a long snake. She loved to feel the weight of it dragging her head back, and she loved to feel it loose, covering her bare arms. 'Yes, my dear, there is no doubt about it, you really are a lovely little thing.'

At the words her bosom lifted; she took a long breath of delight, half closing her eyes.

But even as she looked the smile faded from her lips and eyes. Oh God, there she was, back again, playing the same old game. False – false as ever. False as when she'd written to Nan Pym. False even when she was alone with herself, now.

What had the creature in the glass to do with her, and why was she staring? She dropped down to one side of her bed and buried her face in her arms.

'Oh,' she cried, 'I am so miserable – so frightfully miserable. I know that I'm silly and spiteful and vain; I'm always acting a part. I'm never my real self for a moment.' And plainly, plainly, she saw her false self running up and down the stairs, laughing a special trilling laugh if they had visitors, standing under the lamp if a man came to dinner, so that he should see the light on her hair, pouting and pretending to be a little girl when she was asked to play the guitar. Why? She even kept it up for Stanley's benefit. Only last night when he was reading the paper her false self had stood beside him and leaned against his shoulder on purpose. Hadn't she put her hand over his, pointing out something so that he should see how white her hand was beside his brown one.

How despicable! Despicable! Her heart was cold with rage. 'It's marvellous how you keep it up,' said she to the false self. But then it was only because she was so miserable – so miserable. If she had been happy and leading her own life, her false life would cease to be. She saw the real Beryl – a shadow . . . a shadow. Faint and unsubstantial she shone. What was there of her except the radiance? And for what tiny moments she was really she. Beryl could almost remember every one of them. At those times she had felt: 'Life is rich and mysterious and good, and I am rich and mysterious and good, too.' Shall I ever be that Beryl for ever? Shall I? How can I? And was there ever a time when I did not

have a false self? . . . But just as she had got that far she heard the sound of little steps running along the passage; the door handle rattled. Kezia came in.

'Aunt Beryl, mother says will you please come down? Father is home with a man and lunch is ready.'

Botheration! How she had crumpled her skirt, kneeling in that idiotic way.

'Very well, Kezia.' She went over to the dressing table and powdered her nose.

Kezia crossed too, and unscrewed a little pot of cream and sniffed it. Under her arm she carried a very dirty calico cat.

When Aunt Beryl ran out of the room she sat the cat up on the dressing table and stuck the top of the cream jar over its ear.

'Now look at yourself,' said she sternly.

The calico cat was so overcome by the sight that it toppled over backwards and bumped and bumped on to the floor. And the top of the cream jar flew through the air and rolled like a penny in a round on the linoleum – and did not break.

But for Kezia it had broken the moment it flew through the air, and she picked it up, hot all over, and put it back on the dressing table.

Then she tip-toed away, far too quickly and airily . . .

At the Bay

1

Very early morning. The sun was not yet risen, and the whole of Crescent Bay was hidden under a white sea-mist. The big bush-covered hills at the back were smothered. You could not see where they ended and the paddocks and bungalows began. The sandy road was gone and the paddocks and bungalows the other side of it; there were no white dunes covered with reddish grass beyond them; there was nothing to mark which was beach and where was the sea. A heavy dew had fallen. The grass was blue. Big drops hung on the bushes and just did not fall, the silvery, fluffy toi-toi was limp on its long stalks, and all the marigolds and the pinks in the bungalow gardens were bowed to the earth with wetness. Drenched were the cold fuchsias, round pearls of dew lay on the flat nasturtium leaves. It looked as though the sea had beaten up softly in the darkness, as though one immense wave had come rippling, rippling – how far? Perhaps if you had waked up in the middle of the night you might have seen a big fish flicking in at the window and gone again . . .

Ah-Aah! sounded the sleepy sea. And from the bush there came the sound of little streams flowing, quickly, lightly, slipping between the smooth stones, gushing into ferny basins and out again; and there was the

splashing of big drops on large leaves, and something
else – what was it? – a faint stirring and shaking, the
snapping of a twig and then such silence that it
seemed someone was listening.

Round the corner of Crescent Bay, between the piled-
up masses of broken rock, a flock of sheep came pattering. They were huddled together, a small, tossing,
woolly mass, and their thin, stick-like legs trotted along
quickly as if the cold and the quiet had frightened
them. Behind them an old sheep-dog, his soaking paws
covered with sand, ran along with his nose to the
ground, but carelessly, as if thinking of something else.
And then in the rocky gateway the shepherd himself
appeared. He was a lean, upright old man, in a frieze
coat that was covered with a web of tiny drops, velvet
trousers tied under the knee, and a wide-awake with a
folded blue handkerchief round the brim. One hand
was crammed into his belt, the other grasped a beautifully smooth yellow stick. And as he walked, taking his
time, he kept up a very soft light whistling, an airy,
far-away fluting that sounded mournful and tender.
The old dog cut an ancient caper or two and then drew
up sharp, ashamed of his levity, and walked a few dignified paces by his master's side. The sheep ran forward in
little pattering rushes; they began to bleat, and ghostly
flocks and herds answered them from under the sea.
'Baa! Baaa!' For a time they seemed to be always on
the same piece of ground. There ahead was stretched
the sandy road with shallow puddles; the same soaking
bushes showed on either side and the same shadowy
palings. Then something immense came into view; an
enormous shock-haired giant with his arms stretched
out. It was the big gum-tree outside Mrs Stubbs's shop,
and as they passed by there was a strong whiff of
eucalyptus. And now big spots of light gleamed in the
mist. The shepherd stopped whistling; he rubbed his

red nose and wet beard on his wet sleeve and, screwing up his eyes, glanced in the direction of the sea. The sun was rising. It was marvellous how quickly the mist thinned, sped away, dissolved from the shallow plain, rolled up from the bush and was gone as if in a hurry to escape; big twists and curls jostled and shouldered each other as the silvery beams broadened. The far-away sky – a bright, pure blue – was reflected in the puddles, and the drops, swimming along the telegraph poles, flashed into points of light. Now the leaping, glittering sea was so bright it made one's eyes ache to look at it. The shepherd drew a pipe, the bowl as small as an acorn, out of his breast pocket, fumbled for a chunk of speckled tobacco, pared off a few shavings and stuffed the bowl. He was a grave, fine-looking old man. As he lit up and the blue smoke wreathed his head, the dog, watching, looked proud of him.

'Baa! Baaa!' The sheep spread out into a fan. They were just clear of the summer colony before the first sleeper turned over and lifted a drowsy head; their cry sounded in the dreams of little children . . . who lifted their arms to drag down, to cuddle the darling little woolly lambs of sleep. Then the first inhabitant appeared; it was the Burnells' cat Florrie, sitting on the gatepost, far too early as usual, looking for their milk-girl. When she saw the old sheep-dog she sprang up quickly, arched her back, drew in her tabby head, and seemed to give a little fastidious shiver. 'Ugh! What a coarse, revolting creature!' said Florrie. But the old sheep-dog, not looking up, waggled past, flinging out his legs from side to side. Only one of his ears twitched to prove that he saw, and thought her a silly young female.

The breeze of morning lifted in the bush and the smell of leaves and wet black earth mingled with the sharp smell of the sea. Myriads of birds were singing.

A goldfinch flew over the shepherd's head and, perching on the tiptop of a spray, it turned to the sun, ruffling its small breast feathers. And now they had passed the fisherman's hut, passed the charred-looking little *whare* where Leila the milk-girl lived with her old Gran. The sheep strayed over a yellow swamp and Wag, the sheep-dog, padded after, rounded them up and headed them for the steeper, narrower rocky pass that led out of Crescent Bay and towards Daylight Cove. 'Baa! Baaa!' Faint the cry came as they rocked along the fast-drying road. The shepherd put away his pipe, dropping it into his breast-pocket so that the little bowl hung over. And straightway the soft airy whistling began again. Wag ran out along a ledge of rock after something that smelled, and ran back again disgusted. Then pushing, nudging, hurrying, the sheep rounded the bend and the shepherd followed after out of sight.

2

A few moments later the back door of one of the bungalows opened, and a figure in a broad-striped bathing suit flung down the paddock, cleared the stile, rushed through the tussock grass into the hollow, staggered up the sandy hillock, and raced for dear life over the big porous stones, over the cold, wet pebbles, on to the hard sand that gleamed like oil. Splish-Splosh! Splish-Splosh! The water bubbled round his legs as Stanley Burnell waded out exulting. First man in as usual! He'd beaten them all again. And he swooped down to souse his head and neck.

'Hail, brother! All hail, Thou Mighty One!' A velvety bass voice came booming over the water.

Great Scott! Damnation take it! Stanley lifted up to see a dark head bobbing far out and an arm lifted. It

was Jonathan Trout – there before him! 'Glorious morning!' sang the voice.

'Yes, very fine!' said Stanley briefly. Why the dickens didn't the fellow stick to his part of the sea? Why should he come barging over to this exact spot? Stanley gave a kick, a lunge and struck out, swimming overarm. But Jonathan was a match for him. Up he came, his black hair sleek on his forehead, his short beard sleek.

'I had an extraordinary dream last night!' he shouted. What was the matter with the man? This mania for conversation irritated Stanley beyond words. And it was always the same – always some piffle about a dream he'd had, or some cranky idea he'd got hold of, or some rot he'd been reading. Stanley turned over on his back and kicked with his legs till he was a living waterspout. But even then . . . 'I dreamed I was hanging over a terrifically high cliff, shouting to some one below.' You would be! thought Stanley. He could stick no more of it. He stopped splashing. 'Look here, Trout,' he said, 'I'm in rather a hurry this morning.'

'You're WHAT?' Jonathan was so surprised – or pretended to be – that he sank under the water, then reappeared again blowing.

'All I mean is,' said Stanley, 'I've no time to – to – to fool about. I want to get this over. I'm in a hurry. I've work to do this morning – see?'

Jonathan was gone before Stanley had finished. 'Pass, friend!' said the bass voice gently, and he slid away through the water with scarcely a ripple . . . But curse the fellow! He'd ruined Stanley's bathe. What an unpractical idiot the man was! Stanley struck out to sea again, and then as quickly swam in again, and away he rushed up the beach. He felt cheated.

Jonathan stayed a little longer in the water. He floated, gently moving his hands like fins, and letting

the sea rock his long skinny body. It was curious, but in spite of everything he was fond of Stanley Burnell. True, he had a fiendish desire to tease him sometimes, to poke fun at him, but at bottom he was sorry for the fellow. There was something pathetic in his determination to make a job of everything. You couldn't help feeling he'd be caught out one day, and then what an almighty cropper he'd come! At that moment an immense wave lifted Jonathan, rode past him, and broke along the beach with a joyful sound. What a beauty! And now there came another. That was the way to live – carelessly, recklessly, spending oneself. He got on to his feet and began to wade towards the shore, pressing his toes into the firm, wrinkled sand. To take things easy, not to fight against the ebb and flow of life, but to give way to it – that was what was needed. It was this tension that was all wrong. To live – to live! And the perfect morning, so fresh and fair, basking in the light, as though laughing at its own beauty, seemed to whisper, 'Why not?'

But now he was out of the water Jonathan turned blue with cold. He ached all over; it was as though some one was wringing the blood out of him. And stalking up the beach, shivering, all his muscles tight, he too felt his bathe was spoilt. He'd stayed in too long.

3

Beryl was alone in the living-room when Stanley appeared, wearing a blue serge suit, a stiff collar and a spotted tie. He looked almost uncannily clean and brushed; he was going to town for the day. Dropping into his chair, he pulled out his watch and put it beside his plate.

'I've just got twenty-five minutes,' he said. 'You might go and see if the porridge is ready, Beryl?'

'Mother's just gone for it,' said Beryl. She sat down at the table and poured out his tea.

'Thanks!' Stanley took a sip. 'Hullo!' he said in an astonished voice, 'you've forgotten the sugar.'

'Oh, sorry!' But even then Beryl didn't help him; she pushed the basin across. What did this mean? As Stanley helped himself his blue eyes widened; they seemed to quiver. He shot a quick glance at his sister-in-law and leaned back.

'Nothing wrong, is there?' he asked carelessly, fingering his collar.

Beryl's head was bent; she turned her plate in her fingers.

'Nothing,' said her light voice. Then she too looked up, and smiled at Stanley. 'Why should there be?'

'O-oh! No reason at all as far as I know. I thought you seemed rather – '

At that moment the door opened and the three little girls appeared, each carrying a porridge plate. They were dressed alike in blue jerseys and knickers; their brown legs were bare, and each had her hair plaited and pinned up in what was called a horse's tail. Behind them came Mrs Fairfield with the tray.

'Carefully, children,' she warned. But they were taking the very greatest care. They loved being allowed to carry things. 'Have you said good morning to your father?'

'Yes, grandma.' They settled themselves on the bench opposite Stanley and Beryl.

'Good morning, Stanley!' Old Mrs Fairfield gave him his plate.

'Morning, mother! How's the boy?'

'Splendid! He only woke up once last night. What a perfect morning!' The old woman paused, her hand on the loaf of bread, to gaze out of the open door into the garden. The sea sounded. Through the wide-open

158

window streamed the sun on to the yellow varnished walls and bare floor. Everything on the table flashed and glittered. In the middle there was an old salad bowl filled with yellow and red nasturtiums. She smiled, and a look of deep content shone in her eyes.

'You might *cut* me a slice of that bread, mother,' said Stanley. 'I've only twelve and a half minutes before the coach passes. Has anyone given my shoes to the servant girl?'

'Yes, they're ready for you.' Mrs Fairfield was quite unruffled.

'Oh, Kezia! Why are you such a messy child!' cried Beryl despairingly.

'Me, Aunt Beryl?' Kezia stared at her. What had she done now? She had only dug a river down the middle of her porridge, filled it, and was eating the banks away. But she did that every single morning, and no one had said a word up till now.

'Why can't you eat your food properly like Isabel and Lottie?' How unfair grown-ups are!

'But Lottie always makes a floating island, don't you, Lottie?'

'I don't,' said Isabel smartly. 'I just sprinkle mine with sugar and put on the milk and finish it. Only babies play with their food.'

Stanley pushed back his chair and got up.

'Would you get me those shoes, mother? And, Beryl, if you've finished, I wish you'd cut down to the gate and stop the coach. Run in to your mother, Isabel, and ask her where my bowler hat's been put. Wait a minute—have you children been playing with my stick?'

'No, father!'

'But I put it here,' Stanley began to bluster. 'I remember distinctly putting it in this corner. Now, who's had it? There's no time to lose. Look sharp! The stick's got to be found.'

Even Alice, the servant-girl, was drawn into the chase. 'You haven't been using it to poke the kitchen fire with by any chance?'

Stanley dashed into the bedroom where Linda was lying. 'Most extraordinary thing. I can't keep a single possession to myself. They've made away with my stick, now!'

'Stick, dear? What stick?' Linda's vagueness on these occasions could not be real, Stanley decided. Would nobody sympathize with him?

'Coach! Coach, Stanley!' Beryl's voice cried from the gate.

Stanley waved his arm to Linda. 'No time to say goodbye!' he cried. And he meant that as a punishment to her.

He snatched his bowler hat, dashed out of the house, and swung down the garden path. Yes, the coach was there waiting, and Beryl, leaning over the open gate, was laughing up at somebody or other just as if nothing had happened. The heartlessness of women! The way they took it for granted it was your job to slave away for them while they didn't even take the trouble to see that your walking stick wasn't lost. Kelly trailed his whip across the horses.

'Goodbye, Stanley,' called Beryl, sweetly and gaily. It was easy enough to say goodbye! And there she stood, idle, shading her eyes with her hand. The worst of it was Stanley had to shout goodbye too, for the sake of appearances. Then he saw her turn, give a little skip and run back to the house. She was glad to be rid of him!

Yes, she was thankful. Into the living-room she ran and called 'He's gone!' Linda cried from her room: 'Beryl! Has Stanley gone?' Old Mrs Fairfield appeared, carrying the boy in his little flannel coatee.

'Gone?'

160

'Gone!'

Oh, the relief, the difference it made to have the man out of the house. Their very voices were changed as they called to one another; they sounded warm and loving and as if they shared a secret. Beryl went over to the table. 'Have another cup of tea, mother. It's still hot.' She wanted, somehow, to celebrate the fact that they could do what they liked now. There was no man to disturb them; the whole perfect day was theirs.

'No, thank you, child,' said old Mrs Fairfield, but the way at that moment she tossed the boy up and said 'a-goos-a-goos-a-ga!' to him meant that she felt the same. The little girls ran into the paddock like chickens let out of a coop.

Even Alice, the servant-girl, washing up the dishe in the kitchen, caught the infection and used the precious tank water in a perfectly reckless fashion.

'Oh, these men!' said she, and she plunged the teapot into the bowl and held it under the water even after it had stopped bubbling, as if it too was a man and drowning was too good for them.

4

'Wait for me, Isa-bel! Kezia, wait for me!'

There was poor little Lottie, left behind again, because she found it so fearfully hard to get over the stile by herself. When she stood on the first step her knees began to wobble; she grasped the post. Then you had to put one leg over. But which leg? She never could decide. And when she did finally put one leg over with a sort of stamp of despair – then the feeling was awful. She was half in the paddock still and half in the tussock grass. She clutched the post desperately and lifted up her voice. 'Wait for me!'

'No, don't you wait for her, Kezia!' said Isabel. 'She's such a little silly. She's always making a fuss. Come on!' And she tugged Kezia's jersey. 'You can use my bucket if you come with me,' she said kindly. 'It's bigger than yours.' But Kezia couldn't leave Lottie all by herself. She ran back to her. By this time Lottie was very red in the face and breathing heavily.

'Here, put your other foot over,' said Kezia.

'Where?'

Lottie looked down at Kezia as if from a mountain height.

'Here where my hand is.' Kezia patted the place.

'Oh, *there* do you mean?' Lottie gave a deep sigh and put the second foot over.

'Now – sort of turn round and sit down and slide,' said Kezia.

'But there's nothing to sit down *on*, Kezia,' said Lottie.

She managed it at last, and once it was over she shook herself and began to beam.

'I'm getting better at climbing over stiles, aren't I, Kezia?'

Lottie's was a very hopeful nature.

The pink and the blue sunbonnet followed Isabel's bright red sunbonnet up that sliding, slipping hill. At the top they paused to decide where to go and to have a good stare at who was there already. Seen from behind, standing against the skyline, gesticulating largely with their spades, they looked like minute puzzled explorers.

The whole family of Samuel Josephs was there already with their lady-help, who sat on a camp-stool and kept order with a whistle that she wore tied round her neck, and a small cane with which she directed operations. The Samuel Josephs never played by themselves or managed their own game. If they did, it

ended in the boys pouring water down the girls' necks
or the girls trying to put little black crabs into the
boys' pockets. So Mrs S. J. and the poor lady-help drew
up what she called a 'brogramme' every morning to
keep them 'abused and out of bischief'. It was all
competitions or races or round games. Everything
began with a piercing blast of the lady-help's whistle
and ended with another. There were even prizes –
large, rather dirty paper parcels which the lady-help
with a sour little smile drew out of a bulging string
kit. The Samuel Josephs fought fearfully for the
prizes and cheated and pinched one another's arms –
they were all expert pinchers. The only time the
Burnell children ever played with them Kezia had got
a prize, and when she undid three bits of paper she
found a very small rusty button-hook. She couldn't
understand why they made such a fuss . . .

But they never played with the Samuel Josephs now
or even went to their parties. The Samuel Josephs were
always giving children's parties at the Bay and there
was always the same food. A big wash-hand basin of
very brown fruit-salad, buns cut into four and a wash-
hand jug full of something the lady-help called 'Lim-
monadear'. And you went away in the evening with
half the frill torn off your frock or something spilled
all down the front of your openwork pinafore, leaving
the Samuel Josephs leaping like savages on their lawn.
No! They were too awful.

On the other side of the beach, close down to the
water, two little boys, their knickers rolled up, twinkled
like spiders. One was digging, the other pattered in and
out of the water, filling a small bucket. They were the
Trout boys, Pip and Rags. But Pip was so busy digging
and Rags was so busy helping that they didn't see their
little cousins until they were quite close.

'Look!' said Pip. 'Look what I've discovered.' And

he showed them an old wet, squashed-looking boot. The three little girls stared.

'Whatever are you going to do with it?' asked Kezia.

'Keep it, of course!' Pip was very scornful. 'It's a find – see?'

Yes, Kezia saw that. All the same . . .

'There's lots of things buried in the sand,' explained Pip. 'They get chucked up from wrecks. Treasure. Why – you might find –'

'But why does Rags have to keep on pouring water in?' asked Lottie.

'Oh, that's to moisten it,' said Pip, 'to make the work a bit easier. Keep it up, Rags.'

And good little Rags ran up and down, pouring in the water that turned brown like cocoa.

'Here, shall I show you what I found yesterday?' said Pip mysteriously, and he stuck his spade into the sand. 'Promise not to tell.'

They promised.

'Say, cross my heart straight dinkum.'

The little girls said it.

Pip took something out of his pocket, rubbed it a long time on the front of his jersey, then breathed on it and rubbed it again.

'Now turn round!' he ordered.

They turned round.

'All look the same way! Keep still! Now!'

And his hand opened; he held up to the light something that flashed, that winked, that was a most lovely green.

'It's a nemeral,' said Pip solemnly.

'Is it really, Pip?' Even Isabel was impressed.

The lovely green thing seemed to dance in Pip's fingers. Aunt Beryl had a nemeral in a ring, but it was a very small one. This one was as big as a star and far more beautiful.

164

5

As the morning lengthened whole parties appeared over the sand-hills and came down on the beach to bathe. It was understood that at eleven o'clock the women and children of the summer colony had the sea to themselves. First the women undressed, pulled on their bathing dresses and covered their heads in hideous caps like sponge bags; then the children were unbuttoned. The beach was strewn with little heaps of clothes and shoes; the big summer hats, with stones on them to keep them from blowing away, looked like immense shells. It was strange that even the sea seemed to sound differently when all those leaping, laughing figures ran into the waves. Old Mrs Fairfield, in a lilac cotton dress and a black hat tied under the chin, gathered her little brood and got them ready. The little Trout boys whipped their shirts over their heads, and away the five sped, while their grandma sat with one hand in her knitting-bag ready to draw out the ball of wool when she was satisfied they were safely in.

The firm compact little girls were not half so brave as the tender, delicate-looking little boys. Pip and Rags, shivering, crouching down, slapping the water, never hesitated. But Isabel, who could swim twelve strokes, and Kezia, who could nearly swim eight, only followed on the strict understanding they were not to be splashed. As for Lottie, she didn't follow at all. She liked to be left to go in her own way, please. And that way was to sit down at the edge of the water, her legs straight, her knees pressed together, and to make vague motions with her arms as if she expected to be wafted out to sea. But when a bigger wave than usual, an old whiskery one, came lolloping along in her direction, she scrambled to her feet with a face of horror and flew up the beach again.

'Here, mother, keep those for me, will you?'

Two rings and a thin gold chain were dropped into Mrs Fairfield's lap.

'Yes, dear. But aren't you going to bathe here?'

'No-o,' Beryl drawled. She sounded vague. 'I'm undressing farther along. I'm going to bathe with Mrs Harry Kember.'

'Very well.' But Mrs Fairfield's lips set. She disapproved of Mrs Harry Kember. Beryl knew it.

Poor old mother, she smiled, as she skimmed over the stones. Poor old mother! Old! Oh, what joy, what bliss it was to be young . . .

'You look very pleased,' said Mrs Harry Kember. She sat hunched up on the stones, her arms round her knees, smoking.

'It's such a lovely day,' said Beryl, smiling down at her.

'Oh my *dear*!' Mrs Harry Kember's voice sounded as though she knew better than that. But then her voice always sounded as though she knew something more about you than you did yourself. She was a long, strange-looking woman with narrow hands and feet. Her face, too, was long and narrow and exhausted-looking; even her fair curled fringe looked burnt out and withered. She was the only woman at the Bay who smoked, and she smoked incessantly, keeping the cigarette between her lips while she talked, and only taking it out when the ash was so long you could not understand why it did not fall. When she was not playing bridge – she played bridge every day of her life – she spent her time lying in the full glare of the sun. She could stand any amount of it; she never had enough. All the same, it did not seem to warm her. Parched, withered, cold, she lay stretched on the stones like a piece of tossed-up driftwood. The women at the Bay thought she was very, very fast. Her lack of vanity, her slang, the way she treated men as though she was one of them, and

the fact that she didn't care twopence about her house and called the servant Gladys 'Glad-eyes', was disgraceful. Standing on the veranda steps Mrs Kember would call in her indifferent, tired voice, 'I say, Glad-eyes, you might heave me a handkerchief if I've got one, will you?' And Glad-eyes, a red bow in her hair instead of a cap, and white shoes, came running with an impudent smile. It was an absolute scandal! True, she had no children, and her husband . . . Here the voices were always raised; they became fervent. How can he have married her? How can he, how can he? It must have been money, of course, but even then!

Mrs Kember's husband was at least ten years younger than she was, and so incredibly handsome that he looked like a mask or a most perfect illustration in an American novel rather than a man. Black hair, dark blue eyes, red lips, a slow sleepy smile, a fine tennis player, a perfect dancer, and with it all a mystery. Harry Kember was like a man walking in his sleep. Men couldn't stand him, they couldn't get a word out of the chap; he ignored his wife just as she ignored him. How did he live? Of course there were stories, but such stories! They simply couldn't be told. The women he'd been seen with, the places he'd been seen in . . . but nothing was ever certain, nothing definite. Some of the women at the Bay privately thought he'd commit a murder one day. Yes, even while they talked to Mrs Kember and took in the awful concoction she was wearing, they saw her, stretched as she lay on the beach; but cold, bloody, and still with a cigarette stuck in the corner of her mouth.

Mrs Kember rose, yawned, unsnapped her belt buckle, and tugged at the tape of her blouse. And Beryl stepped out of her skirt and shed her jersey, and stood up in her short white petticoat, and her camisole with ribbon bows on the shoulders.

'Mercy on us,' said Mrs Harry Kember, 'what a little beauty you are!'

'Don't!' said Beryl softly; but, drawing off one stocking and then the other, she felt a little beauty.

'My dear – why not?' said Mrs Harry Kember, stamping on her own petticoat. Really – her underclothes! A pair of blue cotton knickers and a linen bodice that reminded one somehow of a pillow-case ... 'And you don't wear stays, do you?' She touched Beryl's waist, and Beryl sprang away with a small affected cry. Then 'Never!' she said firmly.

'Lucky little creature,' sighed Mrs Kember, unfastening her own.

Beryl turned her back and began the complicated movements of someone who is trying to take off her clothes and to pull on her bathing-dress all at one and the same time.

'Oh, my dear – don't mind me,' said Mrs Harry Kember. 'Why be shy! I shan't eat you. I shan't be shocked like those other ninnies.' And she gave her strange neighing laugh and grimaced at the other women.

But Beryl was shy She never undressed in front of anybody. Was that silly? Mrs Harry Kember made her feel it was silly, even something to be ashamed of. Why be shy indeed! She glanced quickly at her friend standing so boldly in her torn chemise and lighting a fresh cigarette; and a quick, bold, evil feeling started up in her breast. Laughing recklessly, she drew on the limp, sandy-feeling bathing-dress that was not quite dry and fastened the twisted buttons.

'That's better,' said Mrs Harry Kember. They began to go down the beach together. 'Really, it's a sin for you to wear clothes, my dear. Somebody's got to tell you some day.'

The water was quite warm. It was that marvellous

transparent blue, flecked with silver, but the sand at the bottom looked gold; when you kicked with your toes there rose a little puff of gold-dust. Now the waves just reached her breast. Beryl stood, her arms outstretched, gazing out, and as each wave came she gave the slightest little jump, so that it seemed it was the wave which lifted her so gently.

'I believe in pretty girls having a good time,' said Mrs Harry Kember. 'Why not? Don't you make a mistake, my dear. Enjoy yourself.' And suddenly she turned turtle, disappeared, and swam away quickly, quickly, like a rat. Then she flicked round and began swimming back. She was going to say something else. Beryl felt that she was being poisoned by this cold woman, but she longed to hear. But oh, how strange, how horrible! As Mrs Harry Kember came up close she looked, in her black waterproof bathing-cap, with her sleepy face lifted above the water, just her chin touching, like a horrible caricature of her husband.

6

In a steamer chair, under a manuka-tree that grew in the middle of the front grass patch, Linda Burnell dreamed the morning away. She did nothing. She looked up at the dark, close, dry leaves of the manuka, at the chinks of blue between, and now and again a tiny yellowish flower dropped on her. Pretty – yes, if you held one of those flowers on the palm of your hand and looked at it closely, it was an exquisite small thing. Each pale yellow petal shone as if each was the careful work of a loving hand. The tiny tongue in the centre gave it the shape of a bell. And when you turned it over the outside was a deep bronze colour. But as soon as they flowered, they fell and were scattered. You brushed them off your frock as you talked; the horrid

little things got caught in one's hair. Why then, flower at all? Who takes the trouble – or the joy – to make all these things that are wasted, wasted . . . It was uncanny.

On the grass beside her, lying between two pillows, was the boy. Sound asleep he lay, his head turned away from his mother. His fine dark hair looked more like a shadow than like real hair, but his ear was a bright, deep coral. Linda clasped her hands above her head and crossed her feet. It was very pleasant to know that all these bungalows were empty, that everybody was down on the beach, out of sight, out of hearing. She had the garden to herself; she was alone.

Dazzling white the picotees shone; the golden-eyed marigold glittered; the nasturtiums wreathed the veranda poles in green and gold flame. If only one had time to look at these flowers long enough, time to get over the sense of novelty and strangeness, time to know them! But as soon as one paused to part the petals, to discover the under-side of the leaf, along came Life and one was swept away. And, lying in her cane chair, Linda felt so light; she felt like a leaf. Along came Life like a wind and she was seized and shaken; she had to go. Oh dear, would it always be so? Was there no escape?

. . . Now she sat on the veranda of their Tasmanian home, leaning against her father's knee. And he promised, 'As soon as you and I are old enough, Linny, we'll cut off somewhere, we'll escape. Two boys together. I have a fancy I'd like to sail up a river in China.' Linda saw that river, very wide, covered with little rafts and boats. She saw the yellow hats of the boatmen and she heard their high, thin voices as they called . . .

'Yes, papa.'

But just then a very broad young man with bright ginger hair walked slowly past their house, and slowly,

solemnly even, uncovered. Linda's father pulled her ear teasingly, in the way he had.

'Linny's beau,' he whispered.

'Oh, papa, fancy being married to Stanley Burnell!'

Well, she was married to him. And what was more she loved him. Not the Stanley whom everyone saw, not the everyday one; but a timid, sensitive, innocent Stanley who knelt down every night to say his prayers, and who longed to be good. Stanley was simple. If he believed in people – as he believed in her, for instance – it was with his whole heart. He could not be disloyal; he could not tell a lie. And how terribly he suffered if he thought anyone – she – was not being dead straight, dead sincere with him! 'This is too subtle for me!' He flung out the words, but his open, quivering, distraught look was like the look of a trapped beast.

But the trouble was – here Linda felt almost inclined to laugh, though Heaven knows it was no laughing matter – she saw *her* Stanley so seldom. There were glimpses, moments, breathing spaces of calm, but all the rest of the time it was like living in a house that couldn't be cured of the habit of catching on fire, on a ship that got wrecked every day. And it was always Stanley who was in the thick of the danger. Her whole time was spent in rescuing him, and restoring him, and calming him down, and listening to his story. And what was left of her time was spent in the dread of having children.

Linda frowned; she sat up quickly in her steamer chair and clasped her ankles. Yes, that was her real grudge against life; that was what she could not understand. That was the question she asked and asked, and listened in vain for the answer. It was all very well to say it was the common lot of women to bear children. It wasn't true. She, for one, could prove that wrong. She was broken, made weak, her courage was gone,

through child-bearing. And what made it doubly hard to bear was, she did not love her children. It was useless pretending. Even if she had had the strength she never would have nursed and played with the little girls. No, it was as though a cold breath had chilled her through and through on each of those awful journeys; she had no warmth left to give them. As to the boy – well, thank Heaven, mother had taken him; he was mother's, or Beryl's or anybody's who wanted him. She had hardly held him in her arms. She was so indifferent about him that as he lay there . . . Linda glanced down.

The boy had turned over. He lay facing her, and he was no longer asleep. His dark-blue, baby eyes were open; he looked as though he was peeping at his mother. And suddenly his face dimpled; it broke into a wide, toothless smile, a perfect beam, no less.

'I'm here!' that happy smile seemed to say. 'Why don't you like me?'

There was something so quaint, so unexpected about that smile that Linda smiled herself. But she checked herself and said to the boy coldly, 'I don't like babies.'

'Don't like babies?' The boy couldn't believe her. 'Don't like *me*?' He waved his arms foolishly at his mother.

Linda dropped off her chair on to the grass.

'Why do you keep on smiling?' she said severely. 'If you knew what I was thinking about, you wouldn't.'

But he only squeezed up his eyes, slyly, and rolled his head on the pillow. He didn't believe a word she said.

'We know all about that!' smiled the boy.

Linda was so astonished at the confidence of this little creature . . . Ah no, be sincere. That was not what she felt; it was something far different, it was something so new, so . . . The tears danced in her eyes;

she breathed in a small whisper to the boy, 'Hallo, my funny!'

But now the boy had forgotten his mother. He was serious again. Something pink, something soft waved in front of him. He made a grab at it and it immediately disappeared. But when he lay back, another, like the first, appeared. This time he determined to catch it. He made a tremendous effort and rolled right over.

7

The tide was out; the beach was deserted; lazily flopped the warm sea. The sun beat down, beat down hot and fiery on the fine sand, baking the grey and blue and black and white-veined pebbles. It sucked up the little drop of water that lay in the hollow of the curved shells; it bleached the pink convolvulus that threaded through and through the sand-hills. Nothing seemed to move but the small sand-hoppers. Pit-pit-pit! They were never still.

Over there on the weed-hung rocks that looked at low tide like shaggy beasts come down to the water to drink, the sunlight seemed to spin like a silver coin dropped into each of the small rock pools. They danced, they quivered, and minute ripples laved the porous shores. Looking down, bending over, each pool was like a lake with pink and blue houses clustered on the shores; and oh! the vast mountainous country behind those houses – the ravines, the passes, the dangerous creeks and fearful tracks that led to the water's edge. Underneath waved the sea-forest – pink thread-like trees, velvet anemones, and orange berry-spotted weeds. Now a stone on the bottom moved, rocked, and there was a glimpse of a black feeler; now a thread-like creature wavered by and was lost. Something was happening to the pink, waving trees; they were changing

to a cold moonlight blue. And now there sounded the
faintest 'plop'. Who made that sound? What was going
on down there? And how strong, how damp the sea-
weed smelt in the hot sun . . .

The green blinds were drawn in the bungalows of the
summer colony. Over the verandas, prone on the
paddock, flung over the fences, there were exhausted-
looking bathing-dresses and rough striped towels. Each
back window seemed to have a pair of sand-shoes on the
sill and some lumps of rock or a bucket or a collection of
pawa shells. The bush quivered in a haze of heat; the
sandy road was empty except for the Trouts' dog
Snooker, who lay stretched in the very middle of it.
His blue eye was turned up, his legs stuck out stiffly,
and he gave an occasional desperate-sounding puff, as
much as to say he had decided to make an end of it
and was only waiting for some kind cart to come
along.

'What are you looking at, my grandma? Why do you
keep stopping and sort of staring at the wall?'

Kezia and her grandmother were taking their siesta
together. The little girl, wearing only her short drawers
and her under-bodice, her arms and legs bare, lay on
one of the puffed-up pillows of her grandma's bed, and
the old woman, in a white ruffled dressing-gown sat in
a rocker at the window, with a long piece of pink
knitting in her lap. This room that they shared, like
the other rooms of her bungalow, was of light varnished
wood and the floor was bare. The furniture was of the
shabbiest, the simplest. The dressing-table, for instance, was a packing-case in a sprigged muslin petticoat, and the mirror above was very strange; it was as
though a little piece of forked lightning was imprisoned
in it. On the table there stood a jar of seapinks, pressed
so tightly together they looked more like a velvet pin-
cushion, and a special shell which Kezia had given her

grandma for a pin-tray, and another even more special which she had thought would make a very nice place for a watch to curl up in.

'Tell me, grandma,' said Kezia.

The old woman sighed, whipped the wool twice round her thumb, and drew the bone needle through. She was casting on.

'I was thinking of your Uncle William, darling,' she said quietly.

'My Australian Uncle William?' said Kezia. She had another.

'Yes, of course.'

'The one I never saw?'

'That was the one.'

'Well, what happened to him?' Kezia knew perfectly well, but she wanted to be told again.

'He went to the mines, and he got a sunstroke there and died,' said old Mrs Fairfield.

Kezia blinked and considered the picture again . . . A little man fallen over like a tin soldier by the side of a big black hole.

'Does it make you sad to think about him, grandma?' She hated her grandma to be sad.

It was the old woman's turn to consider. Did it make her sad? To look back, back. To stare down the years, as Kezia had seen her doing. To look after *them* as a woman does, long after *they* were out of sight. Did it make her sad? No, life was like that.

'No, Kezia.'

'But why?' asked Kezia. She lifted one bare arm and began to draw things in the air. 'Why did Uncle William have to die? He wasn't old.'

Mrs Fairfield began counting the stitches in threes. 'It just happened,' she said in an absorbed voice.

'Does everybody have to die?' asked Kezia.

'Everybody!'

'*Me?*' Kezia sounded fearfully incredulous.

'Some day, my darling.'

'But, grandma,' Kezia waved her left leg and waggled the toes. They felt sandy. 'What if I just won't?' The old woman sighed again and drew a long thread from the ball.

'We're not asked, Kezia,' she said sadly. 'It happens to all of us sooner or later.'

Kezia lay still thinking this over. She didn't want to die. It meant she would have to leave here, leave everywhere, for ever, leave – leave her grandma. She rolled over quickly.

'Grandma,' she said in a startled voice.

'What, my pet!'

'*You're* not to die.' Kezia was very decided.

'Ah, Kezia' – her grandma looked up and smiled and shook her head – 'don't let's talk about it.'

'But you're not to. You couldn't leave me. You couldn't not be there.' This was awful. 'Promise me you won't ever do it, grandma,' pleaded Kezia.

The old woman went on knitting.

'Promise me! Say never!'

But still her grandma was silent.

Kezia rolled off her bed; she couldn't bear it any longer, and lightly she leapt on to her grandma's knees, clasped her hand round the old woman's throat and began kissing her, under the chin, behind the ear, and blowing down her neck.

'Say never . . . say never . . . say never – ' She gasped between the kisses. And then she began, very softly and lightly, to tickle her grandma.

'Kezia!' The old woman dropped her knitting. She swung back in the rocker. She began to tickle Kezia. 'Say never, say never, say never,' gurgled Kezia, while they lay there laughing in each other's arms. 'Come, that's enough, my squirrel! That's enough, my wild

pony!' said old Mrs Fairfield, setting her cap straight.
'Pick up my knitting.'

Both of them had forgotten what the 'never' was
about.

8

The sun was still full on the garden when the back
door of the Burnells' shut with a bang, and a very gay
figure walked down the path to the gate. It was Alice,
the servant-girl, dressed for her afternoon out. She
wore a white cotton dress with such large red spots on
it, and so many that they made you shudder, white
shoes and a leghorn turned up under the brim with
poppies. Of course she wore gloves, white ones, stained
at the fastenings with iron-mould, and in one hand she
carried a very dashed-looking sunshade which she re-
ferred to as her *perishall*.

Beryl, sitting in the window, fanning her freshly-
washed hair, thought she had never seen such a guy.
If Alice had only blacked her face with a piece of cork
before she started out, the picture would have been
complete. And where did a girl like that go to in a
place like this? The heart-shaped Fijian fan beat scorn-
fully at that lovely bright mane. She supposed Alice
had picked up some horrible common larrikin and
they'd go off into the bush together. Pity to make herself so conspicuous; they'd have hard work to hide with
Alice in that rig-out.

But no, Beryl was unfair. Alice was going to tea
with Mrs Stubbs, who'd sent her an 'invite' by the
little boy who called for orders. She had taken ever
such a liking to Mrs Stubbs ever since the first time she
went to the shop to get something for her mosquitoes.

'Dear heart!' Mrs Stubbs had clapped her hand to
her side. 'I never seen anyone so eaten. You might have
been attacked by canningbals.'

Alice did wish there'd been a bit of life on the road though. Made her feel so queer, having nobody behind her. Made her feel all weak in the spine. She couldn't believe that someone wasn't watching her. And yet it was silly to turn round; it gave you away. She pulled up her gloves, hummed to herself and said to the distant gum-tree, 'Shan't be long now.' But that was hardly company.

Mrs Stubbs's shop was perched on a little hillock just off the road. It had two big windows for eyes, a broad veranda for a hat, and the sign on the roof, scrawled MRS STUBBS'S, was like a little card stuck rakishly in the hat crown.

On the veranda there hung a long string of bathing-dresses, clinging together as though they'd just been rescued from the sea rather than waiting to go in, and beside them there hung a cluster of sand-shoes so extraordinarily mixed that to get at one pair you had to tear apart and forcibly separate at least fifty. Even then it was the rarest thing to find the left that belonged to the right. So many people had lost patience and gone off with one shoe that fitted and one that was a little too big . . . Mrs Stubbs prided herself on keeping something of everything. The two windows, arranged in the form of precarious pyramids, were crammed so tight, piled so high, that it seemed only a conjurer could prevent them from toppling over. In the left-hand corner of one window, glued to the pane by four gelatine lozenges, there was – and there had been from time immemorial – a notice.

LOST! HANSOME GOLE BROOCH

SOLID GOLD

ON OR NEAR BEACH

REWARD OFFERED

Alice pressed open the door. The bell jangled, the red

serge curtains parted, and Mrs Stubbs appeared. With her broad smile and the long bacon knife in her hand, she looked like a friendly brigand. Alice was welcomed so warmly that she found it quite difficult to keep up her 'manners'. They consisted of persistent little coughs and hems, pulls at her gloves, tweaks at her skirt, and a curious difficulty in seeing what was set before her or understanding what was said.

Tea was laid on the parlour table – ham, sardines, a whole pound of butter, and such a large johnny cake that it looked like an advertisement for somebody's baking-powder. But the Primus stove roared so loudly that it was useless to try to talk above it. Alice sat down on the edge of a basket-chair while Mrs Stubbs pumped the stove still higher. Suddenly Mrs Stubbs whipped the cushion off a chair and disclosed a large brown-paper parcel.

'I've just had some new photers taken, my dear,' she shouted cheerfully to Alice. 'Tell me what you think of them.'

In a very dainty, refined way Alice wet her finger and put the tissue back from the first one. Life? How many there were! There were three dozzing at least. And she held hers up to the light.

Mrs Stubbs sat in an arm-chair, leaning very much to one side. There was a look of mild astonishment on her large face, and well there might be. For though the arm-chair stood on a carpet, to the left of it, miraculously skirting the carpet-border, there was a dashing water-fall. On her right stood a Grecian pillar with a giant fern-tree on either side of it, and in the background towered a gaunt mountain, pale with snow.

'It is a nice style, isn't it?' shouted Mrs Stubbs; and Alice had just screamed 'Sweetly' when the roaring of the Primus stove died down, fizzled out, ceased, and she said 'Pretty' in a silence that was frightening.

'Draw up your chair, my dear,' said Mrs Stubbs, beginning to pour out. 'Yes,' she said thoughtfully, as she handed the tea, 'but I don't care about the size. I'm having an enlargemint. All very well for Christmas cards, but I never was the one for small photers myself. You get no comfort out of them. To say the truth, I find them dis'eartening.'

Alice quite saw what she meant.

'Size,' said Mrs Stubbs. 'Give me size. That was what my poor dear husband was always saying. He couldn't stand anything small. Gave him the creeps. And, strange as it may seem my dear' – here Mrs Stubbs creaked and seemed to expand herself at the memory – 'it was dropsy that carried him off at the larst. Many's the time they drawn one and a half pints from 'im at the 'ospital . . . It seemed like a judgemint.'

Alice burned to know exactly what it was that was drawn from him. She ventured, 'I suppose it was water.'

But Mrs Stubbs fixed Alice with her eyes and replied meaningly, 'It was *liquid*, my dear.'

Liquid! Alice jumped away from the word like a cat and came back to it, nosing and wary.

'That's 'im!' said Mrs Stubbs, and she pointed dramatically to the life-size head and shoulders of a burly man with a dead white rose in the button-hole of his coat that made you think of a curl of cold mutting fat. Just below, in silver letters on a red cardboard ground, were the words, 'Be not afraid, it is I.'

'It's ever such a fine face,' said Alice faintly.

The pale-blue bow on the top of Mrs Stubbs's fair frizzy hair quivered. She arched her plump neck. What a neck she had! It was bright pink where it began and then it changed to warm apricot, and that faded to the colour of a brown egg and then to a deep creamy.

'All the same, my dear,' she said surprisingly,

'freedom's best!' Her soft, fat chuckle sounded like a purr. 'Freedom's best,' said Mrs Stubbs again.

Freedom! Alice gave a loud, silly little titter. She felt awkward. Her mind flew back to her own kitching. Ever so queer! She wanted to be back in it again.

9

A strange company assembled in the Burnells' wash-house after tea. Round the table there sat a bull, a rooster, a donkey that kept forgetting it was a donkey, a sheep and a bee. The washhouse was the perfect place for such a meeting because they could make as much noise as they liked, and nobody ever interrupted. It was a small tin shed standing apart from the bungalow. Against the wall there was a deep trough and in the corner a copper with a basket of clothes-pegs on top of it. The little window, spun over with cobwebs, had a piece of candle and a mouse-trap on the dusty sill. There were clothes-lines criss-crossed overhead and, hanging from a peg on the wall, a very big, a huge, rusty horseshoe. The table was in the middle with a form at either side.

'You can't be a bee, Kezia. A bee's not an animal. It's a ninseck.'

'Oh, but I do want to be a bee frightfully,' wailed Kezia . . . A tiny bee, all yellow-furry, with striped legs. She drew her legs up under her and leaned over the table. She felt she was a bee.

'A ninseck must be an animal,' she said stoutly. 'It makes a noise. It's not like a fish.'

'I'm a bull, I'm a bull!' cried Pip. And he gave such a tremendous bellow — how did he make that noise? — that Lottie looked quite alarmed.

'I'll be a sheep,' said little Rags. 'A whole lot of sheep went past this morning.'

'How do you know?'

'Dad heard them. Baa!' He sounded like the little lamb that trots behind and seems to wait to be carried. 'Cock-a-doodle-do!' shrilled Isabel. With her red cheeks and bright eyes she looked like a rooster.

'What'll I be?' Lottie asked everybody, and she sat there smiling, waiting for them to decide for her. It had to be an easy one.

'Be a donkey, Lottie.' It was Kezia's suggestion. 'Hee-haw! You can't forget that.'

'Hee-haw!' said Lottie solemnly. 'When do I have to say it?'

'I'll explain, I'll explain,' said the bull. It was he who had the cards. He waved them round his head. 'All be quiet! All listen!' And he waited for them. 'Look here, Lottie.' He turned up a card. 'It's got two spots on it – see? Now, if you put that card in the middle and somebody else has one with two spots as well, you say "Hee-haw", and the card's yours.'

'Mine?' Lottie was round-eyed. 'To keep?'

'No, silly. Just for the game, see? Just while we're playing.' The bull was very cross with her.

'Oh, Lottie, you *are* a little silly,' said the proud rooster.

Lottie looked at both of them. Then she hung her head; her lip quivered. 'I don't want to play,' she whispered. The others glanced at one another like conspirators. All of them knew what that meant. She would go away and be discovered somewhere standing with her pinny thrown over her head in a corner, or against a wall, or even behind a chair.

'Yes, you *do*, Lottie. It's quite easy,' said Kezia.

And Isabel, repentant, said exactly like a grown-up, 'Watch *me*, Lottie, and you'll soon learn.'

'Cheer up, Lot,' said Pip. 'There, I know what I'll do. I'll give you the first one. It's mine, really, but I'll

give it to you. Here you are.' And he slammed the card down in front of Lottie.

Lottie revived at that. But now she was in another difficulty. 'I haven't got a hanky,' she said; 'I want one badly, too.'

'Here, Lottie, you can use mine.' Rags dipped into his sailor blouse and brought up a very wet-looking one, knotted together. 'Be very careful,' he warned her. 'Only use that corner. Don't undo it. I've got a little star-fish inside I'm going to try and tame.'

'Oh, come on, you girls,' said the bull. 'And mind – you're not to look at your cards. You've got to keep your hands under the table till I say "Go".'

Smack went the cards round the table. They tried with all their might to see, but Pip was too quick for them. It was very exciting, sitting there in the wash-house; it was all they could do not to burst into a little chorus of animals before Pip had finished dealing.

'Now, Lottie, you begin.'

Timidly Lottie stretched out a hand, took the top card off her pack, had a good look at it – it was plain she was counting the spots – and put it down.

'No, Lottie, you can't do that. You mustn't look first. You must turn it the other way over.'

'But then everybody will see it the same time as me,' said Lottie.

The game proceeded. Mooe-ooo-er! The bull was terrible. He charged over the table and seemed to eat the cards up.

Bss-ss! said the bee.

Cock-a-doodle-do! Isabel stood up in her excitement and moved her elbows like wings.

Baa! Little Rags put down the King of Diamonds and Lottie put down the one they called the King of Spain. She had hardly any cards left.

'Why don't you call out, Lottie?'

'I've forgotten what I am,' said the donkey woefully.

'Well, change! Be a dog instead! Bow-wow!'

'Oh yes. That's *much* easier.' Lottie smiled again. But when she and Kezia both had a one Kezia waited on purpose. The others made signs to Lottie and pointed. Lottie turned very red; she looked bewildered, and at last she said, 'Hee-haw! Ke-zia.'

'Ss! Wait a minute!' They were in the very thick of it when the bull stopped them, holding up his hand. 'What's that? What's that noise?'

'What noise? What do you mean?' asked the rooster.

'Ss! Shut up! Listen!' They were mouse-still. 'I thought I heard a – sort of knocking,' said the bull.

'What was it like?' asked the sheep faintly.

No answer.

The bee gave a shudder. 'Whatever did we shut the door for?' she said softly. Oh, why, why had they shut the door?

While they were playing, the day had faded; the gorgeous sunset had blazed and died. And now the quick dark came racing over the sea, over the sandhills, up the paddock. You were frightened to look in the corners of the washhouse, and yet you had to look with all your might. And somewhere, far away, grandma was lighting a lamp. The blinds were being pulled down; the kitchen fire leapt in the tins on the mantelpiece.

'It would be awful now,' said the bull, 'if a spider was to fall from the ceiling on to the table, wouldn't it?'

'Spiders don't fall from ceilings.'

'Yes, they do. Our Min told us she'd seen a spider as big as a saucer, with long hairs on it like a gooseberry.'

Quickly all the little heads were jerked up; all the little bodies drew together, pressed together.

'Why doesn't somebody come and call us?' cried the rooster.

Oh, those grown-ups, laughing and snug, sitting in

184

the lamp-light, drinking out of cups! They'd forgotten about them. No, not really forgotten. That was what their smile meant. They had decided to leave them there all by themselves.

Suddenly Lottie gave such a piercing scream that all of them jumped off the forms, all of them screamed too. 'A face – a face looking!' shrieked Lottie.

It was true, it was real. Pressed against the window was a pale face, black eyes, a black beard.

'Grandma! Mother! Somebody!'

But they had not got to the door, tumbling over one another, before it opened for Uncle Jonathan. He had come to take the little boys home.

10

He had meant to be there before, but in the front garden he had come upon Linda walking up and down the grass, stopping to pick off a dead pink or give a top-heavy carnation something to lean against, or to take a deep breath of something, and then walking on again, with her little air of remoteness. Over her white frock she wore a yellow, pink-fringed shawl from the Chinaman's shop.

'Hallo, Jonathan!' called Linda. And Jonathan whipped off his shabby panama, pressed it against his breast, dropped on one knee, and kissed Linda's hand.

'Greeting, my Fair One! Greeting, my Celestial Peach Blossom!' boomed the bass voice gently. 'Where are the other noble dames?'

'Beryl's out playing bridge and mother's giving the boy his bath . . . Have you come to borrow something?'

The Trouts were for ever running out of things and sending across to the Burnells' at the last moment.

But Jonathan only answered, 'A little love, a little kindness;' and he walked by his sister-in-law's side.

Linda dropped into Beryl's hammock under the manuka-tree, and Jonathan stretched himself on the grass beside her, pulled a long stalk and began chewing it. They knew each other well. The voices of children cried from the other gardens. A fisherman's light cart shook along the sandy road, and from far away they heard a dog barking; it was muffled as though the dog had its head in a sack. If you listened you could just hear the soft swish of the sea at full tide sweeping the pebbles. The sun was sinking.

'And so you go back to the office on Monday, do you, Jonathan?' asked Linda.

'On Monday the cage door opens and clangs to upon the victim for another eleven months and a week,' answered Jonathan.

Linda swung a little. 'It must be awful,' she said slowly.

'Would ye have me laugh, my fair sister? Would ye have me weep?'

Linda was so accustomed to Jonathan's way of talking that she paid no attention to it.

'I suppose,' she said vaguely, 'one gets used to it. One gets used to anything.'

'Does one? Hum!' The 'Hum' was so deep it seemed to boom from underneath the ground. 'I wonder how it's done,' brooded Jonathan; 'I've never managed it.'

Looking at him as he lay there, Linda thought again how attractive he was. It was strange to think that he was only an ordinary clerk, that Stanley earned twice as much money as he. What was the matter with Jonathan? He had no ambition; she supposed that was it. And yet one felt he was gifted, exceptional. He was passionately fond of music; every spare penny he had went on books. He was always full of new ideas, schemes, plans. But nothing came of it all. The new fire blazed in Jonathan; you almost heard it roaring

softly as he explained, described and dilated on the new
thing; but a moment later it had fallen in and there
was nothing but ashes, and Jonathan went about with
a look like hunger in his black eyes. At these times he
exaggerated his absurd manner of speaking, and he
sang in church – he was the leader of the choir – with
such fearful dramatic intensity that the meanest hymn
put on an unholy splendour.

'It seems to me just as imbecile, just as infernal, to
have to go to the office on Monday,' said Jonathan, 'as
it always has done and always will do. To spend all the
best years of one's life sitting on a stool from nine to
five, scratching in somebody's ledger! It's a queer use
to make of one's . . . one and only life, isn't it? Or do I
fondly dream?' He rolled over on the grass and looked
up at Linda. 'Tell me, what is the difference between
my life and that of an ordinary prisoner? The only
difference I can see is that I put myself in jail and
nobody's ever going to let me out. That's a more
intolerable situation than the other. For if I'd been –
pushed in, against my will – kicking, even – once the
door was locked, or at any rate in five years or so, I
might have accepted the fact and begun to take an
interest in the flight of flies or counting the warder's
steps along the passage with particular attention to
variations of tread and so on. But as it is, I'm like an
insect that's flown into a room of its own accord. I dash
against the walls, dash against the windows, flop against
the ceiling, do everything on God's earth, in fact,
except fly out again. And all the while I'm thinking,
like that moth, or that butterfly, or whatever it is, "The
shortness of life! The shortness of life!" I've only one
night or one day, and there's this vast dangerous
garden, waiting out there, undiscovered, unexplored.'

'But, if you feel like that, why – ' began Linda
quickly.

'*Ah!*' cried Jonathan. And that 'Ah!' was somehow almost exultant. 'There you have me. Why? Why indeed? There's the maddening, mysterious question. Why don't I fly out again? There's the window or the door or whatever it was I came in by. It's not hopelessly shut – is it? Why don't I find it and be off? Answer me that, little sister.' But he gave her no time to answer.

'I'm exactly like that insect again. For some reason' – Jonathan paused between the words – 'it's not allowed, it's forbidden, it's against the insect law, to stop banging and flopping and crawling up the pane even for an instant. Why don't I leave the office? Why don't I seriously consider, this moment, for instance, what it is that prevents me leaving? It's not as though I'm tremendously tied. I've two boys to provide for, but, after all, they're boys. I could cut off to sea, or get a job up-country, or – ' Suddenly he smiled at Linda and said in a changed voice, as if he were confiding a secret, 'Weak . . . weak. No stamina. No anchor. No guiding principle, let us call it.' But then the dark velvety voice rolled out:

Would ye hear the story
How it unfolds itself . . .

and they were silent.

The sun had set. In the western sky there were great masses of crushed-up rose-coloured clouds. Broad beams of light shone through the clouds and beyond them as if they would cover the whole sky. Overhead the blue faded; it turned a pale gold, and the bush outlined against it gleamed dark and brilliant like metal. Sometimes when those beams of light show in the sky they are very awful. They remind you that up there sits Jehovah, the jealous God, the Almighty, Whose eye is upon you, ever watchful, never weary. You remember that at His coming the whole earth will shake into one

ruined graveyard; the cold, bright angels will drive you this way and that, and there will be no time to explain what could be explained so simply . . . But tonight it seemed to Linda there was something infinitely joyful and loving in those silver beams. And now no sound came from the sea. It breathed softly as if it would draw that tender, joyful beauty into its own bosom.

'It's all wrong, it's all wrong,' came the shadowy voice of Jonathan. 'It's not the scene, it's not the setting for . . . three stools, three desks, three ink pots and a wire blind.'

Linda knew that he would never change, but she said, 'Is it too late, even now?'

'I'm old – I'm old,' intoned Jonathan. He bent towards her, he passed his hand over his head. 'Look!' His black hair was speckled all over with silver, like the breast plumage of a black fowl.

Linda was surprised. She had no idea that he was grey. And yet, as he stood up beside her and sighed and stretched, she saw him, for the first time, not resolute, not gallant, not careless, but touched already with age. He looked very tall on the darkening grass, and the thought crossed her mind, 'He is like a weed.'

Jonathan stooped again and kissed her fingers.

'Heaven reward thy sweet patience, lady mine,' he murmured. 'I must go seek those heirs to my fame and fortune . . .' He was gone.

11

Light shone in the windows of the bungalow. Two square patches of gold fell upon the pinks and the peaked marigolds. Florrie, the cat, came out on to the veranda, and sat on the top step, her white paws close together, her tail curled round. She looked content, as though she had been waiting for this moment all day.

'Thank goodness, it's getting late,' said Florrie. 'Thank goodness, the long day is over.' Her greengage eyes opened.

Presently there sounded the rumble of the coach, the crack of Kelly's whip. It came near enough for one to hear the voices of the men from town, talking loudly together. It stopped at the Burnells' gate.

Stanley was half-way up the path before he saw Linda. 'Is that you, darling?'

'Yes, Stanley.'

He leapt across the flower-bed and seized her in his arms. She was enfolded in that familiar, eager, strong embrace.

'Forgive me, darling, forgive me,' stammered Stanley, and he put his hand under her chin and lifted her face to him.

'Forgive you?' smiled Linda. 'But whatever for?'

'Good God! You can't have forgotten,' cried Stanley Burnell. 'I've thought of nothing else all day. I've had the hell of a day. I made up my mind to dash out and telegraph, and then I thought the wire mightn't reach you before I did. I've been in tortures, Linda.'

'But, Stanley,' said Linda, 'what must I forgive you for?'

'Linda!' – Stanley was very hurt – 'didn't you realize – you must have realized – I went away without saying goodbye to you this morning? I can't imagine how I can have done such a thing. My confounded temper, of course. But – well' – and he sighed and took her in his arms again – 'I've suffered for it enough today.'

'What's that you've got in your hand?' asked Linda. 'New gloves? Let me see.'

'Oh, just a cheap pair of wash-leather ones,' said Stanley humbly. 'I noticed Bell was wearing some in the coach this morning, so, as I was passing the shop,

I dashed in and got myself a pair. What are you smiling at? You don't think it was wrong of me, do you?'

'On the *con*-trary, darling,' said Linda, 'I think it was most sensible.'

She pulled one of the large, pale gloves on her own fingers and looked at her hand, turning it this way and that. She was still smiling.

Stanley wanted to say, 'I was thinking of you the whole time I bought them.' It was true, but for some reason he couldn't say it. 'Let's go in,' said he.

12

Why does one feel so different at night? Why is it so exciting to be awake when everybody else is asleep? Late – it is very late! And yet every moment you feel more and more wakeful, as though you were slowly almost with every breath, waking up into a new, wonderful, far more thrilling and exciting world than the daylight one. And what is this queer sensation that you're a conspirator? Lightly, stealthily you move about your room. You take something off the dressing-table and put it down again without a sound. And everything, even the bed-posts, knows you, responds, shares your secret . . .

You're not very fond of your room by day. You never think about it. You're in and out, the door opens and slams, the cupboard creaks. You sit down on the side of your bed, change your shoes and dash out again. A dive down to the glass, two pins in your hair, powder your nose and off again. But now – it's suddenly dear to you. It's a darling little funny room. It's yours. Oh, what a joy it is to own things! Mine – my own!

'My very own for ever?'

'Yes.' Their lips met.

No, of course, that had nothing to do with it. That

was all nonsense and rubbish. But, in spite of herself, Beryl saw so plainly two people standing in the middle of her room. Her arms were round his neck; he held her. And now he whispered, 'My beauty, my little beauty!' She jumped off her bed, ran over to the window and kneeled on the window-seat, with her elbows on the sill. But the beautiful night, the garden, every bush, every leaf, even the white palings, even the stars, were conspirators too. So bright was the moon that the flowers were bright as by day; the shadows of the nasturtiums, exquisite lily-like leaves and wide-open flowers, lay across the silvery veranda. The manuka-tree, bent by the southerly winds, was like a bird on one leg stretching out a wing.

But when Beryl looked at the bush, it seemed to her the bush was sad.

'We are dumb trees, reaching up in the night, imploring we know not what,' said the sorrowful bush.

It is true when you are by yourself and you think about life, it is always sad. All that excitement and so on has a way of suddenly leaving you, and it's as though, in the silence, somebody called your name, and you heard your name for the first time. 'Beryl!'

'Yes, I'm here. I'm Beryl. Who wants me?'

'Beryl!'

'Let me come.'

It is lonely living by oneself. Of course, there are relations, friends, heaps of them; but that's not what she means. She wants someone who will find the Beryl they none of them know, who will expect her to be that Beryl always. She wants a lover.

'Take me away from all these other people, my love. Let us go far away. Let us live our life, all new, all ours, from the very beginning. Let us make our fire. Let us sit down to eat together. Let us have long talks at night.'

192

And the thought was almost, 'Save me, my love. Save me!'

. . . 'Oh, go on! Don't be a prude, my dear. You enjoy yourself while you're young. That's my advice.' And a high rush of silly laughter joined Mrs Harry Kember's loud, indifferent neigh.

You see, it's so frightfully difficult when you've nobody. You're so at the mercy of things. You can't just be rude. And you've always this horror of seeming inexperienced and stuffy like the other ninnies at the Bay. And – and it's fascinating to know you've power over people. Yes, that is fascinating . . .

Oh why, oh why doesn't 'he' come soon?

If I go on living here, thought Beryl, anything may happen to me.

'But how do you know he is coming at all?' mocked a small voice within her.

But Beryl dismissed it. She couldn't be left. Other people, perhaps, but not she. It wasn't possible to think that Beryl Fairfield never married, that lovely fascinating girl.

'Do you remember Beryl Fairfield?'

'Remember her! As if I could forget her! It was one summer at the Bay that I saw her. She was standing on the beach in a blue' – no, pink – 'muslin frock, holding on a big cream' – no, black – 'straw hat. But it's years ago now.'

'She's as lovely as ever, more so if anything.'

Beryl smiled, bit her lip, and gazed over the garden. As she gazed, she saw somebody, a man, leave the road, step along the paddock beside their palings as if he was coming straight towards her. Her heart beat. Who was it? Who could it be? It couldn't be a burglar, certainly not a burglar, for he was smoking and he strolled lightly. Beryl's heart leapt; it seemed to turn right over, and then to stop. She recognized him.

'Good evening, Miss Beryl,' said the voice softly.

'Good evening.'

'Won't you come for a little walk?' it drawled.

Come for a walk – at that time of night! 'I couldn't. Everybody's in bed. Everybody's asleep.'

'Oh,' said the voice lightly, and a whiff of sweet smoke reached her. 'What does everybody matter? Do come! It's such a fine night. There's not a soul about.'

Beryl shook her head. But already something stirred in her, something reared its head.

The voice said, 'Frightened?' It mocked, 'Poor little girl!'

'Not in the least,' said she. As she spoke that weak thing within her seemed to uncoil, to grow suddenly tremendously strong; she longed to go!

And just as if this was quite understood by the other, the voice said, gently and softly, but finally, 'Come along!'

Beryl stepped over her low window, crossed the veranda, ran down the grass to the gate. He was there before her.

'That's right,' breathed the voice, and it teased, 'You're not frightened, are you? You're not frightened?'

She was; now she was here she was terrified, and it seemed to her everything was different. The moonlight stared and glittered; the shadows were like bars of iron. Her hand was taken.

'Not in the least,' she said lightly. 'Why should I be?'

Her hand was pulled gently, tugged. She held back.

'No, I'm not coming any farther,' said Beryl.

'Oh, rot!' Harry Kember didn't believe her. 'Come along! We'll just go as far as that fuchsia bush. Come along!'

The fuchsia bush was tall. It fell over the fence in a shower. There was a little pit of darkness beneath.

'No, really, I don't want to,' said Beryl.

194

For a moment Harry Kember didn't answer. Then he came close to her, turned to her, smiled and said quickly, 'Don't be silly! Don't be silly!'

His smile was something she'd never seen before. Was he drunk? That bright, blind, terrifying smile froze her with horror. What was she doing? How had she got here? The stern garden asked her as the gate pushed open, and quick as a cat Harry Kember came through and snatched her to him.

'Cold little devil! Cold little devil!' said the hateful voice.

But Beryl was strong. She slipped, ducked, wrenched free.

'You are vile, vile,' said she.

'Then why in God's name did you come?' stammered Harry Kember.

Nobody answered him.

A cloud, small, serene, floated across the moon. In that moment of darkness the sea sounded deep, troubled. Then the cloud sailed away, and the sound of the sea was a vague murmur, as though it waked out of a dark dream. All was still.

8

The Doll's House

When dear old Mrs Hay went back to town after staying with the Burnells she sent the children a doll's house. It was so big that the carter and Pat carried it into the courtyard, and there it stayed, propped up on two wooden boxes beside the feed-room door. No harm could come to it; it was summer. And perhaps the smell of paint would have gone off by the time it had to be taken in. For, really, the smell of paint coming from that doll's house ('Sweet of old Mrs Hay, of course; most sweet and generous!') – but the smell of paint was quite enough to make anyone seriously ill, in Aunt Beryl's opinion. Even before the sacking was taken off. And when it was . . .

There stood the doll's house, a dark, oily, spinach green, picked out with bright yellow. Its two solid little chimneys, glued on to the roof, were painted red and white, and the door, gleaming with yellow varnish, was like a little slab of toffee. Four windows, real windows, were divided into panes by a broad streak of green. There was actually a tiny porch, too, painted yellow, with big lumps of congealed paint hanging along the edge.

But perfect, perfect little house! Who could possibly mind the smell. It was part of the joy, part of the newness.

'Open it quickly, someone!'

The hook at the side was stuck fast. Pat prized it open with his penknife, and the whole house front swung back, and – there you were, gazing at one and the same moment into the drawing-room and dining-room, the kitchen and two bedrooms. That is the way for a house to open! Why don't all houses open like that? How much more exciting than peering through the slit of a door into a mean little hall with a hatstand and two umbrellas! That is – isn't it? – what you long to know about a house when you put your hand on the knocker. Perhaps it is the way God opens houses at the dead of night when He is taking a quiet turn with an angel . . .

'O-oh!' The Burnell children sounded as though they were in despair. It was too marvellous; it was too much for them. They had never seen anything like it in their lives. All the rooms were papered. There were pictures on the walls, painted on the paper, with gold frames complete. Red carpet covered all the floors except the kitchen; red plush chairs in the drawing-room, green in the dining-room; tables, beds with real bedclothes, a cradle, a stove, a dresser with tiny plates and one big jug. But what Kezia liked more than anything, what she liked frightfully, was the lamp. It stood in the middle of the dining-room table, an exquisite little amber lamp with a white globe. It was even filled all ready for lighting, though, of course, you couldn't light it. But there was something inside that looked like oil and moved when you shook it.

The father and mother dolls, who sprawled very stiff as though they had fainted in the drawing-room, and their two little children asleep upstairs, were really too big for the doll's house. They didn't look as though they belonged. But the lamp was perfect. It seemed to smile at Kezia, to say, 'I live here'. The lamp was real.

The Burnell children could hardly walk to school fast

enough the next morning. They burned to tell everybody, to describe, to – well – to boast about their doll's
house before the school-bell rang.

'I'm to tell,' said Isabel, 'because I'm the eldest. And
you two can join in after. But I'm to tell first.'

There was nothing to answer. Isabel was bossy, but
she was always right, and Lottie and Kezia knew too
well the powers that went with being eldest. They
brushed through the thick buttercups at the road edge
and said nothing.

'And I'm to choose who's to come and see it first.
Mother said I might.'

For it had been arranged that while the doll's house
stood in the courtyard they might ask the girls at
school, two at a time, to come and look. Not to stay to
tea, of course, or to come traipsing through the house.
But just to stand quietly in the courtyard while Isabel
pointed out the beauties, and Lottie and Kezia looked
pleased . . .

But hurry as they might, by the time they had
reached the tarred palings of the boys' playground the
bell had begun to jangle. They only just had time to
whip off their hats and fall into line before the roll was
called. Never mind. Isabel tried to make up for it by
looking very important and mysterious and by whispering behind her hand to the girls near her, 'Got something to tell you at playtime.'

Playtime came and Isabel was surrounded. The girls
of her class nearly fought to put their arms round her,
to walk away with her, to beam flatteringly, to be her
special friend. She held quite a court under the huge
pine trees at the side of the playground. Nudging,
giggling together, the little girls pressed up close. And
the only two who stayed outside the ring were the two
who were always outside, the little Kelveys. They knew
better than to come anywhere near the Burnells.

For the fact was, the school the Burnell children went to was not at all the kind of place their parents would have chosen if there had been any choice. But there was none. It was the only school for miles. And the consequence was all the children of the neighbourhood, the judge's little girls, the doctor's daughters, the store-keeper's children, the milkman's, were forced to mix together. Not to speak of there being an equal number of rude, rough little boys as well. But the line had to be drawn somewhere. It was drawn at the Kelveys. Many of the children, including the Burnells, were not allowed even to speak to them. They walked past the Kelveys with their heads in the air, and as they set the fashion in all matters of behaviour, the Kelveys were shunned by everybody. Even the teacher had a special voice for them, and a special smile for the other children when Lil Kelvey came up to her desk with a bunch of dreadfully common-looking flowers.

They were the daughters of a spry, hard-working little washerwoman, who went about from house to house by the day. This was awful enough. But where was Mr Kelvey? Nobody knew for certain. But everybody said he was in prison. So they were the daughters of a washerwoman and a gaolbird. Very nice company for other people's children! And they looked it. Why Mrs Kelvey made them so conspicuous was hard to understand. The truth was they were dressed in 'bits' given to her by the people for whom she worked. Lil, for instance, who was a stout, plain child, with big freckles, came to school in a dress made from a green art-serge table-cloth of the Burnells', with red plush sleeves from the Logans' curtains. Her hat, perched on top of her high forehead, was a grown-up woman's hat, once the property of Miss Lecky, the postmistress. It was turned up at the back and trimmed with a large scarlet quill. What a little guy she looked! It was

impossible not to laugh. And her little sister, our Else, wore a long white dress, rather like a nightgown, and a pair of little boy's boots. But whatever our Else wore she would have looked strange. She was a tiny wishbone of a child, with cropped hair and enormous solemn eyes – a little white owl. Nobody had ever seen her smile; she scarcely ever spoke. She went through life holding on to Lil, with a piece of Lil's skirt screwed up in her hand. Where Lil went, our Else followed. In the playground, on the road going to and from school, there was Lil marching in front and our Else holding on behind. Only when she wanted anything, or when she was out of breath, our Else gave Lil a tug, a twitch, and Lil stopped and turned round. The Kelveys never failed to understand each other.

Now they hovered at the edge; you couldn't stop them listening. When the little girls turned round and sneered, Lil, as usual, gave her silly, shamefaced smile, but our Else only looked.

And Isabel's voice, so very proud, went on telling. The carpet made a great sensation, but so did the beds with real bedclothes, and the stove with an oven door.

When she finished Kezia broke in. 'You've forgotten the lamp, Isabel.'

'Oh, yes,' said Isabel, 'and there's a teeny little lamp, all made of yellow glass, with a white globe that stands on the dining-room table. You couldn't tell it from a real one.'

'The lamp's best of all,' cried Kezia. She thought Isabel wasn't making half enough of the little lamp. But nobody paid any attention. Isabel was choosing the two who were to come back with them that afternoon and see it. She chose Emmie Cole and Lena Logan. But when the others knew they were all to have a chance, they couldn't be nice enough to Isabel. One by one they put their arms round Isabel's waist and

walked her off. They had something to whisper to her, a secret. 'Isabel's *my* friend.'

Only the little Kelveys moved away forgotten; there was nothing more for them to hear.

Days passed, and as more children saw the doll's house, the fame of it spread. It became the one subject, the rage. The one question was, 'Have you seen Burnells' doll's house? Oh, ain't it lovely!' 'Haven't you seen it? Oh, I say!'

Even the dinner hour was given up to talking about it. The little girls sat under the pines eating their thick mutton sandwiches and big slabs of johnny cake spread with butter. While always, as near as they could get, sat the Kelveys, our Else holding on to Lil, listening too, while they chewed their jam sandwiches out of a newspaper soaked with large red blobs.

'Mother,' said Kezia, 'can't I ask the Kelveys just once?'

'Certainly not, Kezia.'

'But why not?'

'Run away, Kezia; you know quite well why not.'

At last everybody had seen it except them. On that day the subject rather flagged. It was the dinner hour. The children stood together under the pine trees, and suddenly, as they looked at the Kelveys eating out of their paper, always by themselves, always listening, they wanted to be horrid to them. Emmie Cole started the whisper.

'Lil Kelvey's going to be a servant when she grows up.'

'O-oh, how awful!' said Isabel Burnell, and she made eyes at Emmie.

Emmie swallowed in a very meaning way and nodded to Isabel as she'd seen her mother do on those occasions.

'It's true – it's true – it's true,' she said.

Then Lena Logan's little eyes snapped. 'Shall I ask her?' she whispered.

'Bet you don't,' said Jessie May.

'Pooh, I'm not frightened,' said Lena. Suddenly she gave a little squeal and danced in front of the other girls. 'Watch! Watch me! Watch me now!' said Lena. And sliding, gliding, dragging one foot, giggling behind her hand, Lena went over to the Kelveys.

Lil looked up from her dinner. She wrapped the rest quickly away. Our Else stopped chewing. What was coming now?

'Is it true you're going to be a servant when you grow up, Lil Kelvey?' shrilled Lena.

Dead silence. But instead of answering, Lil only gave her silly, shamefaced smile. She didn't seem to mind the question at all. What a sell for Lena! The girls began to titter.

Lena couldn't stand that. She put her hands on her hips; she shot forward. 'Yah, yer father's in prison!' she hissed, spitefully.

This was such a marvellous thing to have said that the little girls rushed away in a body, deeply, deeply excited, wild with joy. Someone found a long rope, and they began skipping. And never did they skip so high, run in and out so fast, or do such daring things as on that morning.

In the afternoon Pat called for the Burnell children with the buggy and they drove home. There were visitors. Isabel and Lottie, who liked visitors, went upstairs to change their pinafores. But Kezia thieved out at the back. Nobody was about; she began to swing on the big white gates of the courtyard. Presently, looking along the road, she saw two little dots. They grew bigger, they were coming towards her. Now she could see that one was in front and one close behind. Now

she could see that they were the Kelveys. Kezia stopped
swinging. She slipped off the gate as if she was going to
run away. Then she hesitated. The Kelveys came
nearer, and beside them walked their shadows, very
long, stretching right across the road with their heads
in the buttercups. Kezia clambered back on the gate;
she had made up her mind; she swung out.

'Hullo,' she said to the passing Kelveys.

They were so astounded that they stopped. Lil gave
her silly smile. Our Else stared.

'You can come and see our doll's house if you want
to,' said Kezia, and she dragged one toe on the ground.
But at that Lil turned red and shook her head quickly.

'Why not?' asked Kezia.

Lil gasped, then she said, 'Your ma told our ma
you wasn't to speak to us.'

'Oh, well,' said Kezia. She didn't know what to
reply. 'It doesn't matter. You can come and see our
doll's house all the same. Come on. Nobody's looking.'

But Lil shook her head still harder.

'Don't you want to?' asked Kezia.

Suddenly there was a twitch, a tug at Lil's skirt. She
turned round. Our Else was looking at her with big,
imploring eyes; she was frowning; she wanted to go.
For a moment Lil looked at our Else very doubtfully.
But then our Else twitched her skirt again. She started
forward. Kezia led the way. Like two little stray cats
they followed across the courtyard to where the doll's
house stood.

'There it is,' said Kezia.

There was a pause. Lil breathed loudly, almost snor-
ted; our Else was still as stone.

'I'll open it for you,' said Kezia kindly. She undid
the hook and they looked inside.

'There's the drawing-room and the dining-room,
and that's the . . .'

'Kezia!'

Oh, what a start they gave!

'Kezia!'

It was Aunt Beryl's voice. They turned round. At the back door stood Aunt Beryl, staring as if she couldn't believe what she saw.

'How dare you ask the little Kelveys into the courtyard?' said her cold, furious voice. 'You know as well as I do, you're not allowed to talk to them. Run away, children, run away at once. And don't come back again,' said Aunt Beryl. And she stepped into the yard and shooed them out as if they were chickens.

'Off you go immediately!' she called, cold and proud.

They did not need telling twice. Burning with shame, shrinking together, Lil huddling along like her mother, our Else dazed, somehow they crossed the big courtyard and squeezed through the white gate.

'Wicked, disobedient little girl!' said Aunt Beryl bitterly to Kezia, and she slammed the doll's house to.

The afternoon had been awful. A letter had come from Willie Brent, a terrifying, threatening letter, saying if she did not meet him that evening in Pulman's Bush, he'd come to the front door and ask the reason why! But now that she had frightened those little rats of Kelveys and given Kezia a good scolding, her heart felt lighter. That ghastly pressure was gone. She went back to the house humming.

When the Kelveys were well out of sight of Burnells', they sat down to rest on a big red drainpipe by the side of the road. Lil's cheeks were still burning; she took off the hat with the quill and held it on her knee. Dreamily they looked over the hay paddocks, past the creek, to the group of wattles where Logan's cows stood waiting to be milked. What were their thoughts?

Presently our Else nudged up close to her sister. But now she had forgotten the cross lady. She put out

a finger and stroked her sister's quill; she smiled her rare smile.

'I seen the little lamp,' she said, softly.

Then both were silent once more.

9

Marriage à la Mode

On his way to the station William remembered with a
fresh pang of disappointment that he was taking nothing down to the kiddies. Poor little chaps! It was hard
lines on them. Their first words always were as they
ran to greet him, 'What have you got for me, daddy?'
and he had nothing. He would have to buy them some
sweets at the station. But that was what he had done
for the past four Saturdays; their faces had fallen last
time when they saw the same old boxes produced
again.

And Paddy had said, 'I had red ribbing on mine *bee-
fore!*'

And Johnny had said, 'It's always pink on mine. I
hate pink.'

But what was William to do? The affair wasn't so
easily settled. In the old days, of course, he would have
taken a taxi off to a decent toyshop and chosen them
something in five minutes. But nowadays they had
Russian toys, French toys, Serbian toys – toys from
God knows where. It was over a year since Isabel had
scrapped the old donkeys and engines and so on because
they were so 'dreadfully sentimental' and 'so appallingly
bad for the babies' sense of form'.

'It's so important,' the new Isabel had explained,
'that they should like the right things from the very
beginning. It saves so much time later on. Really, if

the poor pets have to spend their infant years staring at these horrors, one can imagine them growing up and asking to be taken to the Royal Academy.'

And she spoke as though a visit to the Royal Academy was certain immediate death to anyone . . .

'Well, I don't know,' said William slowly. 'When I was their age I used to go to bed hugging an old towel with a knot in it.'

The new Isabel looked at him, her eyes narrowed, her lips apart.

'*Dear* William! I'm sure you did!' She laughed in the new way.

Sweets it would have to be, however, thought William gloomily, fishing in his pocket for change for the taxi-man. And he saw the kiddies handing the boxes round – they were awfully generous little chaps – while Isabel's precious friends didn't hesitate to help themselves . . .

What about fruit? William hovered before a stall just inside the station. What about a melon each? Would they have to share that, too? Or a pineapple for Pad, and a melon for Johnny? Isabel's friends could hardly go sneaking up to the nursery at the children's meal-times. All the same, as he bought the melon William had a horrible vision of one of Isabel's young poets lapping up a slice, for some reason, behind the nursery door.

With his two very awkward parcels he strode off to his train. The platform was crowded, the train was in. Doors banged open and shut. There came such a loud hissing from the engine that people looked dazed as they scurried to and fro. William made straight for a first-class smoker, stowed away his suit-case and parcels, and taking a huge wad of papers out of his inner pocket, he flung down in the corner and began to read.

'Our client moreover is positive . . . We are inclined

to reconsider . . . in the event of – ' Ah, that was better. William pressed back his flattened hair and stretched his legs across the carriage floor. The familiar dull gnawing in his breast quietened down. 'With regard to our decision – ' He took out a blue pencil and scored a paragraph slowly.

Two men came in, stepped across him, and made for the farther corner. A young fellow swung his golf clubs into the rack and sat down opposite. The train gave a gentle lurch, they were off. William glanced up and saw the hot, bright station slipping away. A red-faced girl raced along by the carriages, there was something strained and almost desperate in the way she waved and called. 'Hysterical!' thought William dully. Then a greasy, black-faced workman at the end of the platform grinned at the passing train. And William thought, 'A filthy life!' and went back to his papers.

When he looked up again there were fields, and beasts standing for shelter under the dark trees. A wide river, with naked children splashing in the shallows, glided into sight and was gone again. The sky shone pale, and one bird drifted high like a dark fleck in a jewel.

'We have examined our client's correspondence files . . .' The last sentence he had read echoed in his mind. 'We have examined . . .' William hung on to that sentence, but it was no good; it snapped in the middle, and the fields, the sky, the sailing bird, the water, all said, 'Isabel'. The same thing happened every Saturday afternoon. When he was on his way to meet Isabel there began those countless imaginary meetings. She was at the station, standing just a little apart from everybody else; she was sitting in the open taxi outside; she was at the garden gate; walking across the parched grass; at the door, or just inside the hall.

And her clear, light voice said, 'It's William,' or

'Hillo, William!' or 'So William has come!' He touched her cool hand, her cool cheek.

The exquisite freshness of Isabel! When he had been a little boy, it was his delight to run into the garden after a shower of rain and shake the rose-bush over him. Isabel was that rose-bush, petal-soft, sparkling and cool. And he was still that little boy. But there was no running into the garden now, no laughing and shaking. The dull, persistent gnawing in his breast started again. He drew up his legs, tossed the papers aside, and shut his eyes.

'What is it, Isabel? What is it?' he said tenderly. They were in their bedroom in the new house. Isabel sat on a painted stool before the dressing-table that was strewn with little back and green boxes.

'What is what, William?' And she bent forward, and her fine hair fell over her cheeks.

'Ah, you know!' He stood in the middle of the strange room and he felt a stranger. At that Isabel wheeled round quickly and faced him.

'Oh, William!' she cried imploringly, and she held up the hair-brush. 'Please! Please don't be so dreadfully stuffy and – tragic. You're always saying or looking or hinting that I've changed. Just because I've got to know really congenial people, and go about more, and am frightfully keen on – on everything, you behave as though I'd – ' Isabel tossed back her hair and laughed – 'killed our love or something. It's so awfully absurd' – she bit her lip – 'and it's so maddening, William. Even this new house and the servants you grudge me.'

'Isabel!'

'Yes, yes, it's true in a way,' said Isabel quickly. 'You think they are another bad sign. Oh, I know you do. I feel it,' she said softly, 'every time you come up the stairs. But we couldn't have gone on living in that other poky little hole, William. Be practical, at least!

Why, there wasn't enough room for the babies even.'

No, it was true. Every morning when he came back from chambers it was to find the babies with Isabel in the back drawing-room. They were having rides on the leopard skin thrown over the sofa back, or they were playing shops with Isabel's desk for a counter, or Pad was sitting on the hearthrug rowing away for dear life with a little brass fire-shovel, while Johnny shot at pirates with the tongs. Every evening they each had a pick-a-back up the narrow stairs to their fat old Nanny.

Yes, he supposed it was a poky little house. A little white house with blue curtains and a window-box of petunias. William met their friends at the door with 'Seen our petunias? Pretty terrific for London, don't you think?'

But the imbecile thing, the absolutely extraordinary thing was that he hadn't the slightest idea that Isabel wasn't as happy as he. God, what blindness! He hadn't the remotest notion in those days that she really hated that inconvenient little house, that she thought the fat Nanny was ruining the babies, that she was desperately lonely, pining for new people and new music and pictures and so on. If they hadn't gone to that studio party at Moira Morrison's – if Moira Morrison hadn't said as they were leaving, 'I'm going to rescue your wife, selfish man. She's like an exquisite little Titania' – if Isabel hadn't gone with Moira to Paris – if – if . . .

The train stopped at another station. Bettingford. Good heavens! They'd be there in ten minutes. William stuffed the papers back into his pockets; the young man opposite had long since disappeared. Now the other two got out. The late afternoon sun shone on women in cotton frocks and little sun-burnt, barefoot children. It blazed on a silky yellow flower with coarse leaves which sprawled over a bank of rock. The air ruffling through the window smelled of the sea. Had Isabel the

same crowd with her this week-end, wondered William?

And he remembered the holidays they used to have, the four of them, with a little farm girl, Rose, to look after the babies. Isabel wore a jersey and her hair in a plait; she looked about fourteen. Lord! how his nose used to peel! And the amount they ate, and the amount they slept in that immense feather bed with their feet locked together . . . William couldn't help a grim smile as he thought of Isabel's horror if she knew the full extent of his sentimentality.

'Hillo, William!' She was at the station after all, standing just as he had imagined, apart from the others, and – William's heart leapt – she was alone.

'Hallo, Isabel!' William stared. He thought she looked so beautiful that he had to say something, 'You look very cool.'

'Do I?' said Isabel. 'I don't feel very cool. Come along, your horrid old train is late. The taxi's outside.' She put her hand lightly on his arm as they passed the ticket collector. 'We've all come to meet you,' she said. 'But we've left Bobby Kane at the sweet shop, to be called for.'

'Oh!' said William. It was all he could say for the moment.

There in the glare waited the taxi, with Bill Hunt and Dennis Green sprawling on one side, their hats tilted over their faces, while on the other, Moira Morrison, in a bonnet like a huge strawberry, jumped up and down.

'No ice! No ice! No ice!' she shouted gaily.

And Dennis chimed in from under his hat. '*Only* to be had from the fishmonger's.'

And Bill Hunt, emerging, added, 'With *whole* fish in it.'

'Oh, what a bore!' wailed Isabel. And she explained

to William how they had been chasing round the town for ice while she waited for him. 'Simply everything is running down the steep cliffs into the sea, beginning with the butter.'

'We shall have to anoint ourselves with the butter,' said Dennis. 'May thy head, William, lack not ointment.'

'Look here,' said William, 'how are we going to sit? I'd better get up by the driver.'

'No, Bobby Kane's by the driver,' said Isabel. 'You're to sit between Moira and me.' The taxi started. 'What have you got in those mysterious parcels?'

'De-cap-it-ated heads!' said Bill Hunt, shuddering beneath his hat.

'Oh, fruit!' Isabel sounded very pleased. 'Wise William! A melon and a pineapple. How too nice!'

'No, wait a bit,' said William, smiling. But he really was anxious. 'I brought them down for the kiddies.'

'Oh, my dear!' Isabel laughed, and slipped her hand through his arm. 'They'd be rolling in agonies if they were to eat them. No' – she patted his hand – 'you must bring them something next time. I refuse to part with my pineapple.'

'Cruel Isabel! Do let me smell it!' said Moira. She flung her arms across William appealingly. 'Oh!' The strawberry bonnet fell forward: she sounded quite faint.

'A Lady in Love with a Pine-apple,' said Dennis, as the taxi drew up before a little shop with a striped blind. Out came Bobby Kane, his arms full of little packets.

'I do hope they'll be good. I've chosen them because of the colours. There are some round things which really look too divine. And just look at this nougat,' he cried ecstatically, 'just look at it! It's a perfect little ballet!'

But at that moment the shopman appeared. 'Oh, I

212

forgot. They're none of them paid for,' said Bobby, looking frightened. Isabel gave the shopman a note, and Bobby was radiant again. 'Hallo, William! I'm sitting by the driver.' And bare-headed, all in white, with his sleeves rolled up to the shoulders, he leapt into his place. '*Avanti!*' he cried . . .

After tea the others went off to bathe, while William stayed and made his peace with the kiddies. But Johnny and Paddy were asleep, the rose-red glow had paled, bats were flying, and still the bathers had not returned. As William wandered downstairs, the maid crossed the hall carrying a lamp. He followed her into the sitting-room. It was a long room, coloured yellow. On the wall opposite William some one had painted a young man, over life-size, with very wobbly legs, offering a wide-eyed daisy to a young woman who had one very short arm and one very long, thin one. Over the chairs and sofa there hung strips of black material, covered with big splashes like broken eggs, and everywhere one looked there seemed to be an ash-tray full of cigarette ends. William sat down in one of the armchairs. Nowadays, when one felt with one hand down the sides, it wasn't to come upon a sheep with three legs or a cow that had lost one horn, or a very fat dove out of the Noah's Ark. One fished up yet another little paper-covered book of smudged-looking poems . . . He thought of the wad of papers in his pocket, but he was too hungry and tired to read. The door was open; sounds came from the kitchen. The servants were talking as if they were alone in the house. Suddenly there came a loud screech of laughter and an equally loud 'Sh!' They had remembered him. William got up and went through the french windows into the garden, and as he stood there in the shadow he heard the bathers coming up the sandy road; their voices rang through the quiet.

'I think it's up to Moira to use her little arts and wiles.'

A tragic moan from Moira.

'We ought to have a gramophone for the week-ends that played "The Maid of the Mountains".'

'Oh no! Oh no!' cried Isabel's voice. 'That's not fair to William. Be nice to him, my children! He's only staying until tomorrow evening.'

'Leave him to me,' cried Bobby Kane. 'I'm awfully good at looking after people.'

The gate swung open and shut. William moved on the terrace; they had seen him. 'Hallo, William!' And Bobby Kane, flapping his towel, began to leap and pirouette on the parched lawn. 'Pity you didn't come, William. The water was divine. And we all went to a little pub afterwards and had sloe gin.'

The others had reached the house. 'I say, Isabel,' called Bobby, 'would you like me to wear my Nijinsky dress tonight?'

'No,' said Isabel, 'nobody's going to dress. We're all starving. William's starving, too. Come along, *mes amis*, let's begin with sardines.'

'I've found the sardines,' said Moira, and she ran into the hall, holding a box high in the air.

'A Lady with a Box of Sardines,' said Dennis gravely.

'Well, William, and how's London?' asked Bill Hunt, drawing the cork out of a bottle of whisky.

'Oh, London's not much changed,' answered William.

'Good old London,' said Bobby, very hearty, spearing a sardine.

But a moment later William was forgotten. Moira Morrison began wondering what colour one's legs really were under water.

'Mine are the palest, palest mushroom colour.'

Bill and Dennis ate enormously. And Isabel filled

214

glasses, and changed plates, and found matches, smiling blissfully. At one moment she said, 'I do wish, Bill, you'd paint it.'

'Paint what?' said Bill loudly, stuffing his mouth with bread.

'Us,' said Isabel, 'round the table. It would be so fascinating in twenty years' time.'

Bill screwed up his eyes and chewed. 'Light's wrong,' he said rudely, 'far too much yellow'; and went on eating. And that seemed to charm Isabel, too.

But after supper they were all so tired they could do nothing but yawn until it was late enough to go to bed . . .

It was not until William was waiting for his taxi the next afternoon that he found himself alone with Isabel. When he brought his suit-case down into the hall, Isabel left the others and went over to him. She stooped down and picked up the suit-case. 'What a weight!' she said, and she gave a little awkward laugh. 'Let me carry it! To the gate.'

'No, why should you?' said William. 'Of course not. Give it to me.'

'Oh, please do let me,' said Isabel. 'I want to, really.' They walked together silently. William felt there was nothing to say now.

'There,' said Isabel triumphantly, setting the suit-case down, and she looked anxiously along the sandy road. 'I hardly seem to have seen you this time,' she said breathlessly. 'It's so short, isn't it? I feel you've only just come. Next time – ' The taxi came into sight. 'I hope they look after you properly in London. I'm so sorry the babies have been out all day, but Miss Neil had arranged it. They'll hate missing you. Poor William, going back to London.' The taxi turned. 'Goodbye!' She gave him a little hurried kiss; she was gone.

Fields, trees, hedges streamed by. They shook through

the empty, blind-looking little town, ground up the steep pull to the station. The train was in. William made straight for a first-class smoker, flung back into the corner, but this time he let the papers alone. He folded his arms against the dull, persistent gnawing, and began in his mind to write a letter to Isabel.

The post was late as usual. They sat outside the house in long chairs under coloured parasols. Only Bobby Kane lay on the turf at Isabel's feet. It was dull, stifling; the day drooped like a flag.

'Do you think there will be Mondays in Heaven?' asked Bobby childishly.

And Dennis murmured, 'Heaven will be one long Monday.'

But Isabel couldn't help wondering what had happened to the salmon they had for supper last night. She had meant to have fish mayonnaise for lunch and now . . .

Moira was asleep. Sleeping was her latest discovery. 'It's *so* wonderful. One simply shuts one's eyes, that's all. It's *so* delicious.'

When the old ruddy postman came beating along the sandy road on his tricycle one felt the handlebars ought to have been oars.

Bill Hunt put down his book. 'Letters,' he said complacently, and they all waited. But, heartless postman – O malignant world! There was only one, a fat one for Isabel. Not even a paper.

'And mine's only from William,' said Isabel mournfully.

'From William – already?'

'He's sending you back your marriage lines as a gentle reminder.'

'Does everybody have marriage lines? I thought they were only for servants.'

'Pages and pages! Look at her! A Lady reading a Letter,' said Dennis.

My darling, precious Isabel. Pages and pages there were. As Isabel read on her feeling of astonishment changed to a stifled feeling. What on earth had induced William . . . ? How extraordinary it was . . . What could have made him . . . ? She felt confused, more and more excited, even frightened. It was just like William. Was it? It was absurd, of course, it must be absurd, ridiculous. 'Ha, ha, ha! Oh dear!' What was she to do? Isabel flung back in her chair and laughed till she couldn't stop laughing.

'Do, tell us,' said the others. 'You must tell us.'

'I'm longing to,' gurgled Isabel. She sat up, gathered the letter, and waved it at them. 'Gather round,' she said. 'Listen, it's too marvellous. A love-letter!'

'A love-letter! But how divine!' *Darling, precious Isabel.* But she had hardly begun before their laughter interrupted her.

'Go on, Isabel, it's perfect.'

'It's the most marvellous find.'

'Oh, do go on, Isabel!'

God forbid, my darling, that I should be a drag on your happiness.

'Oh! oh! oh!'

'Sh! sh! sh!'

And Isabel went on. When she reached the end they were hysterical: Bobby rolled on the turf and almost sobbed.

'You must let me have it just as it is, entire, for my new book,' said Dennis firmly. 'I shall give it a whole chapter.'

'Oh, Isabel,' moaned Moira, 'that wonderful bit about holding you in his arms!'

'I always thought those letters in divorce cases were made up. But they pale before this.'

'Let me hold it. Let me read it, mine own self,' said Bobby Kane.

But, to their surprise, Isabel crushed the letter in her hand. She was laughing no longer. She glanced quickly at them all; she looked exhausted. 'No, not just now,' she stammered.

And before they could recover she had run into the house, through the hall, up the stairs into her bedroom. Down she sat on the side of the bed. 'How vile, odious, abominable, vulgar,' muttered Isabel. She pressed her eyes with her knuckles and rocked to and fro. And again she saw them, but not four, more like forty, laughing, sneering, jeering, stretching out their hands while she read them William's letter. Oh, what a loathsome thing to have done. How could she have done it! *God forbid, my darling, that I should be a drag on your happiness.* William! Isabel pressed her face into the pillow. But she felt that even the grave bedroom knew her for what she was, shallow, tinkling, vain . . .

Presently from the garden below there came voices.

'Isabel, we're all going for a bathe. Do come!'

'Come, thou wife of William!'

'Call her once before you go, call once yet!'

Isabel sat up. Now was the moment, now she must decide. Would she go with them, or stay here and write to William. Which, which should it be? 'I must make up my mind.' Oh, but how could there be any question? Of course she would stay and write.

'Titania!' piped Moira.

'Is-abel?'

No, it was too difficult. 'I'll – I'll go with them, and write to William later. Some other time. Later. Not now. But I shall *certainly* write,' thought Isabel hurriedly.

And, laughing in the new way, she ran down the stairs.

10

A Married Man's Story

It is evening. Supper is over. We have left the small,
cold dining-room, we have come back to the sitting-
room where there is a fire. All is as usual. I am sitting
at my writing table which is placed across a corner so
that I am behind it, as it were, and facing the room.
The lamp with the green shade is alight; I have before
me two large books of reference, both open, a pile of
papers . . . All the paraphernalia, in fact, of an extremely
occupied man. My wife, with her little boy on her lap,
is in a low chair before the fire. She is about to put him
to bed before she clears away the dishes and piles them
up in the kitchen for the servant girl tomorrow morning. But the warmth, the quiet, and the sleepy baby,
have made her dreamy. One of his red woollen boots is
off, one is on. She sits, bent forward, clasping the little
bare foot, staring into the glow, and as the fire quickens,
falls, flares again, her shadow – an immense *Mother
and Child* – is here and gone again upon the wall . . .
Outside it is raining. I like to think of that cold
drenched window behind the blind, and beyond, the
dark bushes in the garden, their broad leaves bright
with rain, and beyond the fence, the gleaming road
with the two hoarse little gutters singing against each
other, and the wavering reflections of the lamps, like
fishes' tails. While I am here, I am there, lifting my
face to the dim sky, and it seems to me it must be

raining all over the world – that the whole earth is drenched, is sounding with a soft quick patter or hard steady drumming, or gurgling and something that is like sobbing and laughing mingled together, and that light playful splashing that is of water falling into still lakes and flowing rivers. And all at one and the same moment I am arriving in a strange city, slipping under the hood of the cab while the driver whips the cover off the breathing horse, running from shelter to shelter, dodging someone, swerving by someone else. I am conscious of tall houses, their doors and shutters sealed against the night, of dripping balconies and sodden flower-pots. I am brushing through deserted gardens and falling into moist smelling summer-houses (you know how soft and almost crumbling the wood of a summer-house is in the rain), I am standing on the dark quayside, giving my ticket into the wet red hand of the old sailor in an oilskin. How strong the sea smells! How loudly the tied-up boats knock against one another! I am crossing the wet stackyard, hooded in an old sack, carrying a lantern, while the house-dog, like a soaking doormat, springs, shakes himself over me. And now I am walking along a deserted road it is impossible to miss the puddles, and the trees are stirring – stirring.

But one could go on with such a catalogue for ever – on and on – until one lifted the single arum lily leaf and discovered the tiny snails clinging, until one counted . . . and what then? Aren't those just the signs, the traces of my feeling? The bright green streaks made by someone who walks over the dewy grass? Not the feeling itself. And as I think that, a mournful glorious voice begins to sing in my bosom. Yes, perhaps that is nearer what I mean. What a voice! What power! What velvety softness! Marvellous!

Suddenly my wife turns round quickly. She knows –

how long has she known? – that I am not 'working'. It is strange that with her full, open gaze, she should smile so timidly – and that she should say in such a hesitating voice, 'What are you thinking?'

I smile and draw two fingers across my forehead in the way I have. 'Nothing,' I answer softly.

At that she stirs, and still trying not to make it sound important, she says, 'Oh, but you must have been thinking of something!'

Then I really meet her gaze, meet it fully, and I fancy her face quivers. Will she never grow accustomed to these simple – one might say – everyday little lies? Will she never learn not to expose herself – or to build up defences?

'Truly, I was thinking of nothing.'

There! I seem to see it dart at her. She turns away, pulls the other red sock off the baby, sits him up, and begins to unbutton him behind. I wonder if that little soft rolling bundle sees anything, feels anything? Now she turns him over on her knee, and in this light, his soft arms and legs waving, he is extraordinarily like a young crab. A queer thing is I can't connect him with my wife and myself; I've never accepted him as ours. Each time when I come into the hall and see the perambulator, I catch myself thinking: 'H'm, someone has brought a baby!' Or, when his crying wakes me at night, I feel inclined to blame my wife for having brought the baby in from outside. The truth is, that though one might suspect her of strong maternal feelings, my wife doesn't seem to me the type of woman who bears children in her own body. There's an immense difference! Where is that . . . animal ease and playfulness, that quick kissing and cuddling one has been taught to expect of young mothers? She hasn't a sign of it. I believe that when she ties its bonnet she feels like an aunt and not a mother. But of course I may

be wrong; she may be passionately devoted . . . I don't
think so. At any rate, isn't it a trifle indecent to feel
like this about one's own wife? Indecent or not, one has
these feelings. And one other thing. How can I reason-
ably expect my wife, *a broken-hearted woman*, to spend
her time tossing the baby? But that is beside the mark.
She never even began to toss when her heart was
whole.

And now she has carried the baby to bed. I hear her
soft, deliberate steps moving between the dining-room
and the kitchen, there and back again, to the tune of
the clattering dishes. And now all is quiet. What is
happening now? Oh, I know just as surely as if I'd
gone to see – she is standing in the middle of the
kitchen facing the rainy window. Her head is bent,
with one finger she is tracing something – nothing – on
the table. It is cold in the kitchen; the gas jumps; the
tap drips; it's a forlorn picture. And nobody is going to
come behind her, to take her in his arms, to kiss her
soft hair, to lead her to the fire and to rub her hands
warm again. Nobody is going to call her or to wonder
what she is doing out there. And she knows it. And
yet, being a woman, deep down, deep down, she really
does expect the miracle to happen; she really could
embrace that dark, dark deceit, rather than live – like
this.

To live like this . . . I write those words, very carefully,
very beautifully. For some reason I feel inclined to
sign them, or to write underneath – Trying a New
Pen. But seriously, isn't it staggering to think what
may be contained in one innocent-looking little phrase?
It tempts me – it tempts me terribly. Scene. The
supper-table. My wife has just handed me my tea. I
stir it, lift the spoon, idly chase and then carefully
capture a speck of tea-leaf, and having brought it

ashore, I murmur, quite gently, 'How long shall we
continue to live – like – this?' And immediately there
is that famous 'blinding flash and deafening roar.
Huge pieces of debris (I must say I like debris) are
flung into the air . . . and when the dark clouds of
smoke have drifted away . . .' But this will never
happen; I shall never know it. It will be found upon
me 'intact' as they say. 'Open my heart and you will
see . . .'

Why? Ah, there you have me! There is the most
difficult question of all to answer. Why do people stay
together? Putting aside 'for the sake of the children'
and 'the habit of years' and 'economic reasons' as
lawyers' nonsense – it's not much more – if one really
does try to find out why it is that people don't leave
each other, one discovers a mystery. It is because they
can't; they are bound. And nobody on earth knows
what are the bonds that bind them except those two. Am
I being obscure? Well, the thing itself isn't so frightfully crystal clear, is it? Let me put it like this.
Supposing you are taken, absolutely, first into his confidence and then into hers. Supposing you know all there
is to know about the situation. And having given it not
only your deepest sympathy but your most honest im-
partial criticism, you declare, very calmly, (but not
without the slightest suggestion of relish – for there is –
I swear there is – in the very best of us – something that
leaps up and cries 'A-ahh!' for joy at the thought of
destroying), 'Well, my opinion is that you two people
ought to part. You'll do no earthly good together. Indeed, it seems to me, it's the duty of either to set the
other free.' What happens then? He – and she – agree.
It is their conviction too. You are only saying what they
have been thinking all last night. And away they go
to act on your advice, immediately . . . And the next
time you hear of them they are still together. You see –

you've reckoned without the unknown quantity – which is their secret relation to each other – and that they can't disclose even if they want to. Thus far you may tell and no further. Oh, don't misunderstand me! It need not necessarily have anything to do with their sleeping together . . . But this brings me to a thought I've often half entertained. Which is that human beings, as we know them, don't choose each other at all. It is the owner, the second self inhabiting them, who makes the choice for his own particular purposes, and – this may sound absurdly far-fetched – it's the second self in the other which responds. Dimly – dimly – or so it has seemed to me – we realize this, at any rate to the extent that we realize the hopelessness of trying to escape. So that, what it all amounts to is – if the impermanent selves of my wife and me are happy – *tant mieux pour nous* – if miserable – *tant pis* . . . But I don't know, I don't know. And it may be that it's something entirely individual in me – this sensation (yes, it is even a sensation) of how extraordinarily *shell-like* we are as we are – little creatures, peering out of the sentry-box at the gate, ogling through our glass case at the entry, wan little servants, who never can say for certain, even, if the master is out or in . . .

The door opens . . . My wife. She says, 'I am going to bed.'

And I look up vaguely, and vaguely say, 'You are going to bed.'

'Yes.' A tiny pause. 'Don't forget – will you? – to turn out the gas in the hall.'

And again I repeat, 'The gas in the hall.'

There was a time – the time before – when this habit of mine – it really has become a habit now – it wasn't one then – was one of our sweetest jokes together. It began, of course, when on several occasions I really was deeply engaged and I didn't hear. I

emerged only to see her shaking her head and laughing at me, 'You haven't heard a word!'

'No. What did you say?'

Why should she think that so funny and charming? She did; it delighted her. 'Oh, my darling, it's so like you! It's so – so – ' And I knew she loved me for it. I knew she positively looked forward to coming in and disturbing me, and so – as one does – I played up. I was guaranteed to be wrapped away every evening at 10.30 pm. But now? For some reason I feel it would be crude to stop my performance. It's simplest to play on. But what is she waiting for tonight? Why doesn't she go? Why prolong this? She is going. No, her hand on the door-knob, she turns round again, and she says in the most curious, small, breathless voice, 'You're not cold?'

Oh, it's not fair to be as pathetic as that! That was simply damnable. I shuddered all over before I managed to bring out a slow 'No-o!' while my left hand ruffles the reference pages.

She is gone; she will not come back again tonight. It is not only I who recognize that; the room changes too. It relaxes, like an old actor. Slowly the mask is rubbed off; the look of strained attention changes to an air of heavy sullen brooding. Every line, every fold breathes fatigue. The mirror is quenched; the ash whitens; only my sly lamp burns on . . . But what a cynical indifference to me it all shows! Or should I perhaps be flattered? No, we understand each other. You know those stories of little children who are suckled by wolves and accepted by the tribe, and how for ever after they move freely among their fleet, grey brothers? Something like that has happened to me. But wait! That about the wolves won't do. Curious! Before I wrote it down, while it was still in my head, I was delighted with it. It seemed to express, and more,

to suggest, just what I wanted to say. But written, I can smell the falseness immediately and the . . . source of the smell is in that word fleet. Don't you agree? Fleet, grey brothers! 'Fleet.' A word I never use. When I wrote 'wolves' it skimmed across my mind like a shadow and I couldn't resist it. Tell me! Tell me! Why is it so difficult to write simply – and not only simply but *sotto voce*, if you know what I mean? That is how I long to write. No fine effects – no bravura. But just the plain truth, as only a liar can tell it.

I light a cigarette, lean back, inhale deeply – and find myself wondering if my wife is asleep. Or is she lying in her cold bed, staring into the dark, with those trustful, bewildered eyes? Her eyes are like the eyes of a cow that is being driven along a road. 'Why am I being driven – what harm have I done?' But I really am not responsible for that look; it's her natural expression. One day, when she was turning out a cupboard, she found a little old photograph of herself, taken when she was a girl at school. In her confirmation dress, she explained. And there were the eyes, even then. I remember saying to her, 'Did you always look so sad?' Leaning over my shoulder, she laughed lightly, 'Do I look sad? I think it's just . . . me.' And she waited for me to say something about it. But I was marvelling at her courage at having shown it to me at all. It was a hideous photograph! And I wondered again if she realized how plain she was, and comforted herself with the idea that people who loved each other didn't criticise but accepted everything, or if she really rather liked her appearance and expected me to say something complimentary.

Oh, that was base of me! How could I have forgotten all the numberless times when I have known her turn away to avoid the light, press her face into my shoul-

ders. And, above all, how could I have forgotten the afternoon of our wedding day when we sat on the green bench in the Botanical Gardens and listened to the band, how, in an interval between two pieces, she suddenly turned to me and said in the voice in which one says, 'Do you think the grass is damp?' or 'Do you think it's time for tea?' . . . 'Tell me, do you think physical beauty is so very important?' I don't like to think how often she had rehearsed that question. And do you know what I answered? At that moment, as if at my command there came a great gush of hard, bright sound from the band, and I managed to shout above it cheerfully, 'I didn't hear what you said.' Devilish! Wasn't it? Perhaps not wholly. She looked like the poor patient who hears the surgeon say, 'It will certainly be necessary to perform the operation – but not now!'

But all this conveys the impression that my wife and I were never really happy together. Not true! Not true! We were marvellously, radiantly happy. We were a model couple. If you had seen us together, any time, any place, if you had followed us, tracked us down, spied, taken us off our guard, you still would have been forced to confess, 'I have never seen a more ideally suited pair.' Until last autumn.

But really to explain what happened then I should have to go back and back, I should have to dwindle until my two hands clutched the bannisters, the stair-rail was higher than my head, and I peered through to watch my father padding softly up and down. There were coloured windows on the landings. As he came up, first his bald head was scarlet; then it was yellow. How frightened I was! And when they put me to bed, it was to dream that we were living inside one of my father's big coloured bottles. For he was a chemist. I was born

nine years after my parents were married. I was an only child, and the effort to produce even me – small, withered bud I must have been – sapped all my mother's strength. She never left her room again. Bed, sofa, window, she moved between the three. Well I can see her, on the window days, sitting, her cheek in her hand, staring out. Her room looked over the street. Opposite there was a wall plastered with advertisements for travelling shows and circuses and so on. I stand beside her, and we gaze at the slim lady in a red dress hitting a dark gentleman over the head with her parasol, or at the tiger peering through the jungle while the clown, close by, balances a bottle on his nose, or at a little golden-haired girl sitting on the knee of an old black man in a broad cotton hat . . . She says nothing. On sofa days there is a flannel dressing gown that I loathe, and a cushion that keeps on slipping off the hard sofa. I pick it up. It has flowers and writing sewn on. I ask what the writing says, and she whispers, 'Sweet Repose!' In bed her fingers plait, in tight little plaits, the fringe of the quilt, and her lips are thin. And that is all there is of my mother, except the last queer 'episode' that comes later.

My father . . . Curled up in the corner on the lid of a round box that held sponges, I stared at my father so long, it's as though his image, cut off at the waist by the counter, has remained solid in my memory. Perfectly bald, polished head, shaped like a thin egg, creased, creamy cheeks, little bags under the eyes, large pale ears like handles. His manner was discreet, sly, faintly amused and tinged with impudence. Long before I could appreciate it, I knew the mixture . . . I even used to copy him in my corner, bending forward, with a small reproduction of his faint sneer. In the evening his customers were, chiefly, young women; some of them came in every day for his famous five-

penny pick-me-up. Their gaudy looks, their voices, their free ways, fascinated me. I longed to be my father, handing them across the counter the little glass of bluish stuff they tossed off so greedily. God knows what it was made of. Years after I drank some, just to see what it tasted like, and I felt as though someone had given me a terrific blow on the head; I felt stunned.

One of those evenings I remember vividly. It was cold; it must have been autumn, for the flaring gas was lighted after my tea. I sat in my corner and my father was mixing something; the shop was empty. Suddenly the bell jangled and a young woman rushed in, crying so loud, sobbing so hard, that it didn't sound real. She wore a green cape trimmed with fur and a hat with cherries dangling. My father came from behind the screen. But she couldn't stop herself at first. She stood in the middle of the shop and wrung her hands and moaned; I've never heard such crying since. Presently she managed to gasp out, 'Give me a pick-me-up!' Then she drew a long breath, trembled away from him and quavered, 'I've had *bad news!*' And in the flaring gaslight I saw the whole side of her face was puffed up and purple; her lip was cut, and her eyelid looked as though it was gummed fast over the wet eye. My father pushed the glass across the counter, and she took the purse out of her stocking and paid him. But she couldn't drink; clutching the glass, she stared in front of her as if she could not believe what she saw. Each time she put her head back the tears spurted out again. Finally she put the glass down. It was no use. Holding the cape with one hand, she ran in the same way out of the shop again. My father gave no sign. But long after she had gone I crouched in my corner, and when I think back it's as though I felt my whole body vibrating – 'So that's what it is outside,' I thought. 'That's what it's like out there.'

Do you remember your childhood? I am always coming across these marvellous accounts by writers who declare that they remember 'everything'. I certainly don't. The dark stretches, the blanks, are much bigger than the bright glimpses. I seem to have spent most of my time like a plant in a cupboard. Now and again, when the sun shone, a careless hand thrust me out on to the window-sill, and a careless hand whipped me in again – and that was all. But what happened in the darkness – I wonder? Did one grow? Pale stem . . . timid leaves . . . white reluctant bud. No wonder I was hated at school. Even the masters shrank from me. I somehow knew that my soft hesitating voice disgusted them. I knew, too, how they turned away from my shocked, staring eyes. I was small and thin, and I smelled of the shop; my nickname was Gregory Powder. School was a tin building, stuck on the raw hillside. There were dark red streaks like blood in the oozing clay banks of the playground. I hide in the dark passage, where the coats hang, and am discovered there by one of the masters. 'What are you doing there in the dark?' His terrible voice kills me; I die before his eyes. I am standing in a ring of thrust-out heads, some are grinning, some look greedy, some are spitting. And it is always cold. Big crushed-up clouds press across the sky; the rusty water in the school tank is frozen; the bell sounds numb. One day they put a dead bird in my overcoat pocket. I found it just when I reached home. Oh, what a strange flutter there was at my heart when I drew out that terribly soft, cold little body, with the legs thin as pins and the claws wrung. I sat on the back door step in the yard and put the bird in my cap. The feathers round the neck looked wet, and there was a tiny tuft just above the closed eyes that stood up too. How tightly the beak was shut! I could not see the mark where it was divided. I stretched out one wing and touched the soft,

secret down underneath; I tried to make the claws curl round my finger. But I didn't feel sorry for it – no! I wondered. The smoke from our kitchen chimney poured downwards, and flakes of soot floated – soft, light in the air. Through a big crack in the cement yard a poor-looking plant with dull, reddish flowers had pushed its way. I looked at the dead bird again . . . And that is the first time that I remember singing – rather . . . listening to a silent voice inside a little cage that was me.

But what has all this to do with my married happiness? How can all this affect my wife and me? Why – to tell what happened last autumn – do I run all this way back into the Past? The Past – what is the Past? I might say the star-shaped flake of soot on a leaf of the poor-looking plant, and the bird lying on the quilted lining of my cap, and my father's pestle and my mother's cushion belong to it. But that is not to say they are any less mine than they were when I looked upon them with my very eyes, and touched them with these fingers. No, they are more; they are a living part of me. Who am I, in fact, as I sit here at this table, but my own past? If I deny that, I am nothing. And if I were to try to divide my life into childhood, youth, early manhood and so on, it would be a kind of affectation; I should know I was doing it just because of the pleasantly important sensation it gives one to rule lines, and to use green ink for childhood, red for the next stage, and purple for the period of adolescence. For, one thing I have learnt, one thing I do believe is, Nothing Happens Suddenly. Yes, that is my religion, I suppose.

My mother's death, for instance. Is it more distant from me today than it was then? It is just as close, as strange, as puzzling, and in spite of all the countless times I have recalled the circumstances, I know no

more now than I did then, whether I dreamed them, or whether they really occurred. It happened when I was thirteen and I slept in a little strip of a room on what was called the half-landing. One night I woke up with a start to see my mother, in her night-gown, without even the hated flannel dressing-gown, sitting on my bed. But the strange thing which frightened me was, she wasn't looking at me. Her head was bent; the short, thin tail of hair lay between her shoulders; her hands were pressed between her knees, and my bed shook; she was shivering. It was the first time I had ever seen her out of her own room. I said, or I think I said, 'Is that you, mother?' And as she turned round, I saw in the moonlight how queer she looked. Her face looked small – quite different. She looked like one of the boys at the school baths, who sits on a step, shivering just like that, and wants to go in and yet is frightened.

'Are you awake?' she said. Her eyes opened; I think she smiled. She leaned towards me. 'I've been poisoned,' she whispered. 'Your father's poisoned me.' And she nodded. Then, before I could say a word, she was gone; I thought I heard the door shut. I sat quite still, I couldn't move, I think I expected something else to happen. For a long time I listened for something; there wasn't a sound. The candle was by my bed, but I was too frightened to stretch out my hand for the matches. But even while I wondered what I ought to do, even while my heart thumped – everything became confused. I lay down and pulled the blankets round me. I fell asleep, and the next morning my mother was found dead of failure of the heart.

Did that visit happen? Was it a dream? Why did she come to tell me? Or why, if she came, did she go away so quickly? And her expression – so joyous under the frightened look – was that real? I believed it fully the

afternoon of the funeral, when I saw my father
dressed up for his part, hat and all. That tall hat so
gleaming black and round was like a cork covered with
black sealing-wax, and the rest of my father was awfully
like a bottle, with his face for the label – *Deadly
Poison*. It flashed into my mind as I stood opposite him
in the hall. And Deadly Poison, or old D. P., was my
private name for him from that day.

Late, it grows late. I love the night. I love to feel the
tide of darkness rising slowly and slowly washing,
turning over and over, lifting, floating, all that lies
strewn upon the dark beach, all that lies hid in rocky
hollows. I love, I love this strange feeling of drifting –
whither? After my mother's death I hated to go to bed.
I used to sit on the window-sill, folded up, and watch
the sky. It seemed to me the moon moved much faster
than the sun. And one big, bright green star I chose for
my own. My star! But I never thought of it beckoning
to me, or twinkling merrily for my sake. Cruel, indifferent, splendid – it burned in the airy night. No
matter – it was mine! But, growing close up against the
window, there was a creeper with small, bunched-up
pink and purple flowers. These did know me. These,
when I touched them at night, welcomed my fingers;
the little tendrils, so weak, so delicate, knew I would
not hurt them. When the wind moved the leaves I felt
I understood their shaking. When I came to the window, it seemed to me the flowers said among themselves, 'The boy is here.'
As the months passed, there was often a light in my
father's room below. And I heard voices and laughter.
'He's got some woman with him,' I thought. But it
meant nothing to me. Then the gay voice, the sound of
laughter, gave me the idea it was one of the girls who
used to come to the shop in the evenings – and

gradually I began to imagine which girl it was. It was the dark one in the red coat and skirt, who once had given me a penny. A merry face stooped over me – warm breath tickled my neck – there were little beads of black on her long lashes, and when she opened her arms to kiss me, there came a marvellous wave of scent! Yes, that was the one.

Time passed, and I forgot the moon and my green star and my shy creeper – I came to the window to wait for the light in my father's window, to listen for the laughing voice, until one night I dozed and I dreamed she came again – again she drew me to her, something soft, scented, warm and merry hung over me like a cloud. But when I tried to see, her eyes only mocked me, her red lips opened and she hissed, 'Little sneak! Little sneak!' But not as if she were angry – as if she understood, and her smile somehow was like a rat – hateful!

The night after, I lighted the candle and sat down at the table instead. By and by, as the flame steadied, there was a small lake of liquid wax, surrounded by a white, smooth wall. I took a pin and made little holes in this wall and then sealed them up faster than the wax could escape. After a time I fancied the candle flame joined in the game; it leapt up, quivered, wagged; it even seemed to laugh. But while I played with the candle and smiled and broke off the tiny white peaks of wax that rose above the wall and floated them on my lake, a feeling of awful dreariness fastened on me – yes, that's the word. It crept up from my knees to my thighs, into my arms; I ached all over with misery. And I felt so strangely that I couldn't move. Something bound me there by the table – I couldn't even let the pin drop that I held between my finger and thumb. For a moment I came to a stop, as it were.

Then the shrivelled case of the bud split and fell,

the plant in the cupboard came into flower. 'Who am I?' I thought. 'What is all this?' And I looked at my room, at the broken bust of the man called Hahnemann on top of the cupboard, at my little bed with the pillow like an envelope. I saw it all, but not as I had seen before . . . Everything lived, everything. But that was not all. I was equally alive and – it's the only way I can express it – the barriers were down between us – I had come into my own world!

The barriers were down. I had been all my life a little outcast; but until that moment no one had 'accepted' me; I had lain in the cupboard – or the cave forlorn. But now I was taken, I was accepted, claimed. I did not consciously turn away from the world of human beings; I had never known it; but I from that night did beyond words consciously turn towards my silent brothers . . .

11

The Daughters of the Late Colonel

1

The week after was one of the busiest weeks of their
lives. Even when they went to bed it was only their
bodies that lay down and rested; their minds went on,
thinking things out, talking things over, wondering,
deciding, trying to remember where . . .

Constantia lay like a statue, her hands by her sides,
her feet just overlapping each other, the sheet up to
her chin. She stared at the ceiling.

'Do you think father would mind if we gave his top-
hat to the porter?'

'The porter?' snapped Josephine. 'Why ever the
porter? What a very extraordinary idea!'

'Because,' said Constantia slowly, 'he must often
have to go to funerals. And I noticed at – at the
cemetery that he only had a bowler.' She paused. 'I
thought then how very much he'd appreciate a top-hat.
We ought to give him a present too. He was always
very nice to father.'

'But,' cried Josephine, flouncing on her pillow and
staring across the dark at Constantia, 'father's head!'
And suddenly, for one awful moment, she nearly
giggled. Not, of course, that she felt in the least like
giggling. It must have been habit. Years ago, when
they had stayed awake at night talking, their beds had

236

simply heaved. And now the porter's head, disappearing, popped out, like a candle, under father's hat . . .
The giggle mounted, mounted; she clenched her hands;
she fought it down; she frowned fiercely at the dark
and said 'Remember' terribly sternly.

'We can decide tomorrow,' she said.

Constantia had noticed nothing; she sighed.

'Do you think we ought to have our dressing-gowns
dyed as well?'

'Black?' almost shrieked Josephine.

'Well, what else?' said Constantia. 'I was thinking –
it doesn't seem quite sincere, in a way, to wear black
out of doors and when we're fully dressed, and then
when we're at home – '

'But nobody sees us,' said Josephine. She gave the
bedclothes such a twitch that both her feet became uncovered, and she had to creep up the pillows to get
them well under again.

'Kate does,' said Constantia. 'And the postman very
well might.'

Josephine thought of her dark red slippers, which
matched her dressing-gown, and of Constantia's favourite indefinite green ones which went with hers. Black!
Two black dressing-gowns and two pairs of black woolly
slippers, creeping off to the bathroom like black cats.

'I don't think it's absolutely necessary,' said she.

Silence. Then Constantia said, 'We shall have to post
the papers with the notice in them tomorrow to catch
the Ceylon mail . . . How many letters have we had up
till now?'

'Twenty-three.'

Josephine had replied to them all, and twenty-three
times when she came to 'We miss our dear father so
much' she had broken down and had to use her handkerchief, and on some of them even to soak up a very
light blue tear with an edge of blotting-paper. Strange!

She couldn't have put it on — but twenty-three times. Even now, though, when she said over to herself sadly 'We miss our dear father *so* much,' she could have cried if she'd wanted to.

'Have you got enough stamps?' came from Constantia.

'Oh, how can I tell?' said Josephine crossly. 'What's the good of asking me that now?'

'I was just wondering,' said Constantia mildly.

Silence again. There came a little rustle, a scurry, a hop.

'A mouse,' said Constantia.

'It can't be a mouse because there aren't any crumbs,' said Josephine.

'But it doesn't know there aren't,' said Constantia.

A spasm of pity squeezed her heart. Poor little thing! She wished she'd left a tiny piece of biscuit on the dressing-table. It was awful to think of it not finding anything. What would it do?

'I can't think how they manage to live at all,' she said slowly.

'Who?' demanded Josephine.

And Constantia said more loudly than she meant to, 'Mice.'

Josephine was furious. 'Oh, what nonsense, Con!' she said. 'What have mice got to do with it? You're asleep.'

'I don't think I am,' said Constantia. She shut her eyes to make sure. She was.

Josephine arched her spine, pulled up her knees, folded her arms so that her fists came under her ears, and pressed her cheek hard against the pillow.

2

Another thing which complicated matters was they had Nurse Andrews staying on with them that week. It was their own fault; they had asked her. It was

Josephine's idea. On the morning – well, on the last morning, when the doctor had gone, Josephine had said to Constantia, 'Don't you think it would be rather nice if we asked Nurse Andrews to stay on for a week as our guest?'

'Very nice,' said Constantia.

'I thought,' went on Josephine quickly, 'I should just say this afternoon, after I've paid her, "My sister and I would be very pleased, after all you've done for us, Nurse Andrews, if you would stay on for a week as our guest." I'd have to put that in about being our guest in case – '

'Oh, but she could hardly expect to be paid!' cried Constantia.

'One never knows,' said Josephine sagely.

Nurse Andrews had, of course, jumped at the idea. But it was a bother. It meant they had to have regular sit-down meals at the proper times, whereas if they'd been alone they could just have asked Kate if she wouldn't have minded bringing them a tray wherever they were. And meal-times now that the strain was over were rather a trial.

Nurse Andrews was simply fearful about butter. Really they couldn't help feeling that about butter, at least, she took advantage of their kindness. And she had that maddening habit of asking for just an inch more bread to finish what she had on her plate, and then, at the last mouthful, absent-mindedly – of course it wasn't absent-mindedly – taking another helping. Josephine got very red when this happened, and she fastened her small, bead-like eyes on the tablecloth as if she saw a minute strange insect creeping through the web of it. But Constantia's long, pale face lengthened and set, and she gazed away – away – far over the desert, to where that line of camels unwound like a thread of wool . . .

239

'When I was with Lady Tukes,' said Nurse Andrews, 'she had such a dainty little contrayvance for the buttah. It was a silvah Cupid balanced on the – on the bordah of a glass dish, holding a tayny fork. And when you wanted some buttah you simply pressed his foot and he bent down and speared you a piece. It was quite a gayme.'

Josephine could hardly bear that. But 'I think those things are very extravagant' was all she said.

'But whey?' asked Nurse Andrews, beaming through her eyeglasses. 'No one, surely, would take more buttah than one wanted – would one?'

'Ring, Con,' cried Josephine. She couldn't trust herself to reply.

And proud young Kate, the enchanted princess, came in to see what the old tabbies wanted now. She snatched away their plates of mock something or other and slapped down a white, terrified blancmange.

'Jam, please, Kate,' said Josephine kindly.

Kate knelt and burst open the sideboard, lifted the lid of the jam-pot, saw it was empty, put it on the table, and stalked off.

'I'm afraid,' said Nurse Andrews a moment later, 'there isn't any.'

'Oh, what a bother!' said Josephine. She bit her lip. 'What had we better do?'

Constantia looked dubious. 'We can't disturb Kate again,' she said softly.

Nurse Andrews waited, smiling at them both. Her eyes wandered, spying at everything behind her eyeglasses. Constantia in despair went back to her camels. Josephine frowned heavily – concentrated. If it hadn't been for this idiotic woman she and Con would, of course, have eaten their blancmange without. Suddenly the idea came.

'I know,' she said. 'Marmalade. There's some marmalade in the sideboard. Get it, Con.'

'I hope,' laughed Nurse Andrews, and her laugh was like a spoon tinkling against a medicine-glass – 'I hope it's not very bittah marmalade.'

3

But, after all, it was not long now, and then she'd be gone for good. And there was no getting over the fact that she had been very kind to father. She had nursed him day and night at the end. Indeed, both Constantia and Josephine felt privately she had rather overdone the not leaving him at the very last. For when they had gone in to say goodbye Nurse Andrews had sat beside his bed the whole time, holding his wrist and pretending to look at her watch. It couldn't have been necessary. It was so tactless, too. Supposing father had wanted to say something – something private to them. Not that he had. Oh, far from it! He lay there, purple, a dark, angry purple in the face, and never even looked at them when they came in. Then, as they were standing there, wondering what to do, he had suddenly opened one eye. Oh, what a difference it would have made, what a difference to their memory of him, how much easier to tell people about it, if he had only opened both! But no – one eye only. It glared at them a moment and then . . . went out.

4

It had made it very awkward for them when Mr Farolles, of St John's, called the same afternoon.

'The end was quite peaceful, I trust?' were the first words he said as he glided towards them through the dark drawing-room.

'Quite,' said Josephine faintly. They both hung their heads. Both of them felt certain that eye wasn't at all a peaceful eye.

'Won't you sit down?' said Josephine.

'Thank you, Miss Pinner,' said Mr Farolles gratefully. He folded his coat-tails and began to lower himself into father's arm-chair, but just as he touched it he almost sprang up and slid into the next chair instead.

He coughed. Josephine clasped her hands; Constantia looked vague.

'I want you to feel, Miss Pinner,' said Mr Farolles, 'and you, Miss Constantia, that I'm trying to be helpful. I want to be helpful to you both, if you will let me. These are the times,' said Mr Farolles, very simply and earnestly, 'when God means us to be helpful to one another.'

'Thank you very much, Mr Farolles,' said Josephine and Constantia.

'Not at all,' said Mr Farolles gently. He drew his kid gloves through his fingers and leaned forward. 'And if either of you would like a little Communion, either or both of you, here *and* now, you have only to tell me. A little Communion is often very help – a great comfort,' he added tenderly.

But the idea of a little Communion terrified them. What! In the drawing-room by themselves   with no no altar or anything! The piano would be much too high, thought Constantia, and Mr Farolles could not possibly lean over it with the chalice. And Kate would be sure to come bursting in and interrupt them, thought Josephine. And supposing the bell rang in the middle? It might be somebody important – about their mourning. Would they get up reverently and go out, or would they have to wait . . . in torture?

'Perhaps you will send round a note by your good Kate if you would care for it later,' said Mr Farolles.

'Oh yes, thank you very much!' they both said.

Mr Farolles got up and took his black straw hat from the round table.

'And about the funeral,' he said softly. 'I may arrange that – as your dear father's old friend and yours, Miss Pinner – and Miss Constantia?'

Josephine and Constantia got up too.

'I should like it to be quite simple,' said Josephine firmly, 'and not too expensive. At the same time, I should like – '

'A good one that will last,' thought dreamy Constantia, as if Josephine were buying a nightgown. But of course Josephine didn't say that. 'One suitable to our father's position.' She was very nervous.

'I'll run round to our good friend Mr Knight,' said Mr Farolles soothingly. 'I will ask him to come and see you. I am sure you will find him very helpful indeed.'

5

Well, at any rate, all that part of it was over, though neither of them could possibly believe that father was never coming back. Josephine had had a moment of absolute terror at the cemetery, while the coffin was lowered, to think that she and Constantia had done this thing without asking his permission. What would father say when he found out? For he was bound to find out sooner or later. He always did. 'Buried. You two girls had me *buried*!' She heard his stick thumping. Oh, what would they say? What possible excuse could they make? It sounded such an appallingly heartless thing to do. Such a wicked advantage to take of a person because he happened to be helpless at the moment. The other people seemed to treat it all as a matter of course. They were strangers; they couldn't be expected to understand that father was the very last person for such a thing to happen to. No, the entire blame for it all would fall on her and Constantia. And the expense, she thought, stepping into the tight-buttoned cab. When

she had to show him the bills. What would he say then?
She heard him absolutely roaring, 'And do you
expect me to pay for this gimcrack excursion of yours?'

'Oh,' groaned poor Josephine aloud, 'we shouldn't
have done it, Con!'

And Constantia, pale as a lemon in all that blackness,
said in a frightened whisper, 'Done what, Jug?'

'Let them bu-bury father like that,' said Josephine,
breaking down and crying into her new queer-smelling
mourning handkerchief.

'But what else could we have done?' asked Constantia
wonderingly. 'We couldn't have kept him, Jug – we
couldn't have kept him unburied. At any rate, not in
a flat that size.'

Josephine blew her nose; the cab was dreadfully stuffy.

'I don't know,' she said forlornly. 'It is all so dreadful.
I feel we ought to have tried to, just for a time at least.
To make perfectly sure. One thing's certain' – and her
tears sprang out again – 'father will never forgive us
for this – never!'

6

Father would never forgive them. That was what they
felt more than ever when, two mornings later, they
went into his room to go through his things. They had
discussed it quite calmly. It was even down on Josephine's list of things to be done. *Go through father's
things and settle about them.* But that was a very different matter from saying after breakfast:

'Well, are you ready, Con?'

'Yes, Jug – when you are.'

'Then I think we'd better get it over.'

It was dark in the hall. It had been a rule for years
never to disturb father in the morning, whatever happened. And now they were going to open the door

without knocking even . . . Constantia's eyes were enormous at the idea; Josephine felt weak in the knees.

'You – you go first,' she gasped, pushing Constantia.

But Constantia said, as she always had said on those occasions, 'No Jug, that's not fair. You're eldest.'

Josephine was just going to say – what at other times she wouldn't have owned to for the world – what she kept for her very last weapon, 'But you're tallest,' when they noticed that the kitchen door was open, and there stood Kate . . .

'Very stiff,' said Josephine, grasping the door-handle and doing her best to turn it. As if anything ever deceived Kate!

It couldn't be helped. That girl was . . . Then the door was shut behind them, but – but they weren't in father's room at all. They might have suddenly walked through the wall by mistake into a different flat altogether. Was the door just behind them? They were too frightened to look. Josephine knew that if it was it was holding itself tight shut; Constantia felt that, like the doors in dreams, it hadn't any handle at all. It was the coldness which made it so awful. Or the whiteness – which? Everything was covered. The blinds were down, a cloth hung over the mirror, a sheet hid the bed; a huge fan of white paper filled the fire-place. Constantia timidly put out her hand; she almost expected a snow-flake to fall. Josephine felt a queer tingling in her nose, as if her nose was freezing. Then a cab klop-klopped over the cobbles below, and the quiet seemed to shake into little pieces.

'I had better pull up a blind,' said Josephine bravely.

'Yes, it might be a good idea,' whispered Constantia.

They only gave the blind a touch, but it flew up and the cord flew after, rolling round the blind-stick, and the little tassel tapped as if trying to get free. That was too much for Constantia.

245

'Don't you think – don't you think we might put it off another day?' she whispered.

'Why?' snapped Josephine, feeling, as usual, much better now that she knew for certain that Constantia was terrified. 'It's got to be done. But I do wish you wouldn't whisper, Con.'

'I didn't know I was whispering,' whispered Constantia.

'And why do you keep on staring at the bed?' said Josephine, raising her voice almost defiantly. 'There's nothing *on* the bed.'

'Oh, Jug, don't say so!' said poor Connie. 'At any rate, not so loudly.'

Josephine felt herself that she had gone too far. She took a wide swerve over to the chest of drawers, put out her hand, but quickly drew it back again.

'Connie!' she gasped, and she wheeled round and leaned with her back against the chest of drawers.

'Oh, Jug – what?'

Josephine could only glare. She had the most extraordinary feeling that she had just escaped something simply awful. But how could she explain to Constantia that father was in the chest of drawers? He was in the top drawer with his handkerchiefs and neckties, or in the next with his shirts and pyjamas, or in the lowest of all with his suits. He was watching there, hidden away – just behind the door-handle – ready to spring.

She pulled a funny old-fashioned face at Constantia, just as she used to in the old days when she was going to cry.

'I can't open,' she nearly wailed.

'No, don't, Jug,' whispered Constantia earnestly. 'It's much better not to. Don't let's open anything. At any rate, not for a long time.'

'But – but it seems so weak,' said Josephine, breaking down.

'But why not be weak for once, Jug?' argued Constantia, whispering quite fiercely. 'If it is weak.' And her pale stare flew from the locked writing-table – so safe – to the huge glittering wardrobe, and she began to breathe in a queer, panting way. 'Why shouldn't we be weak for once in our lives, Jug? It's quite excusable. Let's be weak – be weak, Jug. It's much nicer to be weak than to be strong.'

And then she did one of those amazingly bold things that she'd done about twice before in their lives; she marched over to the wardrobe, turned the key, and took it out of the lock. Took it out of the lock and held it up to Josephine, showing Josephine by her extraordinary smile that she knew what she'd done, she'd risked deliberately father being in there among his overcoats.

If the huge wardrobe had lurched forward, had crashed down on Constantia, Josephine wouldn't have been surprised. On the contrary, she would have thought it the only suitable thing to happen. But nothing happened. Only the room seemed quieter than ever, and bigger flakes of cold air fell on Josephine's shoulders and knees. She began to shiver.

'Come, Jug,' said Constantia, still with that awful callous smile, and Josephine followed just as she had that last time, when Constantia had pushed Benny into the round pond.

7

But the strain told on them when they were back in the dining-room. They sat down, very shaky, and looked at each other.

'I don't feel I can settle to anything,' said Josephine, 'until I've had something. Do you think we could ask Kate for two cups of hot water?'

'I really don't see why we shouldn't,' said Constantia

carefully. She was quite normal again. 'I won't ring. I'll go to the kitchen door and ask her.'

'Yes, do,' said Josephine, sinking down into a chair. 'Tell her, just two cups, Con, nothing else – on a tray.'

'She needn't even put the jug on, need she?' said Constantia, as though Kate might very well complain if the jug had been there.

'Oh no, certainly not! The jug's not at all necessary. She can pour it direct out of the kettle,' cried Josephine, feeling that would be a labour-saving indeed.

Their cold lips quivered at the greenish brims. Josephine curved her small red hands round the cup; Constantia sat up and blew on the wavy steam, making it flutter from one side to the other.

'Speaking of Benny,' said Josephine.

And though Benny hadn't been mentioned Constantia immediately looked as though he had.

'He'll expect us to send him something of father's, of course. But it's so difficult to know what to send to Ceylon.'

'You mean things get unstuck so on the voyage,' murmured Constantia.

'No, lost,' said Josephine sharply. 'You know there's no post. Only runners.'

Both paused to watch a black man in white linen drawers running through the pale fields for dear life, with a large brown-paper parcel in his hands. Josephine's black man was tiny; he scurried along glistening like an ant. But there was something blind and tireless about Constantia's tall, thin fellow, which made him, she decided, a very unpleasant person indeed . . . On the veranda, dressed all in white and wearing a cork helmet, stood Benny. His right hand shook up and down, as father's did when he was impatient. And behind him, not in the least interested, sat Hilda, the unknown sister-in-law. She swung in a cane rocker and

flicked over the leaves of the *Tatler*.

'I think his watch would be the most suitable present,' said Josephine.

Constantia looked up; she seemed surprised.

'Oh, would you trust a gold watch to a native?'

'But of course I'd disguise it,' said Josephine. 'No one would know it was a watch.' She liked the idea of having to make a parcel such a curious shape that no one could possibly guess what it was. She even thought for a moment of hiding the watch in a narrow cardboard corset-box that she'd kept by her for a long time, waiting for it to come in for something. It was such beautiful firm cardboard. But, no, it wouldn't be appropriate for this occasion. It had lettering on it: *Medium Women's* 28. *Extra Firm Busks*. It would be almost too much of a surprise for Benny to open that and find father's watch inside.

'And of course it isn't as though it would be going – ticking, I mean,' said Constantia, who was still thinking of the native love of jewellery. 'At least,' she added, 'it would be very strange if after all that time it was.'

8

Josephine made no reply. She had flown off on one of her tangents. She had suddenly thought of Cyril. Wasn't it more usual for the only grandson to have the watch? And then dear Cyril was so appreciative, and a gold watch meant so much to a young man. Benny, in all probability, had quite got out of the habit of watches; men so seldom wore waistcoats in those hot climates. Whereas Cyril in London wore them from year's end to year's end. And it would be so nice for her and Constantia, when he came to tea, to know it was there. 'I see you've got on grandfather's watch, Cyril.' It would be somehow so satisfactory.

Dear boy! What a blow his sweet, sympathetic little note had been! Of course they quite understood; but it was most unfortunate.

'It would have been such a point, having him,' said Josephine.

'And he would have enjoyed it so,' said Constantia, not thinking what she was saying.

However, as soon as he got back he was coming to tea with his aunties. Cyril to tea was one of their rare treats.

'Now, Cyril, you mustn't be frightened of our cakes. Your Auntie Con and I bought them at Buszard's this morning. We know what a man's appetite is. So don't be ashamed of making a good tea.'

Josephine cut recklessly into the rich dark cake that stood for her winter gloves or the soling and heeling of Constantia's only respectable shoes. But Cyril was most unmanlike in appetite.

'I say, Aunt Josephine, I simply can't. I've only just had lunch, you know.'

'Oh, Cyril, that can't be true! It's after four,' cried Josephine. Constantia sat with her knife poised over the chocolate-roll.

'It is, all the same,' said Cyril. 'I had to meet a man at Victoria, and he kept me hanging about till . . . there was only time to get lunch and to come on here. And he gave me – phew' – Cyril put his hand to his forehead – 'a terrific blow-out,' he said.

It was disappointing – today of all days. But still he couldn't be expected to know.

'But you'll have a meringue, won't you, Cyril?' said Aunt Josephine. 'These meringues were bought specially for you. Your dear father was so fond of them. We were sure you are, too.'

'I *am*, Aunt Josephine,' cried Cyril ardently. 'Do you mind if I take half to begin with?'

'Not at all, dear boy; but we musn't let you off with that.'

'Is your dear father still so fond of meringues?' asked Auntie Con gently. She winced faintly as she broke through the shell of hers.

'Well, I don't quite know, Auntie Con,' said Cyril breezily.

At that they both looked up.

'Don't know?' almost snapped Josephine. 'Don't know a thing like that about your own father, Cyril?'

'Surely,' said Auntie Con softly.

Cyril tried to laugh it off. 'Oh, well,' he said, 'it's such a long time since – ' He faltered. He stopped. Their faces were too much for him.

'Even *so*,' said Josephine.

And Auntie Con looked.

Cyril put down his teacup. 'Wait a bit,' he cried. 'Wait a bit, Aunt Josephine. What am I thinking of?'

He looked up. They were beginning to brighten. Cyril slapped his knee.

'Of course,' he said, 'it was meringues. How could I have forgotten? Yes, Aunt Josephine, you're perfectly right. Father's most frightfully keen on meringues.'

They didn't only beam. Aunt Josephine went scarlet with pleasure; Auntie Con gave a deep, deep sigh.

'And now, Cyril, you must come and see father,' said Josephine. 'He knows you were coming today.'

'Right,' said Cyril, very firmly and heartily. He got up from his chair; suddenly he glanced at the clock.

'I say, Auntie Con, isn't your clock a bit slow? I've got to meet a man at – at Paddington just after five. I'm afraid I shan't be able to stay very long with grandfather.'

'Oh, he won't expect you to stay *very* long!' said Aunt Josephine.

Constantia was still gazing at the clock. She couldn't make up her mind if it was fast or slow. It was one or the other, she felt almost certain of that. At any rate, it had been.

Cyril still lingered. 'Aren't you coming along, Auntie Con?'

'Of course,' said Josephine, 'we shall all go. Come on, Con.'

9

They knocked at the door, and Cyril followed his aunts into grandfather's hot, sweetish room.

'Come on,' said Grandfather Pinner. 'Don't hang about. What is it? What've you been up to?'

He was sitting in front of a roaring fire, clasping his stick. He had a thick rug over his knees. On his lap there lay a beautiful pale yellow silk handkerchief.

'It's Cyril, father,' said Josephine shyly. And she took Cyril's hand and led him forward.

'Good afternoon, grandfather,' said Cyril, trying to take his hand out of Aunt Josephine's. Grandfather Pinner shot his eyes at Cyril in the way he was famous for. Where was Auntie Con? She stood on the other side of Aunt Josephine; her long arms hung down in front of her; her hands were clasped. She never took her eyes off grandfather.

'Well,' said Granfather Pinner, beginning to thump, 'what have you got to tell me?'

What had he, what had he got to tell him? Cyril felt himself smiling like a perfect imbecile. The room was stifling, too.

But Aunt Josephine came to his rescue. She cried brightly, 'Cyril says his father is still very fond of meringues, father dear.'

'Eh?' said Grandfather Pinner, curving his hand like

a purple meringue-shell over one ear.

Josephine repeated, 'Cyril says his father is still very fond of meringues.'

'Can't hear,' said Old Colonel Pinner. And he waved Josephine away with his stick, then pointed with his stick to Cyril. 'Tell me what she's trying to say,' he said.

(My God!) 'Must I?' said Cyril, blushing and staring at Aunt Josephine.

'Do, dear,' she smiled. 'It will please him so much.'

'Come on, out with it!' cried Colonel Pinner testily, beginning to thump again.

And Cyril leaned forward and yelled, 'Father's still very fond of meringues.'

At that Grandfather Pinner jumped as though he had been shot.

'Don't shout!' he cried. 'What's the matter with the boy? *Meringues*! What about 'em?'

'Oh, Aunt Josephine, must we go on?' groaned Cyril desperately.

'It's quite all right, dear boy,' said Aunt Josephine, as though he and she were at the dentist's together. 'He'll understand in a minute.' And she whispered to Cyril, 'He's getting a bit deaf, you know.' Then she leaned forward and really bawled at Grandfather Pinner, 'Cyril only wanted to tell you, father, dear, that *his* father is still very fond of meringues.'

Colonel Pinner heard that time, heard and brooded, looking Cyril up and down.

'What an esstrordinary thing!' said old Grandfather Pinner. 'What an esstrordinary thing to come all this way here to tell me!'

And Cyril felt it *was*.

'Yes, I shall send Cyril the watch,' said Josephine.

'That would be very nice,' said Constantia. 'I seem

to remember last time he came there was some little
trouble about the time.'

10

They were interrupted by Kate bursting through the
door in her usual fashion, as though she had discovered
some secret panel in the wall.

'Fried or boiled?' asked the bold voice.

Fried or boiled? Josephine and Constantia were quite
bewildered for the moment. They could hardly take it
in.

'Fried or boiled what, Kate?' asked Josephine, trying
to begin to concentrate.

Kate gave a loud sniff. 'Fish.'

'Well, why didn't you say so immediately?' Josephine reproached her gently. 'How could you expect
us to understand, Kate? There are a great many things
in this world, you know, which are fried or boiled.'
And after such a display of courage she said quite
brightly to Constantia, 'Which do you prefer, Con?'

'I think it might be nice to have it fried,' said Constantia. 'On the other hand, of course, boiled fish is very
nice. I think I prefer both equally well . . . Unless
you . . . In that case – '

'I shall fry it,' said Kate, and she bounced back,
leaving their door open and slamming the door of her
kitchen.

Josephine gazed at Constantia; she raised her pale
eyebrows until they rippled away into her pale hair.
She got up. She said in a very lofty, imposing way,
'Do you mind following me into the drawing-room,
Constantia? I've something of great importance to
discuss with you.'

For it was always to the drawing-room they retired
when they wanted to talk over Kate.

254

Josephine closed the door meaningly. 'Sit down, Constantia,' she said, still very grand. She might have been receiving Constantia for the first time. And Con looked round vaguely for a chair, as though she felt indeed quite a stranger.

'Now the question is,' said Josephine, bending forward, 'whether we shall keep her or not.'

'That is the question,' agreed Constantia.

'And this time,' said Josephine firmly, 'we must come to a definite decision.'

Constantia looked for a moment as though she might begin going over all the other times, but she pulled herself together and said, 'Yes, Jug.'

'You see, Con,' explained Josephine, 'everything is so changed now.' Constantia looked up quickly. 'I mean,' went on Josephine, 'we're not dependent on Kate as we were.' And she blushed faintly. 'There's not father to cook for.'

'That is perfectly true,' agreed Constantia. 'Father certainly doesn't want any cooking now whatever else – '

Josephine broke in sharply, 'You're not sleepy, are you, Con?'

'Sleepy, Jug?' Constantia was wide-eyed.

'Well, concentrate more,' said Josephine sharply, and she returned to the subject. 'What it comes to is, if we did' – and this she barely breathed, glancing at the door – 'give Kate notice' – she raised her voice again – 'we could manage our own food.'

'Why not?' cried Constantia. She couldn't help smiling. The idea was so exciting. She clasped her hands. 'What should we live on, Jug?'

'Oh, eggs in various forms!' said Jug, lofty again. 'And besides, there are all the cooked foods.'

'But I've always heard,' said Constantia, 'they are considered so very expensive.'

255

'Not if one buys them in moderation,' said Josephine. But she tore herself away from this fascinating by path and dragged Constantia after her.

'What we've got to decide now, however, is whether we really do trust Kate or not.'

Constantia leaned back. Her flat little laugh flew from her lips.

'Isn't it curious, Jug,' said she, 'that just on this one subject I've never been able to quite make up my mind?'

11

She never had. The whole difficulty was to prove anything. How did one prove things, how could one? Suppose Kate had stood in front of her and deliberately made a face. Mightn't she very well have been in pain? Wasn't it impossible, at any rate, to ask Kate if she was making a face at her? If Kate answered 'No' – and of course she would say 'No' – what a position! How undignified! Then again Constantia suspected, she was almost certain that Kate went to her chest of drawers when she and Josephine were out, not to take things but to spy. Many times she had come back to find her amethyst cross in the most unlikely places, under her lace ties or on top of her evening Bertha. More than once she had laid a trap for Kate. She had arranged things in a special order and then called Josephine to witness.

'You see, Jug?'

'Quite, Con.'

'Now we shall be able to tell.'

But, oh dear, when she did go to look, she was as far off from a proof as ever! If anything was displaced, it might so very well have happened as she closed the drawer; a jolt might have done it so easily.

'You come, Jug, and decide. I really can't. It's too
difficult.'

But after a pause and a long glare Josephine would
sigh, 'Now you've put the doubt into my mind, Con,
I'm sure I can't tell myself.'

'Well, we can't postpone it again,' said Josephine.
'If we postpone it this time – '

12

But at that moment in the street below a barrel-organ
struck up. Josephine and Constantia sprang to their
feet together.

'Run, Con,' said Josephine. 'Run quickly. There's
sixpence on the – '

Then they remembered. It didn't matter. They
would never have to stop the organ-grinder again.
Never again would she and Constantia be told to make
that monkey take his noise somewhere else. Never
would sound that loud, strange bellow when father
thought they were not hurrying enough. The organ-
grinder might play there all day and the stick would
not thump.

> *It never will thump again,*
> *It never will thump again,*

played the barrel-organ.

What was Constantia thinking? She had such a
strange smile; she looked different. She couldn't be
going to cry.

'Jug, Jug,' said Constantia softly, pressing her hands
together. 'Do you know what day it is? It's Saturday.
It's a week today, a whole week.'

> *A week since father died,*
> *A week since father died,*

cried the barrel-organ. And Josephine, too, forgot to be
practical and sensible; she smiled faintly, strangely.
On the Indian carpet there fell a square of sunlight,
pale red; it came and went and came – and stayed,
deepened – until it shone almost golden.

'The sun's out,' said Josephine, as though it really
mattered.

A perfect fountain of bubbling notes shook from the
barrel-organ, round, bright notes, carelessly scattered.

Constantia lifted her big, cold hands as if to catch
them, and then her hands fell again. She walked over
to the mantelpiece to her favourite Buddha. And the
stone and gilt image, whose smile always gave her such
a queer feeling, almost a pain and yet a pleasant pain,
seemed today to be more than smiling. He knew something; he had a secret. 'I know something that you
don't know,' said her Buddha. Oh, what was it, what
could it be? And yet she had always felt there was . . .
something.

The sunlight pressed through the windows, thieved
its way in, flashed its light over the furniture and the
photographs. Josephine watched it. When it came to
mother's photograph, the enlargement over the piano,
it lingered as though puzzled to find so little remained
of mother, except the ear-rings shaped like tiny pagodas
and a black feather boa. Why did the photographs of
dead people always fade so? wondered Josephine. As
soon as a person was dead their photograph died too.
But, of course, this one of mother was very old. It was
thirty-five years old. Josephine remembered standing
on a chair and pointing out that feather boa to Constantia and telling her that it was a snake that had
killed their mother in Ceylon . . . Would everything
have been different if mother hadn't died? She didn't
see why. Aunt Florence had lived with them until they
had left school, and they had moved three times and

had their yearly holiday and . . . and there'd been changes of servants, of course.

Some little sparrows, young sparrows they sounded, chirped on the window-ledge. *Yeep – eyeep – yeep.* But Josephine felt they were not sparrows, not on the window-ledge. It was inside her, that queer little crying noise. *Yeep – eyeep – yeep.* Ah, what was it crying, so weak and forlorn?

If mother had lived, might they have married? But there had been nobody for them to marry. There had been father's Anglo-Indian friends before he quarrelled with them. But after that she and Constantia never met a single man except clergymen. How did one meet men? Or even if they'd met them, how could they have got to know men well enough to be more than strangers? One read of people having adventures, being followed, and so on. But nobody had ever followed Constantia and her. Oh yes, there had been one year at Eastbourne a mysterious man at their boarding-house who had put a note on the jug of hot water outside their bedroom door! But by the time Connie had found it the steam had made the writing too faint to read; they couldn't even make out to which of them it was addressed. And he had left next day. And that was all. The rest had been looking after father, and at the same time keeping out of father's way. But now? But now? The thieving sun touched Josephine gently. She lifted her face. She was drawn over to the window by gentle beams . . .

Until the barrel-organ stopped playing Constantia stayed before the Buddha, wondering, but not as usual, not vaguely. This time her wonder was like longing. She remembered the times she had come in here, crept out of bed in her nightgown when the moon was full, and lain on the floor with her arms outstretched, as though she was crucified. Why? The big, pale moon

259

had made her do it. The horrible dancing figures on the carved screen had leered at her and she hadn't minded. She remembered too how, whenever they were at the seaside, she had gone off by herself and got as close to the sea as she could, and sung something, something she had made up, while she gazed all over that restless water. There had been this other life, running out, bringing things home in bags, getting things on approval, discussing them with Jug, and taking them back to get more things on approval, and arranging father's trays and trying not to annoy father. But it all seemed to have happened in a kind of tunnel. It wasn't real. It was only when she came out of the tunnel into the moonlight or by the sea or into a thunderstorm that she really felt herself. What did it mean? What was it she was always wanting? What did it all lead to? Now? Now?

She turned away from the Buddha with one of her vague gestures. She went over to where Josephine was standing. She wanted to say something to Josephine, something frightfully important, about – about the future and what . . .

'Don't you think perhaps – ' she began.

But Josephine interrupted her. 'I was wondering if now – ' she murmured. They stopped; they waited for each other.

'Go on Con,' said Josephine.

'No, no, Jug; after you,' said Constantia.

'No, say what you were going to say. You began,' said Josephine.

'I . . . I'd rather hear what you were going to say first,' said Constantia.

'Don't be absurd, Con.'

'Really, Jug.'

'Connie!'

'Oh, *Jug*!'

A pause. Then Constantia said faintly, 'I can't say what I was going to say, Jug, because I've forgotten what it was . . . that I was going to say.'

Josephine was silent for a moment. She stared at a big cloud where the sun had been. Then she replied shortly, 'I've forgotten too.'

12

The Fly

◊ ◊ ◊
◊ ◊
◊

'Y'are very snug in here,' piped old Mr Woodifield,
and he peered out of the great, green leather armchair
by his friend the boss's desk as a baby peers out of its
pram. His talk was over; it was time for him to be off.
But he did not want to go. Since he had retired, since
his . . . stroke, the wife and the girls kept him boxed
up in the house every day of the week except Tuesday.
On Tuesday he was dressed and brushed and allowed to
cut back to the City for the day. Though what he did
there the wife and girls couldn't imagine. Make a
nuisance of himself to his friends, they supposed . . .
Well, perhaps so. All the same, we cling to our last
pleasures as the tree clings to its last leaves. So there
sat old Woodifield, smoking a cigar and staring almost
greedily at the boss, who rolled in his office chair, stout,
rosy, five years older than he, and still going strong,
still at the helm. It did one good to see him.

Wistfully, admiringly, the old voice added, 'It's
snug in here, upon my word!'

'Yes, it's comfortable enough,' agreed the boss, and
he flipped the *Financial Times* with a paper-knife. As a
matter of fact he was proud of his room; he liked to
have it admired, especially by old Woodifield. It gave
him a feeling of deep, solid satisfaction to be planted
there in the midst of it in full view of that frail old
figure in the muffler.

262

'I've had it done up lately,' he explained, as he had explained for the past – how many? – weeks. 'New carpet,' and he pointed to the bright red carpet with a pattern of large white rings. 'New furniture,' and he nodded towards the massive bookcase and the table with legs like twisted treacle. 'Electric heating!' He waved almost exultantly towards the five transparent, pearly sausages glowing so softly in the tilted copper pan.

But he did not draw old Woodifield's attention to the photograph over the table of a grave-looking boy in uniform standing in one of those spectral photographers' parks with photographers' storm-clouds behind him. It was not new. It had been there for over six years.

'There was something I wanted to tell you,' said old Woodifield, and his eyes grew dim remembering. 'Now what was it? I had it in my mind when I started out this morning.' His hands began to tremble, and patches of red showed above his beard.

Poor old chap, he's on his last pins, thought the boss. And, feeling kindly, he winked at the old man, and said jokingly, 'I tell you what. I've got a little drop of something here that'll do you good before you go out into the cold again. It's beautiful stuff. It wouldn't hurt a child.' He took a key off his watch-chain, unlocked a cupboard below his desk, and drew forth a dark squat bottle. 'That's the medicine,' said he. 'And the man from whom I got it told me on the strict Q.T. it came from the cellars at Windsor Castle.'

Old Woodifield's mouth fell open at the sight. He couldn't have looked more surprised if the boss had produced a rabbit.

'It's whisky, ain't it?' he piped, feebly.

The boss turned the bottle and lovingly showed him the label. Whisky it was.

'D'you know,' said he, peering up at the boss wonder-

ingly, 'they won't let me touch it at home.' And he looked as though he was going to cry.

'Ah, that's where we know a bit more than the ladies,' cried the boss, swooping across for two tumblers that stood on the table with the water-bottle, and pouring a generous finger into each. 'Drink it down. It'll do you good. And don't put any water with it. It's sacrilege to tamper with stuff like this. Ah!' He tossed off his, pulled out his handkerchief, hastily wiped his moustaches, and cocked an eye at old Woodifield, who was rolling his in his chaps.

The old man swallowed, was silent a moment, and then said faintly, 'It's nutty!'

But it warmed him; it crept into his chill old brain – he remembered.

'That was it,' he said, heaving himself out of his chair. 'I thought you'd like to know. The girls were in Belgium last week having a look at poor Reggie's grave, and they happened to come across your boy's. They're quite near each other, it seems.'

Old Woodifield paused, but the boss made no reply. Only a quiver in his eyelids showed that he heard.

'The girls were delighted with the way the place is kept,' piped the old voice. 'Beautifully looked after. Couldn't be better if they were at home. You've not been across, have yer?'

'No, no!' For various reasons the boss had not been across.

'There's miles of it,' quavered old Woodifield, 'and it's all as neat as a garden. Flowers growing on all the graves. Nice broad paths.' It was plain from his voice how much he liked a nice broad path.

The pause came again. Then the old man brightened wonderfully.

'D'you know what the hotel made the girls pay for a pot of jam?' he piped. 'Ten francs! Robbery, I call

it. It was a little pot, so Gertrude says, no bigger than
a half-crown. And she hadn't taken more than a spoon-
ful when they charged her ten francs. Gertrude brought
the pot away with her to teach 'em a lesson. Quite
right, too; it's trading on our feelings. They think
because we're over there having a look round we're
ready to pay anything. That's what it is.' And he turned
towards the door.

'Quite right, quite right!' cried the boss, though
what was quite right he hadn't the least idea. He came
round by his desk, followed the shuffling footsteps to
the door, and saw the old fellow out. Woodifield was
gone.

For a long moment the boss stayed, staring at nothing, while the grey-haired office messenger, watching
him, dodged in and out of his cubby hole like a dog that
expects to be taken for a run. Then: 'I'll see nobody
for half an hour, Macey,' said the boss. 'Understand?
Nobody at all.'

'Very good, sir.'

The door shut, the firm heavy steps recrossed the
bright carpet, the fat body plumped down in the
spring chair, and leaning forward, the boss covered his
face with his hands. He wanted, he intended, he had
arranged to weep . . .

It had been a terrible shock to him when old Woodifield sprang that remark upon him about the boy's
grave. It was exactly as though the earth had opened
and he had seen the boy lying there with Woodifield's
girls staring down at him. For it was strange. Although
over six years had passed away, the boss never thought
of the boy except as lying unchanged, unblemished in
his uniform, asleep for ever. 'My son!' groaned the
boss. But no tears came yet. In the past, in the first
months and even years after the boy's death, he had
only to say those words to be overcome by such grief

that nothing short of a violent fit of weeping could relieve him. Time, he had declared then, he had told everybody, could make no difference. Other men perhaps might recover, might live their loss down, but not he. How was it possible? His boy was an only son. Ever since his birth the boss had worked at building up this business for him; it had no other meaning if it was not for the boy. Life itself had come to have no other meaning. How on earth could he have slaved, denied himself, kept going all those years without the promise for ever before him of the boy's stepping into his shoes and carrying on where he left off?

And that promise had been so near being fulfilled. The boy had been in the office learning the ropes for a year before the war. Every morning they had started off together; they had come back by the same train. And what congratulations he had received as the boy's father! No wonder; he had taken to it marvellously. As to his popularity with the staff, every man jack of them down to old Macey couldn't make enough of the boy. And he wasn't in the least spoilt. No, he was just his bright, natural self, with the right word for everybody, with that boyish look and his habit of saying, 'Simply splendid!'

But all that was over and done with as though it never had been. The day had come when Macey had handed him the telegram that brought the whole place crashing about his head. 'Deeply regret to inform you . . .' And he had left the office a broken man, with his life in ruins.

Six years ago, six years . . . How quickly time passed! It might have happened yesterday. The boss took his hands from his face; he was puzzled. Something seemed to be wrong with him. He wasn't feeling as he wanted to feel. He decided to get up and have a look at the boy's photograph. But it wasn't a favourite photo-

graph of his; the expression was unnatural. It was cold, even stern-looking. The boy had never looked like that.

At that moment the boss noticed that a fly had fallen into his broad inkpot, and was trying feebly but desperately to clamber out again. Help! help! said those struggling legs. But the sides of the inkpot were wet and slippery; it fell back again and began to swim. The boss took up a pen, picked the fly out of the ink, and shook it on to a piece of blotting paper. For a fraction of a second it lay still on the dark patch that oozed round it. Then the front legs waved, took hold, and, pulling its small, sodden body up it began the immense task of cleaning the ink from its wings. Over and under, over and under, went a leg along a wing, as the stone goes over and under the scythe. Then there was a pause, while the fly, seeming to stand on the tips of its toes, tried to expand first one wing and then the other. It succeeded at last, and, sitting down, it began, like a minute cat, to clean its face. Now one could imagine that the little front legs rubbed against each other lightly, joyfully. The horrible danger was over; it had escaped; it was ready for life again.

But just then the boss had an idea. He plunged his pen back into the ink, leaned his thick wrist on the blotting paper, and as the fly tried its wings down came a great heavy blot. What would it make of that? What indeed! The little beggar seemed absolutely cowed, stunned, and afraid to move because of what would happen next. But then, as if painfully, it dragged itself forward. The front legs waved, caught hold, and, more slowly this time, the task began from the beginning.

He's a plucky little devil, thought the boss, and he felt a real admiration for the fly's courage. That was the way to tackle things; that was the right spirit. Never say die; it was only a question of . . . But the fly had again finished its laborious task, and the boss had

just time to refill his pen, to shake fair and square on the new-cleaned body yet another dark drop. What about it this time? A painful moment of suspense followed. But behold, the front legs were again waving; the boss felt a rush of relief. He leaned over the fly and said to it tenderly, 'You artful little b . . .' And he actually had the brilliant notion of breathing on it to help the drying process. All the same, there was something timid and weak about its efforts now, and the boss decided that this time should be the last, as he dipped the pen deep into the inkpot.

It was. The last blot fell on the soaked blotting-paper, and the draggled fly lay in it and did not stir. The back legs were stuck to the body; the front legs were not to be seen.

'Come on,' said the boss. 'Look sharp!' And he stirred it with his pen – in vain. Nothing happened or was likely to happen. The fly was dead.

The boss lifted the corpse on the end of the paper-knife and flung it into the waste-paper basket. But such a grinding feeling of wretchedness seized him that he felt positively frightened. He started forward and pressed the bell for Macey.

'Bring me some fresh blotting-paper,' he said, sternly, 'and look sharp about it.' And while the old dog padded away he fell to wondering what it was he had been thinking about before. What was it? It was . . . He took out his handkerchief and passed it inside his collar. For the life of him he could not remember.

Set in 12 Didot Walbaum type
leaded 1 point
and printed by
W & J MACKAY LTD, CHATHAM
the text in letterpress
and the illustrations
by lithography
on Clan Book Extra paper.
Bound by Mackays
using Scholco Brillanta cloth
and specially printed
paper sides